A SPY AT THE HIGHLAND COURT

THE HIGHLAND LADIES BOOK TWO

CELESTE BARCLAY

OLIVER HEBER BOOKS
GNARLY WOOL PUBLISHING
EST. 2014

To those who find their lives split between two cultures,
assimilating to one and then the other.
We are richer for the resilience.

SUBSCRIBE TO CELESTE'S NEWSLETTER

Subscribe to Celeste's bimonthly newsletter to receive exclusive insider perks.

Have you read *Leif, Viking Glory Book One*? This FREE first in series is available to all new subscribers to Celeste's monthly newsletter. Subscribe on her website.
Subscribe Now

Have you chatted with Celeste's hunky heroes? Are you new to Celeste's books or want insider exclusives before anyone else? Subscribe for free to chat with the men of Celeste's *The Highland Ladies* series.
Chat Now

THE HIGHLAND LADIES

A Spinster at the Highland Court

A Spy at the Highland Court

A Wallflower at the Highland Court

A Rogue at the Highland Court

A Rake at the Highland Court

An Enemy at the Highland Court

A Saint at the Highland Court

A Beauty at the Highland Court

A Sinner at the Highland Court

A Hellion at the Highland Court

An Angel at the Highland Court

A Harlot at the Highland Court

ONE

Dedric Hartley watched as the English king continued his royal rage as courtiers and advisors eased away from their irate sovereign. His Majesty's face was mottled with red splotches that only accentuated his fair complexion, and spittle formed at the corners of his mouth as his rant amplified. King Edward stalked about the chamber on the long legs that earned him the moniker "Longshanks."

"I don't give a bloody damn who oversaw the attack. It failed!" He railed against the last advisor who tried to reassure him that the recent loss was not the end of his campaign against the Scots. "Failure is failure. That usurper believes he's gotten the upper hand, and he will continue worming his way further into England now that he thinks he has outsmarted me. I should have killed him when I had the chance."

King Edward muttered his final comments as he sank back into the engraved and carved chair that sat on a dais. His bile spewed, the king retreated into his own thoughts as the rest of the chamber was left wondering what to do next.

Dedric had seen this pattern countless times

over the course of his life. He was all too familiar with the king's mercurial temper and unpredictable outbursts, but he also knew Edward was one of the best strategists and logisticians to have ever lived. While he might not like the man, he respected him. At times. Ric watched as the king scanned the crowd, assessing each knight present until his eyes settled on Ric, who wished he could melt into the curtains and watch the people in the gardens below.

"Sir Dedric, approach."

Ric stifled his groan, knowing from experience that the king would construe even the slightest hesitation as a personal, punishable offense. Ric approached the dais and bent into a low bow, awaiting the slight flick of Edward's fingers that would indicate he could rise. He knew it was the king's intention to make him wait.

When the signal finally came, Ric stood to his full height with his shoulders back and spine straight, just as had been hammered into him since the days when he was a page in the royal household.

"You were there." It was more an accusation than an observation. "What the hell went wrong?"

Dedric did not shift or squirm like he wanted, and he did not avert his gaze. Instead he weighed his words and chose them judiciously.

"There were simply more of them than us."

Ric did not miss the collective gasp that his curt answer elicited. He waited for the king to explode again, but this time Edward laughed. It was a hearty laugh, but Ric did not miss the lack of mirth in the king's eyes. "So, it was as simple as that? How did I not realize?" Edward stood once more and left the dais, this time placing himself directly in front of Ric.

"Sir Dedric, since I'd already deduced the insufficient numbers on our side, I had hoped you might have more insight than to state the obvious!" What started as a reasonable tone ended in a bellow.

"Your Majesty, the clans put aside their enmity toward one another, not just neighbors but Highlanders and Lowlanders, and showed up in great force. There was a great conviction to defeat us and not just for their land."

"Ah, yes. The great Scottish pride. The same pride I have spent a lifetime hammering out of them." Edward sized up Ric, and Ric knew whatever came next would be something he would dread. "You're a Scot."

The king paused, purposely though silently encouraging the whispers that spread through the chamber, grimacing when Ric did not blink. Edward had hoped to garner some reaction from the knight standing before him, but he had underestimated what Dedric Hartley had learned over a lifetime of serving the English king.

"Half, Your Majesty. I'm a Hartley." The name of the well-respected English family made many in the chamber take notice, but the king's mention of his Scottish heritage was a stigma Ric could never get past.

"Yes, and like your father Hallam, you are one of my best knights. You have been part of my household since I took you in as a page. I just hope you don't make the same mistake as your father and go falling in love with a Scot, then getting yourself killed. I'm not raising any more half-Hartleys."

The alliteration garnered the snickers Edward wanted. Dedric had heard the phrase countless times over the twenty-plus years he had been in the king's service. His father had been the illustrious Hallam Hartley, a knight in the king's service sent to the border to wage war against the MacLellan and Maxwell clans. Hallam ended up falling in love with

Emelote MacLellan. They married and were content to make a life for themselves with her people, but a former friend who never accepted Hallam's decision to side with the Scots was his betrayer. Hallam and Emelote's marriage only lasted six years, ending abruptly when the English killed Hallam in a border skirmish. Dedric had few memories of his father, but he clung tightly to them. They had driven him his entire life, earning him the title of a knight.

When Dedric was seven, the English—led by his father's former friend—raided and burned their home. The man assaulted Emelote before murdering her and dragging Ric to King Edward. They forced him to become a page, and by the time he became a squire at age fourteen, he was sure Edward ordered the attack to ensure they took him from his mother. He was payment for the wrong Edward believed his father committed. His mother was retribution. The king had not taken him in but rather stolen him, and he had not raised him but intimidated him.

Ric remained silent, not having missed the real meaning of the king's words. He was being sent back to Scotland when he had only just returned a week earlier. He was still tired, not to mention battered and bruised, from the last campaign. He had hoped for a longer reprieve, mostly so he could soak in countless hot baths before riding his horse again.

"Which men would you have me lead, Sire?"

"Not men. Just you. And I suppose your squire. You shall make use of that MacLellan blood and be of greater use to me."

Ric's stomach dropped to his boots. He had seen none of his mother's people since he was a child. He knew next to nothing about them other than they lived along the border. His missions had been to the eastern border while the MacLellans' land laid to the west near the Stewarts, Maxwells, and Dunbars.

He knew marginally more about his father, but his life and death were stories best kept far from King Edward's ears. As a nine-year-old, he had once gone nearly a week on bread and water for asking one too many questions about his parents. The king had banished Ric to a storage room, where he sat in the dark and feared they would never release him. He learned then that Longshanks had a sadistic and vengeful streak. It had been at the queen's mercy that the king forgave and reinstated Ric as a page.

Queen Eleanor had taken pity on the orphan, having lost several of her own children. She used her influence on her husband to ensure Dedric received the tutelage he needed to become first a squire, then a knight. Dedric appreciated that Eleanor had the ability to tame her belligerent husband from a roaring bear to a docile lapdog, so great was their love.

The king's ongoing monologue brought Ric back to the present, and he caught the last of the king's orders. "You leave in the morning for the Bruce's court. You had better not fail me. I will rely upon the information you send back to destroy these heathenous Scots."

The king clapped his hand on Ric's shoulder and gave it a squeeze. There was an element of pride in the king's eyes that made Ric wonder if Edward saw more to him than he revealed in public.

"Aye, Sire. I will not fail you."

———

Ric wound his way through the corridors and passageways until he came to the knights' quarters. He had no intention of being seen again before morning. He would summon his squire, order a bath, and soak until goosebumps drove him from the tub into bed. He also intended to have his squire pack their belongings and squirrel away any food the kitchens could spare. Ric was not as tall as the king, but he stood over six feet and was a large man. His squire was a youth of seventeen who still seemed to be made up of hollow arms and legs. They both ate a significant amount, and the supplies given to a traveling knight would barely last them the first two days.

"The king seems to favor you after all." The honeyed voice made the hairs on the back of Ric's neck stand up. He knew who it belonged to, and he longed to bolt in the opposite direction from its owner.

"Good eve, Lady Bella." Ric dipped his head but continued on.

"We have much to plan for. We should refresh our memories on how well we suit one another."

Ric came to a halt as he looked down at the stunning woman he had made the mistake of bedding several times shortly after receiving his spurs. He had not even turned twenty-one and was still in awe that he had earned the title of a knight. The woman had appeared out of nowhere and filled his head with compliments and flirtation. As a landless orphan, he was unprepared for such an enticing woman to take an interest in him. Lady Bella had flattered him all the way into her bed.

It was only after a month of sneaking off with her that he learned she was sneaking off with several other men and did not share his feelings. Feelings he understood now had been puppy love and infatuation, but realizing she would never marry him was enough to teach him to keep all women at arm's length. He also knew that Lady Arabella Fitz-Bigod answered to Bella because she believed her looks warranted her being called beautiful as her name, not just as a descriptor. Lady Bella was the illegitimate daughter of a courtier, and King Edward often used her to seduce men into telling their secrets. Ric was not interested, and he had no secrets to tell.

"I see the king didn't inform you that I will be your go-between. You will give your messages to me, and I will ensure they make it to the king."

"Thank you for bringing that to my attention." Ric tried to step past her, but Bella pressed her body against his. He leaned away, refusing the temptation after being celibate for the past several months while entrenched in battles against the Scots. He did not trust his body to cooperate with his mind. Bella knew that and pressed more firmly against him, her hand trailing over his chest to his waist then reaching even further down. His body reacted just as she wanted, and she purred as she stroked his arousal.

"I can tell you remember. Traveling together will be entertaining." Bella pressed harder against Ric, and she tempted him to give in to her clear invitation. However, her words that they would travel together was the final bucket of cold water he needed. It irritated him to learn that he would have to rely on her for this mission, but to travel with her was unacceptable. He knew he would make a swift change in plans.

"If memory serves me as well as you believe, I recall you are currently tied to both the Earl of Salisbury and the Earl of Essex, not to mention the Earls of Hertford and Lancaster. I'm sure you haven't time." He grasped her wrist and pulled it from his hardened cock, stifling the groan as his body rejected his sense of honor, preferring the release he knew she offered.

Bella was not easily deterred and once again leaned forward, offering him a view of the top of her nipples and the supple flesh of her breasts. Ric looked over her head and spotted his squire, Robbie, standing in front of his chamber.

"You would do well to remember those names since your future rests in the messages the king receives and who delivers them," Bella warned.

Ric did not look at her as he nodded once more and stepped around her at last. He made his way to his chamber without looking back. He opened the door and pushed his squire inside. "Begin packing. We leave during the evening meal. I intend to be far from this country by the time the sun rises."

"Lady Bella seemed pleased to see you," Robbie mused.

"You shouldn't have been looking," Ric chastised his squire, but there was no bite to his words.

"She's rather hard to miss."

Ric thought of something else that was hard. "Precisely. That is why we are riding out tonight rather than in the morning. If we wait, we won't be able to miss her."

"Where to, my lord?"

"Scotland."

Robbie's unimpressed smirk ended abruptly when Ric clarified. "Robert the Bruce's court."

TWO

I t took three days for Dedric and Robbie to reach the Scottish border, but rather than cross into Kerr territory, they kept off the main roads and paths while they traveled another day and a half to MacLellan lands. The rolling hills and vistas of Cumberland and Northumberland impressed Ric, and the landscape continued into the Southern Uplands across the border. Ric considered the north a wild and beautiful place, and as a young knight, he had hoped to one day earn a piece of land in the northern counties. He had survived more than one frigid and blustery winter there, but the other seasons made up for it.

As they traveled further west, approaching his mother's clan territory, his heart felt at home. It was an inexplicable and irrational emotion, but a peace of mind and body settled over him. He had never felt it to this extent along other parts of the border or even in the heart of the English north. The land was not drastically different from one side of the border to the other, but he realized that he was returning to the place of his birth and his family. That created this longing.

Robbie rode in silence, and Ric was grateful that

the squire had learned early in his service to curb his natural penchant for chatter. Ric appreciated the young man's company, and Robbie impressed him with his innate abilities with horses in and near battle. The more agitated other horses became before battle, the calmer those Robbie managed remained. He possessed insight into the people they traveled and camped with, and Ric knew he had remained alive more than once due to the information Robbie squirreled away to him.

"I believe we are near to Kirkcudbright, where the laird's family lives. We should come to it before the River Dee."

"Have you decided what you shall say when we arrive?" Robbie asked. "You don't sound very Scottish, and I certainly don't."

"I have. Anyone who knows my story will know the English took me as a child. I was angry for most of my childhood and most of the time I spent as a squire. Becoming a knight forced me to let it go or I wouldn't have survived the first fight along the border. But that anger is still within me. I'll tell them King Edward released me from his service once my tenure came to an end, and I've come home. I'll tell them the truth: I never wanted to be there. I'll let a little of that anger show, and it shouldn't take much to convince them I'm telling the truth."

"And you brought an English squire?"

"You're in my service until I deem you ready to earn your spurs, at which time you must return to serve the king if you don't wish to remain with me. That's true enough."

What the two men would leave out was that Robbie was the son of the Earl of Northumberland and second in line to inherit the title. There was little chance that Robbie would remain with Ric once he was knighted.

Another hour passed as they plodded along, in no hurry to reach their destination. Ric knew that for his squire, the willingness to trot rather than canter or gallop was apprehension, but Ric wanted to enjoy this sense of peace before diving into the lies that would consume him for the foreseeable future.

The sun was inching toward the western horizon when they reined in and looked at the MacLellan keep. The stone structure was impressive and sat on a rise near the shore of the River Dee. The well-fortified bailey wall stood higher than any needed in England. It was proof that the ongoing strife required a castle built for battle. The village that lay beyond the keep was larger than most, and there was activity as people moved about and smoke rose from rooftops.

"I'm sure they've seen us, so we would do well to arrive on our own, rather than with an escort," Ric nodded toward the men that were small blurs along the battlements. They spurred their horses and approached the village, then the keep.

"Who goes?" came the demand once they were within earshot.

"Dedric Hartley, son of Hallam Hartley and Emelote MacLellan Hartley, second cousin to the laird."

Ric sat as he heard voices, but the words were unintelligible. He tried to keep his nervousness from transferring to his horse. He would not give away his mood with a horse that danced about. It was not long before the portcullis opened wide enough for five men to stand beneath it. The man in the center was the laird, and his guard did not look welcoming.

"There is no Dedric Hartley in the MacLellan clan," the laird announced.

Dedric heard the man speak, but he was struck with a vivid memory as he peered into the bailey. He raised his arm and pointed just to the right of the laird.

"There. To your left once stood the armory. It was too close to the gate, and when the English raided, they stormed the armory and gathered the weapons before the laird's men could arm themselves. It was the reason they were able to kill so many, including my mother." Ric looked up and remembered a woman who stood in the window of a third-story chamber, waving at him as he played. "The second window from the far end was my mother's chamber growing up, and it became my parents' until my father died. I had a trundle bed with a horse carved into the head."

Memories flooded back as Ric swept his eyes over the castle and the surrounding buildings. He had not seen the place since he was seven, but it was as though he was a little boy again, playing in the corner near the kitchens.

"Aline was the cook, and she would slip me apricot tarts while I played with the other children. She made me share with my cousin." Ric looked at the man more closely. "You."

The final word came out closer to a whisper. Both men sized one another up before the laird nodded. "Some of that you could have learned from anyone who heard of the raid twenty years ago, but you couldn't have known aboot the trundle bed my own son sleeps in, nor would you have known aboot the pies." Even with the acknowledgment that they were family, there was no invitation to enter the castle. "Why are you here? It's been a long time, and we heard that you served the English bastard."

"I did." Ric would get that admission out of the way from the beginning. "He had me stolen. He believed my father owed him my service after choosing my mother over him. They raised me at court before I earned my way to being a knight. My service is now through, and I do not wish to remain fighting for the man who killed both of my parents."

Ric knew there would never be a confession from the king that he arranged the two battles that killed first his father, then his mother. But he was certain Edward knew and condoned it; after all, it was the Longshanks' order to fight along the border.

The laird continued to assess Ric before he stepped aside and turned his back to Ric and Robbie, but not before he gave the signal for the guards to raise the portcullis all the way. Ric nudged his horse, and Robbie followed. They entered the bailey, and Ric felt awash with more memories. Memories raced before his eyes, memories of his early childhood that he had not thought about since he became a squire and forced himself to only look forward. Ric and Robbie handed their reins over to a stable boy and dismounted. As they did, a woman came to stand at the top of the steps, and it was clear she was the laird's mother. The sun shone in Ric's eyes, but as he approached the laird who now stood below his mother, Ric's step faltered. He felt the blood leach from his face, and he was sure he was looking at a ghost. He shook his head before taking a step back.

"We could have been twins," came the woman's soft voice. She moved down the steps until she could pass her son, who put his arm up to block her advance. She gently pushed it away. "As much as I looked like your mother, you are the image of your father."

The woman stopped in front of Ric and took his large, rough hands in her tiny smooth ones. "I'm your mother's cousin, Emelyn."

Emelyn and Emelote.

"I still have the scar on my knee you stitched when Malcolm and I jumped from the rocks into the river. You promised to fix it before we showed my mother."

Ric swallowed several times as he watched his aunt's smile broaden, and she pulled him into her embrace. It had been years since the queen had embraced him, and the motherly comfort was too much for him. When Emelyn pulled away, she cupped his cheek with one hand and placed the other over his heart.

"You will not have a warm welcome here, but anyone who is auld enough to remember my son as a child will know who you are on sight," she murmured for only Ric to hear.

She wound her arm through his and turned back to her son. When she stepped forward, Ric had no choice but to follow. Emelyn reached her other hand to her son. The three walked into the Great Hall and toward the dais. Ric felt the eyes staring at him, judging him, and finding him wanting. He swept his eyes around the large chamber, taking in the swords above the fireplace and the heraldic shield that sat over them. The tapestries swayed from the breeze of the main door opening and closing. Ric paused before one depicting a knight on horseback leaning over to grasp a woman's arm in preparation to pull her onto the horse. They were in a meadow filled with bright flowers and a beaming sun. Ric looked closer and saw that a child rode in front of the man.

"Your mother made that in honor of your father's life. She hadn't finished before the raid, so my mother finished it and hung it in a place of honor." Those were the first words the laird spoke to Ric after admitting that they were indeed family. "I was raised on stories of your parents' great love. It rivaled that of my own parents."

Ric could only nod as he took in the scene of his family memorialized upon the wall. He had never seen an image of his father before, and he understood why Emelyn said he resembled his father. It was like looking at himself on the wall. He knew he could not remain gawking at the tapestry now that Emelyn and Malcolm sat at the dais, along with a woman noticeably with child. Malcolm rested a protective arm around her shoulders as she leaned into him. Ric approached the dais and bowed to the woman, who was clearly the lady of the keep and Malcolm's wife. He stepped onto the dais and took the seat to the laird's right, between Malcolm and Emelyn. It surprised him that was the seat they showed him, but he supposed it was so Malcolm could drill him with questions.

"You must have traveled a long way to reach us. Unless you already had business along the border." Malcolm's tone did not hide his distaste, and his implication that Ric had been fighting along the border was near to the truth.

"I was with the royal court in Yorkshire when the day of my tenure ended. I departed that evening and rode here."

"You are familiar with this land, but we have never seen you before." Malcolm referred to the other English troops that had harried the MacLellan clan along with their other western border neighbors.

"I haven't been this far west since I was seven."

"So, you have been to the east," Malcolm continued to press.

"Yes." Ric offered nothing more. He looked Malcolm squarely in the eye before taking a long draw from the chalice placed before him. Even over the rim, Ric continued to meet his cousin's gaze.

"Malcolm," the woman who still went without a

name whispered. The laird looked down at his wife's pleading face. "Not in front of your mother."

Malcolm nodded but looked back at Ric, and it was clear the conversation had only been paused. However, Emelyn was not so willing to wait.

"You fought along the eastern border. I take it you fought the Kerrs and Elliots." Emelyn's words were plain and without rancor, even though they made Ric uncomfortable.

"When the king ordered me there."

Malcolm could not hold back. "Ordered to fight your own people?"

"I was sworn in fealty to the king. He may be the reason my parents are dead, but like it or not, he housed me, fed me, and clothed me, not to mention educated me, when I became an orphan. I had a duty to repay that and so I swore my oath. If I hadn't followed the orders, what type of honor would I have had?" Ric's voice was soft, but the iron was there. He would not have his cousin intimidate him or mock him. If his time among his mother's people was short, then Ric would move on to Robert the Bruce's court. But the mention of oaths given and honor placated Malcolm. It was something the man could understand.

The two warriors came to a truce of sorts and Emelyn drove the rest of the conversation, finally introducing Malcolm's wife as Lady Rosalind. That afternoon, Emelyn took Ric on a tour of the castle and its grounds while Rosalind rested, and Malcolm handled clan affairs in his solar. Ric was only too glad to escape to his chamber before the evening meal for a bath and fresh clothing.

"It seems your family welcomes you, if not with open arms, then at least not with a sword in your belly," Robbie mused as he laid out Ric's fresh surcoat and leggings. Once Ric shed his travel-stained clothes and stepped into the tub, Robbie sat with his back turned as he polished the knight's boots.

"It was odd, to say the least, to walk about the place. I hadn't thought of it in years. More faded memories came back to me. I could remember doing things better than I could people's names and faces. There were many in the bailey who remembered my parents, and my resemblance to my father is un-canny, or so it seems. A few welcomed me in his memory, but most were standoffish knowing that I served their enemy and fought their people."

Ric submerged his entire body and held his breath as the hot water washed over him. For a mo-ment he felt like he would float away, but the tub was far too small for that. When he surfaced, he drew a bar of soap over a linen cloth and scrubbed his body before attending to his hair. He signaled for Robbie to pour the pitcher of clean water over his head and wiped the suds from his eyes. He was in his parents' chamber, and little had changed in the years that passed since he was last there. The only thing missing was the trundle bed he slept in, now in use by the laird's children. When he could no longer stand sit-ting in the filthy water, he rose and dried off. A knock on the door startled both Robbie and Ric. Robbie drew a knife as Ric wrapped a towel around his waist and grabbed his sword. Most attackers would not knock before entering, but they were not precisely honored guests. Ric gestured for Robbie to open the door; both were unprepared for Bella to waltz in.

"My timing is impeccable," she purred. She waved her hand in Robbie's direction as if to shoo him from the chamber.

"What're you doing here? And how did you make your way above stairs?" Ric demanded.

"Why wouldn't they allow your companion to join you?" Bella's skirts swished around her as she walked about the room.

"You told them you're my mistress?" While it was a question, it was more of a hissed recrimination. "No. Absolutely not. You will leave here, and you will not make a peep about it, Bella. I am not having my family believe I brought my English mistress to live amongst them."

Ric did not realize he was pointing his sword toward her until she brushed it aside and came to stand in front of him. She reached out her hand just as she had done in the passageway before Ric departed the royal household, but this time, Ric was faster.

"It's too late. They already believe I'm your lover."

"Then they will un-believe it."

"And just how will you do that?"

"Do you intend to test me? I think you would rather depart on your own terms with dignity."

"But I'm not going anywhere. The king expects me to serve as a liaison of sorts between you and his messengers, so you have no choice but to allow me to stay."

"If the king wanted you to be present for whatever I see and hear, then he would have made you the spy and not the liaison."

"As I said, I'm here now. Where would I go as an unaccompanied English woman in Scotland?"

"You should have thought of that before you crossed the border, Bella. I am not having my family believe I am romantically engaged with you. Do you believe they will think me aught but a spy with an English mistress and an English squire? Why would I bring half my life with me from England if that's what I'm trying to leave behind to become a Scot? You have overstepped, and you will bring this whole mission down about our ears because you are far too entitled for one of your station."

Ric bit his tongue before he said anything else. He was a landless orphan. He was in no place to put the illegitimate daughter of a favorite courtier in her place, even if what he said was true. He knew he would regret his words, but he would not regret his decision. When Bella swung at him, he grabbed her wrist and marched to the door. He swung it open so hard and so wide that it slammed against the wall, and they were barely through it before it bounced back closed.

"You are in a drying linen and naught else," Bella hissed. "You will humiliate us both."

"I have naught to hide that others haven't seen before." Ric dragged her to the stairs and only slowed to keep her from falling. He wanted her away from him, not dead. They reached the Great Hall to gasps as people sprang out of their way. They watched in a mixture of horror and curiosity as Ric continued to lead Bella through the large double doors, down the steps, and across the bailey. One hand clung to her as the other held the linen in place. He did not notice the rocks and pebbles that bit into his feet or the chill air that whispered about his legs. He continued their march to the gate.

"Open it," he demanded as they approached. The men in the gatehouse stared at him, but the air of fury that radiated from him told the guardsmen to comply. Once the gate was open, he swung Bella around and pushed her through. "Close it."

"You bastard."

"That's where you are wrong. My father made his home here with his wife, my mother. You will not disgrace me or their memory with your lies. Find somewhere else, anywhere else, beyond this village. I will not see you again until I arrive at court, and even there, you do not know me. You would do well to find somewhere in Stirling to stay. Do not approach the castle," he spat.

The gate slammed shut before Bella could squeeze in another word. Ric spun on his heels and faced most of the clan staring at him. He stomped back to the steps, throwing over his shoulder, "I left England for a reason. You just saw it."

He would allow the people who stood agog to interpret the scene however they wanted.

THREE

The evening progressed without incident. No one asked about Bella's abrupt arrival or departure, but Ric could tell he had done the right thing by making her leave. He was under scrutiny by most of the clan. Emelyn kept a steady stream of conversation going, and it was clear that at his wife's behest, Malcolm was making more of an effort.

"How long have you been a knight?" Rosalind looked past her husband and smiled shyly at Ric.

"Eight years, my lady." Ric answered around a mouth full of lamb stew.

"What do you think you'll do now that you don't have to fight?" Rosalind's questions sounded innocent, but Ric was sure Malcolm had prompted her to ask, as it would seem unassuming from her.

"Find a parcel of land and live on it, if possible."

"You don't intend to stay with us?" Emelyn's question conveyed her shock and hurt. "You've only just arrived."

"I cannot impose, Cousin." The word felt strange on his tongue, but he was willing to try it.

"It's not an imposition when it is family."

Ric smiled and nodded, but he did not back down. "I think it might be the worst imposition when it's family. I've shown up on your doorstep, and I can see many of the clan are not as quick to have me here as you are. I won't be the source of trouble for Malcolm or your family."

"And just who do you think will grant you this land?" Malcolm demanded.

Ric shrugged. "I imagine somewhere there is land I can buy where no one will care where I grew up."

"And how do you plan to survive in the middle of nowhere?" Malcolm scoffed.

"I can hunt as well as any man, and I can tend a garden. That's all I need."

Malcolm narrowed his eyes as he considered his next words. "Why come all the way here to avoid being around people?"

"Kirkcudbright was but a stopping point. I have spent every day of the past twenty years being around other people. I'm looking forward to some solitude."

"Then why bring a squire?" Malcolm would not relent.

"He is bound to me until he earns his spurs, at which time he can remain with me or enter the service of the king."

"How can he become a knight with nowhere to train?"

"I haven't forgotten a lifetime of training just because I don't wear the king's insignia. If need be, we will travel to tournaments. I am looking for a life with less bloodshed and death."

"Then you have come to the wrong place. The borderlands are naught but bloodshed and death," Malcolm grumbled.

"Perhaps King Robert would accept your service for a short time in exchange for land," Emelyn offered.

"Mother! That's outrageous. The king would never accept an English knight in his midst."

"He would if one of his lairds vouched for the mon."

Mother and son stared off at one another. While Emelyn had a soft voice and seemed to glide everywhere she went, she had an iron will to match her son's. It had been necessary to survive along the ever-shifting landscape and to serve as the laird's wife. Eventually, Malcolm relented.

"You may stay here as long as you like, and when you are ready to travel to court, I will send a missive with you, vouching that you are my cousin."

"Thank you," Ric's gratitude was sincere. He had not imagined it would be so easy to gain entry to the royal court, and he did want to spend time with his family.

The next fortnight was spent learning more about his parents and the history of Clan MacLellan. During the day, he trained in the lists and taught the warriors maneuvers and tricks that the English used in battle. He felt sharing what he knew was not a betrayal to Edward, but a small token for the hospitality his clan offered. No one was overtly rude to him, and many began to smile and acknowledge him as they watched him train their laird's guardsmen. The evenings were spent discussing the current state of affairs along the border. Ric shared with Malcolm what he knew of the fight further east. When they did not discuss politics, they played chess and games of chance.

Once Malcolm was willing to lower his guard, they fell into a rhythm that reminded both men of their childhoods. Malcolm was a year older than Ric, but they had been close playmates before Ric left the clan. It was only at night, when Dedric lay in bed, that guilt niggled at his mind. He knew he would betray the MacLellans with the information he sent back to the king. Bella would be expecting a report as soon as he arrived in Stirling. He did not doubt that she had already beguiled a man with her charms and made herself comfortable while she waited. She would appear before he could find her.

I don't have to tell the truth. Bella isn't here to see whether what I say is real or something I've made up. I have the chance to help my people if I give Bella falsehoods.

It surprised Ric how attached he felt to other people for the first time in years. Before arriving, he had not considered whether he would feel such strong loyalty to the MacLellans. He had assumed he would have the same sense of obligation that he felt for the king. He had anticipated feeling torn, but he did not expect to be compelled to protect the Mac-Lellans.

I can tell her that they believe the fight won't come back to them since so much of it has been to the east. I can tell her that they have grown complacent since there has been peace in the area for more than a year. Longshanks will jump at the opportunity to attempt a siege, but he will be surprised to find such a fortified and well-provisioned keep. Malcolm could lay waste to the king's men.

Or do I just tell the truth? Do I tell Bella that they are more than adequately prepared for an attack that could come at any time? Perhaps that would deter Edward from thinking he would prevail. Perhaps it would keep him away.

Ric knew the latter was the wrong choice. Edward would want to prove that he could defeat them as violently as possible. Defeating a strong clan would only make him appear more powerful. Ric prayed that telling the king that the MacLellans were an easy target would fool the king into sending a smaller force that the clan could easily overcome. He could not risk another raid like the one that had killed his mother and changed his life forever. He wrestled with the dilemma night after night until he decided he would only know what to do when the moment came, and the words tumbled from his mouth.

When dawn broke on the morning that he was to depart, Ric found he was in no hurry. He wished he could stay longer, and he wanted to visit more with his mother's cousin. She had shared stories about his mother that he had never imagined. Emelyn and Emelote were only a month apart in age, and they were inseparable. They grew up in a lesser house of the MacLellan clan, but it was in a strategic location. Emelyn's father arranged a marriage with the previous laird, William, and Emelote came with Emelyn. Hallam Hartley was wounded during a battle not far from Kirkcudbright. He was taken prisoner by the laird, and Emelote was charged with healing him enough for William to learn the English's battle plans. Emelote was a skilled healer, and Hallam was soon well enough to move about.

During his recovery, he and Emelote spent a great deal of time talking, and it was not long before they realized they were in love. Hallam renounced his fealty and sent his ring and his surcoat back to King Edward. He swore never to lift a sword against the English, but neither would he fight for them. He spent his time much as Ric had, training the Scots to anticipate and counter the English tactics. Hallam died in a skirmish against another clan that sided with the English. He had not killed any Englishmen, but he had still killed Scots.

Ric and Robbie stood in the bailey as Rosalind ensured enough food was given to them, and Emelyn embraced Ric.

"Your squire is not half bad. If he decides he'd

like to remain in Scotland, then he can make his home here if he likes. He will be a fine addition." Malcolm cracked one of his rare smiles as he looked past Ric to a beaming Robbie. He clasped forearms with Ric, and they shared a hearty shake before both relented and embraced.

"You are welcome here, Cousin," Malcolm whispered.

"Thank you, Cousin. Until we meet again."

Emelyn stepped forward for one more quick embrace and a peck on Ric's cheek before he and Robbie mounted and rode out of the bailey.

"Do you think we will receive such a warm welcome in the Bruce's home?" Robbie's dry humor made Ric grin.

"I doubt it. I would be sure to have your doublet on. It'll keep the pinpricks from the swords pointed at us from breaking the skin."

"And how soon do you believe Lady Bella will find you?"

"Before I reach the castle, I would guess. She'll already have a network of spies in place for her. Mostly lads your age who are too taken with her and will do her bidding."

"You needn't worry about me falling in that category. The woman makes my skin crawl."

"I wish I had been as wise as you all those years ago."

They chatted off and on throughout the four days it took them to ride from Kirkcudbright to Stirling. They took turns at watch during the night and were back on the road as the first pinks and purples touched the horizon. They arrived only half as tired and dirty as they had at Kirkcudbright. Robbie remained silent, and Ric spoke in low tones as he acquired a room along with two meals and baths at the inn just within the city walls. This time when a knock came at the door, Ric was prepared to see Bella.

"Took you long enough," Bella's tone was decidedly frostier than it had been during their last two encounters. The woman had not forgiven him for manhandling and humiliating her. He knew there would be a pound of flesh to pay before she warmed to him again. As long as she did nothing to sabotage him, Ric preferred the distance.

"I had plenty to observe and learn. Besides, I needed them to warm to me enough to receive a missive to the king vouching for me. It's not as though they will open their arms to an English knight."

"And just what did you learn?"

"They were not what I expected," Ric tested. He had no idea how soon after her removal from the keep she made her way to Stirling. He would approach his lies slowly, so he could retract them if it seemed she knew more than he presumed.

"And how is that? Not the heathens you thought."

"Most assuredly not. They were very welcoming to me."

"That's nice. Now to the point, please."

"That is part of the point. They welcomed me and after being shown about, I was given free roam." Bella's ears perked up as she leaned toward him, but this time it was to listen rather than seduce. "I watched them train and saw their armory."

Bella nodded as she waited for him to continue.

"As I said, it was not what I expected. Their level of training and preparedness came as a surprise."

"To the point, Ric."

"I thought you would see my point already. They aren't like the Kerrs and Elliots."

"That's fortunate since they trounced Edward's last campaign. Your last campaign."

Ric nodded as he took in Bella's comment. She assumed he meant they were less prepared. She had jumped to that conclusion with little pressure from him, and he was relieved. Perhaps he could mislead her without actually speaking any lies.

"They definitely wouldn't conduct a fight like their eastern neighbors." Because their eastern neighbors didn't have an English knight to share all the battle strategies and formations that the mounted knights and foot soldiers used.

"Edward will be happy to receive this news. Surely, he will want a win, and if the western clans are the ones to allow him further inroads into Scotland, then your time with your family will be a success." Bella turned back to the door but paused before opening it. "However, I'm sure it will be your head if you're mistaken."

She slipped through the doorway before Ric could say anything, and he realized he had nothing more to say. She had made her own assumptions, and he was content to let her share them with her band of messengers. A perverse part of him hoped that Edward marched his troops to Malcolm's door. It would shock them to encounter a well-trained force that had strategies to counter each of the English moves. Dedric did not want any of his family harmed, but he was finding he understood how his father switched allegiances.

FOUR

Another morning approached. It was still dark in the chamber, and Robbie's light snores told Ric that he, too, should still be asleep. He could feel the butterflies flapping in his belly as he mentally prepared himself for arriving at the castle. He was just as nervous as he had been in his first battle. He had been a squire for six years before he earned his spurs, but he had never been allowed in an actual battle. The first time he experienced the sweat and grime along with the noise, he had been sure he would be ill. He was nearly certain he could never do it again, but the next morning dawned just as this one had, and he rode back into battle. He shut his eyes as he pictured how he would approach the gate and how he would request an audience with Robert the Bruce. He knew the truth of his family's past was what would grant him any chance. Without his history and that of his parents, there was no reason to believe him. He just prayed he could retell it without his nerves showing. That would only make him look suspicious and cagey.

Ric rolled over and gained a couple more hours of sleep before Robbie was moving about the chamber. The young man was efficient, setting out a plain green surcoat that was well tailored, with embroidery at the cuffs and hem and intricate stitching across the entire front. It showed that Ric was a man of some means, but the lack of insignia indicated that he was not a man of consequence. Robbie assisted him with his boots before he gathered the few things that needed returning to his satchel.

They broke their fast in the tavern dining room, and Ric spent the time listening to the conversations going on around him. The accents had grown much thicker as they progressed north, and some patrons even spoke Gaelic. There were only a few people he could understand. One of whom was a barmaid who flirted with him as she brought two bowls of porridge to their table.

"Ye don't strike me as a Scot, even one from the Lowlands," her lilting tones hinted at a burr. Ric shook his head and quickly shoveled a spoonful into his mouth. "Where might ye be heading?"

"Court," he mumbled as he stuffed a chunk of bread in after the porridge.

"Aye, well it's market day today, so there will be plenty of outsiders and foreigners milling aboot. Ye won't be the only ones." She smiled, and Ric noticed several of her teeth were chipped, but she had a pretty enough face and an ample bosom he had caught Robbie staring at more than once.

"When does the market open?" he asked around the food he still chewed. He knew Eleanor would be aghast, as would Emelyn, to see him speaking with his mouth full, but it disguised his voice better.

"It already has. The gates open at sunrise for the vendors to wheel their carts in. People will begin trickling in within the next hour or so."

"Thank you." Ric placed a few coins on the table and nudged Robbie, who had devoured his own bowl and one he snagged from another woman walking by.

They stepped into the morning mist and looked about as the sounds of the market filled the air. They decided to leave their horses at the inn; they would scout the town on foot as inconspicuously as they could. They moved past the food vendors into the millinery goods, and Ric was ready to turn toward the weapons stalls when a head of the fairest blonde hair he had ever seen caught his eye. It was nearly white as it shone in the sunlight that kept breaking through the clouds. He paused and watched as its owner haggled with a vendor. The man in the stall said something that annoyed her, because he watched a woman who could have passed for a country maid transform into a regal lady-in-waiting. He had met enough of them in Edward's court to recognize one. The young woman's chin went up while her back went stiff. The expression on her face had gone from an easy and jovial smile to an imperious one, with a blonde eyebrow cocked in challenge. Ric inched forward to hear their conversation, listening to a tone that sounded refined but obviously irritated.

"I understand you have mouths to feed and children to clothe, but I also know that your family is far from starving. I saw your children pinching apples, figs, and even a loaf of bread earlier, and your wife's booth with the ribbons is entertaining half the ladies-in-waiting. You will not perish." She paused and inched her chin higher. "Unless you refuse to honor the deal we struck last week. We agreed to three shillings for the smaller illuminaries and five shillings for the larger ones."

"That's robbery, my lady."

"That's what we agreed upon. If you couldn't afford it, then you shouldn't have shaken on it. If you don't want my work, then I will find a vendor who does."

"Ye won't find anyone to pay as much as ye're asking."

"I will, and we both know it."

"Nay, my lady. Not as a woman, ye won't."

"And now we come to the real reason you won't pay what was agreed upon. You believe to filch from me the money these are worth and then resell them at twice what you are willing to pay me. Because I am a woman. Perhaps I will find my own mon to set up a cart for me, right next to yours, and sell the vellums directly. I pay him a portion of my earnings, and I come out well ahead." Ric was now close enough to hear everything that was said between the two, and he watched as the woman tapped a long, well-manicured finger against her chin. "Hmm. I'm so happy we talked, mercer. You have given me a glorious idea."

The vellums that had been spread across the makeshift counter were quickly and efficiently rolled and a ribbon tied around them. The woman began to back away, but the man reached out, catching himself before actually touching. Her eyebrow twitched, but she waited.

"Nay, my lady. There is no need for that. I only needed my memory jogged. It was three shillings for the smaller ones and five for the larger ones."

"It was, mercer. But now it isn't. I've realized that having my own stall will be far better for me."

"But I depend upon yer work, my lady. It is a favorite among the other members of court."

"I'm aware. That's how I know that I will do very well with a cart of my own."

"But ye won't be able to get one. Ye must have a

mon to purchase a stall and to run it. Ye certainly can't be seen."

"I was resourceful enough to find you. If you truly want these, I've reconsidered my prices. I must make it worth the effort I would otherwise spend setting up that cart. The larger ones are now eight shillings, and the smaller ones are five."

"That's robbery, my lady."

"You've said that already. I will be on my way."

"My lady," the vendor had sweat trickling along his temples that he attempted to mop away with his sleeve. His face had grown red as the woman's mind ran laps around his. "I can't afford that."

"And I can't afford less. Not now that I'll be opening my own stall. Good day, sir."

The vendor attempted one last tactic as he narrowed his eyes. "Yer secret will be out the moment ye open that cart."

The woman had turned away, but at the threat, she turned back and leaned forward, so only the man and Ric could hear.

"I only have one blind eye." The woman looked to three children who ran toward the stall, and the man's flushed face lost all its color.

"Ye would threaten my children?"

"I don't recall doing that."

"Ye're blackmailing me," he hissed.

"No more than you are me. Now do we have a deal or not? I shall freckle if I remain out here much longer." Her imperious voice once more back in place, reminding the man of her status.

"Ye win, my lady." The man handed a purse over as the woman handed him the parchments.

"Thank you. Until next time, neighbor." The woman had the audacity to wink while the man spluttered.

She walked away with the poise and grace that set her apart as a lady-in-waiting. Ric watched her as she lifted her hood and tucked her hair back underneath it. Something urged him to follow her as she blended into the crowd. He assumed Robbie would keep up or know to meet him back at the stables. He followed the hood until it suddenly disappeared. Ric pushed through the crowd until he nearly stumbled over the woman as she bent over to hand several of her hard-earned coins to children who clearly needed food. Their hollow cheeks and sallow skin spoke of their situation.

"Thank ye, my lady. If ye didn't find us each week, my sisters and I wouldn't eat. We would have starved by now." The oldest boy spoke as he held three younger girls against his side.

"I know, love. That's why I do it. Be careful not to have anyone nick the coins from you."

Ric was mesmerized as she used a handkerchief to wipe away snot that ran down the youngest one's nose and lip. When she was done, she folded it over and stuffed it into a hidden pocket. "Watch out for one another."

The woman moved on, but Ric was struck by the children. He knew what it was to be an orphan, and he suspected these children were the same. Had he not been taken, he would have been raised in the keep alongside his cousin. But he also knew that had the king's whim changed, there would have been little difference between him and the four children standing before him. He looked back over his shoulder at Robbie.

"Take them to wash their hands and faces, then take them to the inn for a proper meal. See if the innkeeper will hire them for any odd jobs. The little one may be too young, but the other three should be able to do something." Ric spoke softly lest his voice travel.

"You want me to speak?" Robbie murmured.

"You've heard enough people speak to pretend to sound like them, or use your French accent." Robbie nodded, and Ric handed him several coins. The children stood wide-eyed as the two men discussed them, then they followed Robbie, only looking back at Ric twice.

"That was very kind of you."

Ric was unprepared for the woman to be standing at his side when he stood up. Her hood was still covering her head, but he noticed she was tall for a woman, even a willowy one. She tilted her head back just enough for him to see eyes that were a mixture of green and gray, reminding him of Italian marble he had seen while traveling with Edward in Europe. She did have a smattering of freckles across her nose, but the shadow of her hood hid her cheeks.

"No more so than you, my lady."

"English." It was not an accusation but more an observation.

"Yes, my lady. But only half."

Her eyes raked over him, and he felt a heat surge through him that began in his bollocks. It was not a seductive or provocative gaze—at least Ric was sure she did not intend it to be—but he prayed his cock would desist before she saw far more than she intended. Fortunately, her eyes returned to his before he made a fool of himself. "Which half?"

Ric cleared his throat and blinked several times before he realized she meant which half of his family, and not which half of him. "My father."

Ric watched her eyes shutter as she nodded and prepared to turn away. He suspected she believed his father had been an English knight who raped his Scottish mother. He could not let her leave with that misperception. He felt compelled to make sure she understood.

"My father married into the MacLellan clan. They lived there until they both died."

"My condolences. Is that why you sound English? Even though you were raised in Scotland."

"I wasn't raised here, my lady. Unfortunately, that was not a choice given to me. I was taken to England where I was raised."

She gasped, and a look of sympathy pushed away the distaste. "Your father's family took you from your home."

"No, my lady. That's not it either. I don't know much about my father's family. He had a brother, but he left to fight the Saracens, and I know not whether he ever returned." Ric was entering dangerous water confessing so much about himself before having an audience with the king. He needed to steer the conversation back to safer ground.

"An English knight in Scotland is a mon who doesn't plan to live long. You had better conduct your business and speak as little as you can." The woman looked up at the castle and then at the sun. "I must be on my way. Thank you for what you did for those children. I surmise you realized they are orphans. If they can find work, then they may survive the winter. I wish I had thought to do as you sent your squire to do."

"You couldn't have taken them to an inn, my lady. It's not for lack of care on your part. We all have limitations, some placed upon us." Ric watched as she scanned the crowd, her gaze finally resting on the group of ladies-in-waiting he noticed earlier. "May I ask your name, my lady?"

"Isabella Dunbar," and with that, she blended into the crowd, and Ric watched her go. She had not asked for his name in return, but neither had she refused to give hers.

FIVE

R ic returned to the inn to find Robbie had secured the children's employment, and the innkeeper's wife took pity on the youngest child. The couple had not been able to have children of their own, and Ric was struck by the kindness they both showed the children. He suspected they would treat the children well, and that their kindness was not just a display.

He and Robbie retrieved their horses and walked through the town until they reached the gates of Stirling Castle. Unlike the city gates, these were closed to anyone who did not have a purpose within the castle grounds.

"State your business," a guard demanded.

Ric knew this would be the first test of many within the next few hours. "Sir Dedric Hartley sent with a letter of voucher from Laird Malcolm Mac-Lellan, my cousin. I am here to hire out my services as a knight."

"English."

"Half."

"Which half?"

This time Ric knew the question did not refer to his parents. "The half that doesn't like bannocks or haggis." Ric and Robbie waited a long moment before the guard grunted and stepped aside.

"We don't have knights in Scotland. We have men."

Ric nodded and shuffled Robbie through the gate and toward the stables.

"Now what?" Robbie asked.

"I'm not sure. We shall see if I can get an audience with the king."

"What would you have me do while you attempt that?"

"See what you can find out but keep quiet. I heard your attempt at a Scottish accent. It was miserable. Muck out stalls if you have to, but keep your ears open and your gob shut."

Ric turned toward the castle, but not without a glance over his shoulder. Robbie was leading their horses into the stables. He made his way inside with little trouble until he arrived at the king's solar. There was a line of men waiting outside, and no one seemed in a hurry to call them within. Ric stood for nearly two hours before the doors opened and a thin man with a booming voice announced the king was finished with his audience, and that they would have to return tomorrow. Ric had no intention of waiting until the next day. If he did, it meant another night at the inn. After what he gave the children, he did not have enough to spend on another night if he and Robbie could find accommodations here, even if they were in the barracks. The men lingering in the hallway filed past him, but he stood rooted in his place.

"I said the king was not holding any further audiences until tomorrow. Be on your way," the man sniffed.

"Since I have nowhere else to be, I shall wait. Perhaps the king shall find he has time after all."

"English."

Ric was becoming tired of how "English" was always an accusation and never an observation. Except for Isabella Dunbar. She had not meant it derisively, but curiously.

"My father was English, and my mother was the cousin of Lady Emelyn MacLellan. I am the son of Hallam Hartley and Emelote MacLellan Hartley."

"Hartley, you say?" The man inched closer as though frightened that Ric would attack. "You have the look of him."

"You knew my father?" Ric was stunned.

"Not well, mind you. But he was presented at court shortly after marrying your mother. The king wanted to meet the English knight who renounced his king for a Scottish lass."

"Then you might understand why I have returned to Scotland after being kept away for so long."

"What does that have to do with the king? You haven't been summoned."

"That is true. I doubt he knows of me. I have left England behind, but that doesn't mean I have left my skills there. I bear a voucher of confidence from my cousin, Laird Malcolm MacLellan. I would offer my sword to the king. The rightful king."

Ric found it was not as difficult to acknowledge Robert the Bruce as king of Scotland now that he had been here for more than a fortnight. Before arriving in Scotland, he had not cared whether Robert had a legitimate claim to the throne. He had only cared about the missions and the battles and staying alive. Now, with distance from King Edward, he admitted to himself that the man who demanded his fealty was a man he detested and no longer feared. Distance did not make the heart grow fonder, at least not Ric's.

"Wait here." The man banged upon the door, and it opened immediately.

It was nearly another hour before Ric was finally admitted. He looked around the solar, surprised at how small it was compared to the chambers Edward selected for his throne. The chamber was barely larger than Malcolm's solar, but had a similar oblong wooden table in the center with parchments strewn across it. A man with russet hair sat at the head with a crown slightly askew as he reviewed the document before him.

"Sire, may I present Sir Hallam Hartley." The man from the passageway stepped forward. Ric bent his knee and lowered his head as he heard the king lay the vellum on the table.

"Rise."

"Your Majesty, if I may, I'm Sir Dedric Hartley. Sir Hallam's son."

King Robert scowled first at him for speaking out of turn, then at his advisor for the incorrect introduction. "The resemblance is strong. I suppose I can see the confusion, though your father would have been close to my age." Ric did not move, knowing from years with Edward that Robert's comments were not meant to draw a response. "What brings you to my court?" King Robert wasted no time with formalities.

"My tenure as a knight is done, and I chose to return to my home."

"Tenure as whose knight and what home? If I recall correctly, your father died fighting another clan on behalf of the MacLellan, and your mother died a few years later during a raid led by the English."

Ric forced his face to remain neutral when he wanted to grimace. "I was taken from my home during that raid and handed over to King Edward. I served as a page, then became a squire to one of his knights before earning my own spurs. I was indebted to the king and forced to swear my oath. I have served my time and do not wish to remain with the man who ruined my life." Ric found each word was true, and the bitterness that crept into his voice was not forced. He did not wish to return to Edward, and dreaded the day when he would have to.

"And so you thought to appear before me." The king's voice remained impassive as he cast an assessing eye over Ric from the top of his head to the tip of his boots.

"I have been to my mother's people and spent a fortnight with them; however, I would not wear out my welcome."

"They are your family. How could you not be welcome?"

Ric recognized the test and knew that King Robert had spent time in King Edward's service, too. Ric had been too young to know there would be any significance to that connection. It was the type of question Edward would have asked. "I have been away most of my life. To appear and expect the laird's family and clan to house me and feed me simply because my mother was one of them seems rather brazen and presumptuous."

"So you appear here instead, and expect my household to house you and feed you." It was not a question.

"I request a position among your guardsmen. I bear a missive from Laird Malcolm attesting to my time spent training his warriors and the knowledge I can offer."

"And why would you do that?"

"The English king killed my family and ruined my life. I thought to say thank you." Ric's bitterness was genuine and caused King Robert to stare harder.

"How long do you intend to remain in my employ? Do you intend to swear your loyalty to me? Did you not once do that to Edward?"

"I swore it out of compulsion, whereas I would swear mine to you out of choice. I will remain as long as I am useful, but I would ask for a piece of land that I might retire to afterward. I would like to have a home where I can live in peace."

"Peace?" The king's laugh held no mirth. "And just where would you plan to find that? Why not return to the MacLellans?"

"I would not ask my cousin to share his land with me. I have no right to inheritance, and I do not presume to believe I will have an unlimited invitation to stay."

"But you are family. You are one of the Mac-Lellans."

Ric shrugged. "If Malcolm sees fit to offer me something, then I shall be thankful. Perhaps I will need to prove myself first."

"And that is where I come in." Ric did not speak. It was a comment not a question, and Ric had learned long ago that one only spoke when spoken to when it came to conversations with sovereigns. "Are you prepared to swear your oath today?"

"I am prepared to serve you at your leisure, Your Majesty."

"Hmmm." The king looked him over once more, noticing the evasion. "Mayhap I will test you out and then decide whether I wish to keep you."

Ric felt like a horse about to be put through its paces, but if it offered him the opportunity to stay, then he would not look a gift horse in the mouth. "Thank you, Your Majesty."

"Don't thank me quite yet. You may join the court for the evening meal." The king returned his attention to the documents before him, and Ric bowed, knowing he had been dismissed. To be included in the evening meal meant that Ric was being treated with the deference of a knight and would not be spending the night sleeping in the barracks with the regular guardsmen. He would need to find Robbie and then the chamber he would be assigned.

It took Ric the better part of half an hour to track his squire down, finally finding him flirting with a servant near the doors to the kitchen. The young woman looked to be the same age as Robbie, and Ric could not help but smile as he remembered being that age. He had discovered women later than some of his counterparts, but he soon realized that they had noticed him for quite some time. It was the sour experience with Bella that taught Ric to keep his attachments short and inconsequential.

As he reminded himself of that, a flash of white-blonde hair passed through his mind, and he pictured the woman from the market with the haughty and expressive eyebrow who had blackmailed the merchant so she could give part of her money to the orphans. As quickly as she came to mind, he pushed her aside. He did not dally with virgins, which she undoubtedly was or was supposed to be, and he did not dally with ladies-in-waiting. He kept his interludes to widows. He did not want to catch the pox, so he only accepted certain services from tavern whores. He did not pursue married women no matter how unhappy their marriage, even if the marriage was in name only. He did not want to wake up at the end of an angry husband's sword.

"Squire," he called out. Robbie scrambled away from the wall, but not before he whispered something that made the woman blush and smile. The squire jogged over to Ric and the two went back into the keep.

"I have been included in the evening meal, which means a chamber within the keep. I would like to find the chamber and then conveniently get lost in the passageways to see if I can learn aught."

"I learned guards change four times each night, and the southern wall is the least watched since it is the hardest to attack. I know that there are guards posted throughout the keep at night, but primarily along any approach to the king and queen's chambers. I know that the guards, along with everyone else but the servants, are expected to attend Mass each morning before considering breaking their fast."

"And just how do you know so much?"

"Millie told me."

"The servant?"

"She works in the buttery."

"She seemed to have told you things that are only useful if you are planning an assignation."

"Or murdering," Robbie mouthed the second word, "the king."

Ric sent him a quelling look, but he had to admit that his squire, while planning a romp with the pretty maid, had learned more than he had. They found the seneschal and were shown their chamber. Robbie set to work brushing and airing out the formal sur-coat Ric would be required to wear to the evening meal. Ric made use of the pitcher of water and the soap as he refreshed himself, then departed for his exploration of the castle. He kept to the shadows in the passageways and ducked into more than one alcove when he heard footsteps or voices, once stumbling upon a couple in the midst of a tryst. He slipped out of the alcove as quickly as he entered, but not before he received an eyeful of a lovely breast and an ample backside.

Lucky bastard. Perhaps I will find a widow after all. It has been far too long, and my hand is far from satisfying.

As the thought crossed his mind, the blonde woman once more floated back to the surface.

Why do I keep thinking of her? She was intriguing, but I doubt I will see much more of her.

Ric inched a door open and peered within another chamber. He could hear soft voices, but he could not see anyone within what looked like a scriptorium. He peered back over his shoulder and eased into the room, pressing the door closed silently. He listened for the direction in which the voices came. He crept toward the Mary altar with candles flickering in the draft of air his entry created. The eyes painted on the icons of long-dead saints seemed to follow him as he moved closer to the wall that divided the chamber where he stood from wherever the conversation was taking place.

"The king is still trying to discover what happened to Elizabeth Fraser's carriage. Hopefully the last snow has fallen, and spring has taken hold. He and his brother sent men out to recover it, but there was little left after sitting exposed during the entire winter. They found the broken axle." A man's muffled voice carried through the thin partition wall. It was made of wood but was little more than a screen. Ric realized the chamber he was in had been divided at some point, and the wooden partition had been placed rather than summoning a mason to install a stone wall.

"You had better hope they don't find aught else that can tie that crash back to either of us." A second man's voice, more strident than the first, came through the partition clearly. Ric smirked at the irony that the man who was more concerned about being caught would not be concerned enough to keep his voice down.

"Shh. You know the walls in this part of the keep are not stone. Someone will hear you."

Ric's smirk widened as the first man read his mind.

"No one but that featherbrained Dunbar lass comes around here. And I know the ladies are with the queen in the royal antechamber."

Ric's smirk slipped when he heard the surname he recognized from earlier that day. He was aggravated by the lady's description, suspecting it was the same woman he met in the market.

"Don't underestimate Isabella. She may be focused on her pet projects that the queen allows her to entertain, but she is astute. And beyond that, her clan is ever loyal to the king. She would not hesitate to hear that someone plotted to kill the king's brother's bride. We may want Edward Bruce to return to Ireland, but we don't want the king to know we have a hand in it."

The voices moved away, and Ric was left wondering what the men meant. Last he had heard, the Scottish king's younger brother was still in Ireland and had not left in over a year. The conversation made it seem as though the man was married and living in Scotland.

"The king has two brothers named Edward. One by blood and one his family took in."

Ric's head jerked up as he recognized the hushed voice. Ric whispered, "Lady Isabella?"

"Yes. We seem to have caught each other where neither of us should be."

Ric watched as the figure materialized from a shadow nearly within arm's length of where he stood. As she stepped closer, he caught a waft of her honeysuckle scent, and he wondered how he could have missed it when it seemed to fill the chamber now. She put her finger to her lips and stepped beside him, pointing to the wall. She used the same finger to point to a notch in the wood that was hollow. She touched her eye and then pointed to the notch again. Ric leaned forward, but the other chamber was empty. He leaned away, but Isabella shook her head and pointed again, angling her finger. Ric looked once more in time to see two men leaving the chamber next door. He did not know who either of them were, but he had a memory for faces.

"What are you doing in here?" Isabella demanded, their conspiratorial time suddenly over.

"I wandered in here because I thought I smelled incense." Which he did, now that he looked around once more. "I thought perhaps I'd found the chapel."

Isabella narrowed her eyes before nodding. "You are in the wrong wing of the castle. But I meant what are you doing inside the keep?"

"The king invited me."

Isabella's green-gray eyes swept over him, assessing him, just as they had in the market. And just as before, Ric's body responded. This time, he was thankful that they remained in the shadows, because his body refused to listen when he told it to relax. It was not just Isabella's eyes and pale hair that caught his attention. It was her plump lower lip that he found himself suddenly craving to nibble. He wanted a better view of the gown that was cut modestly but gave him an enticing hint of a bosom that did not seem to match her willowy frame.

"Why are you staring at me?" Isabella asked bluntly.

"I was wondering the same about you."

"But I asked first."

"So it wasn't just the merchant that you're testy with."

"I know you heard most of my conversation with the mon, but there was little I could do to shoo you away, lest I bring more attention to my negotiation."

"Shoo me? I'm rather large to be treated like a gnat."

Once again, Isabella's eyes raked over him, and Ric's cock twitched. He was thankful that his surcoat hung to his mid-thigh and was loose over his bulge, or he was sure Isabella would be questioning that too. "Too large to be inconspicuous, certainly. Please excuse me. I came to gather something I left here earlier."

Ric's hand caught her waist as he moved to block her. A current raced up his arm, and Isabella's gasp told him she felt the same. Their eyes locked as Ric's hand tightened slightly, and she turned more toward him. "Isa, it's dangerous to be moving about the castle alone, to be in chambers like this alone. What if those men had heard you and came to investigate? What if some other man found you here alone?"

Isabella's eyes flared at the shortening of her name, but she had to admit that she preferred it to the usual diminutive.

"That's not my name," she breathed. "People call me Bella."

Ric stepped back, letting go of her when he heard that name. He shook his head, refusing to associate the name of the repugnant woman he could not seem to escape with a woman whose honeysuckle scent was drawing him in like a drunken bee. "I know someone I do not care for, and her name is Bella. I could never think of you as such."

Isabella's mouth formed a perfect circle, shocked that he mentioned a woman she could only assume was a former lover and that he said he thought of her.

"I like Isa better," she murmured. "It's less pressure."

Ric stepped back toward her, and his knees brushed against her skirts. "I understand why people would call you that. The name suits you. I just don't want to think of someone else when I'm looking at you."

"I don't even know your name. We shouldn't have spoken in the market and certainly not here. We haven't been introduced."

Ric grinned as her sense of propriety tried to gain a foothold, but she did not push him away or try to move past him. "Dedric Hartley, but those who know me best call me Ric."

"Sir Dedric," Isabella spoke as if she was testing out the name on her tongue.

"It's Ric, Isa." Ric wondered if she heard the same beseeching need in his voice as he did.

She nodded, then shook her head. "But I don't know you at all, so how can I be someone who knows you best?"

Ric shrugged as his hand reached for her waist again. "That's what I want you to call me," he admitted.

"Ric," she exhaled.

"Isa."

Ric watched as her pupils dilated, and he recognized the look in her eyes as he was sure she saw the same thing in his. He knew he should pull away, leave her where he found her, and mind his own business—which was spying on the king—but none of that was as strong as the pull he felt bringing him closer to her. He slid his arm around Isa's waist, and she stepped into his embrace.

"You shouldn't be here alone," Ric said for a second time.

"I know. I can never be sure who I might encounter." Isa placed her hands on his arms and gasped as the muscles jumped under her touch. She looked down at where her hands rested before looking back into Ric's topaz eyes. She felt herself falling into the depths of the golden starbursts that ringed his pupil, and the tip of her tongue pressed between her lips.

"Promise me you won't do this again. Even if you've done so since long before I arrived. Isa, it makes me frightened for you."

"You, frightened?" She attempted to scoff, but her voice caught as his sincerity registered.

"Yes. I find the idea of you coming to harm bothers me more than I can justify."

Isa slid her hands up his arms, feeling her fingers wrap around his biceps before reaching his shoulders. "I don't understand what's happening, but I feel as though I couldn't walk away even if I wanted to," Isa admitted.

"Has no man ever held you like this? Made you aware of how badly he wants to kiss you?"

Isa shook her head before responding. "No mon has ever dared. My father has not always been in the king's good graces."

"Knowing I am the only man who has held you in his arms brings me a happiness I know I have no right to possess." Ric lifted her chin and looked into her eyes, his question clear. Isa gave the barest nod before mouthing the word "please."

Ric went slowly, as much to savor the moment he knew he could never repeat and so as not to frighten her. He brushed his lips against hers as their noses rubbed. She lifted her chin further, and their lips pressed together. Ric pulled away before diving in, over and over, until Isa's fingers clutched the material at his shoulders. He swept his tongue over the seam of her lips, and when she gasped at the sinful feel, he slid his tongue into her mouth. Her moan began as another gasp of surprise but quickly melted into a sound of pure pleasure. She opened wider as the feel of Ric's tongue grazing along hers lit a fire in her belly that she had never felt before.

A restlessness settled over her, and she pressed against Ric, feeling the bulge resting at the juncture of her thighs. She understood what it was, and it only increased a need she did not know how to control. She moaned again, and Ric pressed her body more tightly against his, and her arms wrapped around his neck as the kiss deepened.

When both of them could not last any longer without drawing air into their lungs, Ric scorched a trail of kisses along her jaw until he reached the spot behind her ear that made her shiver. She ran her fingers through his jet-black locks as the other hand clutched his shoulder. She twisted her head, bringing their lips back together. Ric's own groan elicited a sigh from Isa as his hands cupped her backside. He backed them against the partition, pressing them into the shadows in which they both had hidden.

"Isa, we should stop."

"I know." But it was her turn to kiss along his throat as she nuzzled the stubble on his jaw.

"Isa, my beard shall leave marks, and people will know what you have been doing."

This made her pull away long enough to search for something in his eyes. Whatever it was, Ric was not sure if she was relieved because she found it, or perhaps she was happy it was not there. Either way, she pulled his head back down to hers.

"One more, please."

Ric groaned again as the heat burst into a roaring fire between them. He chanted to himself that she was a virgin, that she had never even been kissed before. It was the only thing that kept him from hiking her skirts up and delving his fingers into her sheath. He was sure they would be coated with her dew as she pressed her mons against his rod. Isa finally pulled away and pressed her fingers against her lips. She shook her head slightly before her eyes drifted closed for a long heartbeat.

"I don't know if thank you is the right thing to say, but I feel like I should." She swept a lock of Ric's hair from his forehead and tucked it back with the other ones. "I may never experience passion like that again. I'm grateful to have done so at least once before I'm married off."

Ric froze as his heart lurched to a stop. The idea of any man, especially a husband who had rights to Isa, touching her built a different fire in his belly. It was one of fury, jealousy, and possessiveness. While he had experienced each emotion independently, he had never experienced such a scalding mixture.

"Are you betrothed?" he spit out. Isa eye's opened so wide, Ric was sure he could see every inch of white. She shook her head furiously.

"No. Not even remotely. I would never kiss a mon if I'm promised to another. I just meant in the future. At some point. My father will have to marry me to someone. I'm not expecting it to be anyone I desire. It may not be anyone I even know. He will most likely be far aulder than I am and nowhere nearly as handsome as you." Isa slammed her mouth shut as she rambled a confession she should have kept to herself.

"Handsome," Ric growled as he pulled her in for another kiss. This one was different. It was not the gentle exploration that the first kiss had begun as, or even the passionate one it turned into. This was a kiss meant to brand Isa as his, but as much as he attempted to leave his mark on her soul, she did the same to him.

"Yes, handsome. More so than any mon I have ever met," she panted before tugging at his surcoat and pulling him back for another kiss. "What are you doing to me, Ric? I never imagined that men and women could kiss like this, and yet I cannot seem to stop."

"I could ask the same of you. You make me lose control, Isa."

"I know I shouldn't say this, I shouldn't even think of it, but part of me wishes we could both lose control."

"You don't know what you're saying. Isa, do you know what happens between a man and a woman? How their bodies can join?"

"Of course. I grew up in a large keep. It was impossible not to stumble upon people, and many have no discretion at court. What I haven't seen, I have heard the aulder women discuss."

"Then perhaps you can imagine what I want to do to you, with you."

"I can. I'm imagining the same thing."

"Isa," Ric hissed. "We must go. Now."

He took her hand and turned to the door, adjusting himself and relieved she could not see him. He opened the door a crack and looked both ways before sliding out and pausing. When he did not see or hear anything, he pulled Isa into the passageway.

"Which way to the ladies' quarters?"

Isa pointed, and they slipped along the shadows until they reached the corner that led to where Isa's chamber was situated amongst those of the other young women. Ric cupped her cheek and gave her a brief kiss on the forehead before brushing his lips against hers, much the way their initial kiss started. He spun on his heels and made his way to the stairs they had just climbed. He looked back and caught Isa doing the same as she rushed down the passageway. He waited until she reached her door before going inside.

SIX

Isa sat among the ladies-in-waiting, but her mind felt like a hummingbird that flew from one idea to the next, never settling long enough to slow down. She thought about her encounter with Ric in the market, which made her think of the other illuminated manuscripts she needed to finish, then it dashed from their tryst to what she would do if anyone, particularly her parents, discovered what they had done.

Then it danced back to the tryst and settled there until she noticed the hum of voices grow around her, and she turned to follow the other ladies' stares. Her stomach went concave, but she did not utter a sound. She listened to the young women around her ooh and ah over the man she had been tucked away kissing only a couple hours earlier. Isa listened as the ladies speculated about who he was and why he was suddenly at court. She kept her mouth shut and tried to make her interest match the others without giving anything away.

After the meal, the tables were cleared away, and the musicians began to play. Isa joined the other ladies-in-waiting as they lined up for the first dance. It was one that would force her to change partners several times before finally settling with one. She knew who she wished she could partner with, but there was little chance. Instead, she would have to hear later from the other ladies who did end up dancing with Ric. She went through the motions but kept her eyes averted, appearing to be concentrating on the music, but really it was to keep her disappointment from showing.

"Will you not look at me now that I've managed to partner with you?" Ric murmured by Isa's ear. She turned her head and their mouths nearly touched.

"How did you?" She could not offer a complete thought as her eyes glanced over the couples near them and noticed that none seemed to be paying attention to them.

"I recognized the tune and counted the positions until I was sure I would be matched with you once the changes were done."

"You did?"

"Were you hoping for someone else, Isa? Did I take you away from someone you'd rather partner with?" Ric did not want to hear the answers to those questions if they were what he feared, but her quick denial reassured him.

"No. No. There's no one else. I just am surprised you would put such effort into dancing with me."

"Isa, I don't want to see you dancing with another man. I admit the idea of seeing another man touch you after this afternoon—" Ric shrugged. "It would be too soon."

"I didn't like hearing the other ladies talk aboot you when you entered. I don't want to hear any of them discussing what it feels like to be in your arms."

"Then we are much in the same way." Ric looked at her cheeks and chin and wanted to run the pad of his thumb over her skin where there was still a hint of pink from where his stubble had rubbed against her skin.

"It still prickles," she murmured. Ric's arm tightened slightly and pulled her closer, but he was careful to remain within the bounds of propriety. He would not be accused his first night of mauling a lady-in-waiting, even if that was what he had been doing earlier that afternoon. "Ric? Are you—are you thinking aboot this afternoon?"

"How could I not? Your chin may still prickle, but my fingers have itched to touch you ever since the moment we parted."

Isa had several more questions, but she kept them to herself. She had only met the man that afternoon, and she had allowed him to kiss her in ways she never knew existed, and the desire he lit within her still made her body ache with unspent lust. But there was something more about him that drew her. She was aware that there could never be anything more between them than that afternoon and perhaps a few more dances; after all, she was the daughter of a border laird who was a staunch supporter of the Scottish king. The man she danced with might have had a mother who was from a border clan too, but he had been the English king's knight. There was no chance that her father would ever condone a match.

"You seem to have gone somewhere far away, Isa?"

"Hmm? I was enjoying the dance. I don't want to think of aught else than just this."

Ric nodded, but he was certain he knew that she was thinking the same thing he was. This would be their only chance to be together. He might be fortunate enough to partner with her again, but he would have to be careful not to show she was a favorite. The couple continued to twirl about the floor, each lost in thoughts of what they could not have while trying to absorb every moment of what they did have.

"That young knight seems quite taken with our Lady Isabella," Queen Elizabeth spoke softly to her husband.

"I'd noticed as much. He was quite subtle in how he arranged for them to partner, but I noticed nonetheless."

"And why is that?" The queen already knew the answer but nudged her husband's knee to answer.

"I did the same with you more than once." The king cast his gaze at his wife and slid his hand beneath the table. Their tumultuous relationship had seen Elizabeth captured and imprisoned for eight years by King Edward, a man to whom her father still swore loyalty. A fondness developed between the royal couple once Elizabeth returned to the Scottish court. Robert squeezed his wife's knee as she giggled softly.

"It would seem Lady Isabella has eyes for the young knight, too. I wonder how they could have already met." The queen continued to speak quietly to her husband.

"I doubt they could have. He must have seen her during the meal and taken an interest. She's a pretty young woman, and he's a healthy young mon."

"If that is what you think, then you cannot see what I do."

"And what is that, my queen?"

"That there is a spark between them that did not start with the music. There is a familiarity between them, but it seems new. As though neither knows quite what to do with it."

"You see all of that?" The king's skepticism was

evident in his tone as well as the look he cast his wife before looking back at the young couple.

"You spend your days with stuffy auld men. I spend mine with young women who like to gossip and read poetry aboot love. Besides, I was young like Lady Isabella once."

"You are still young, my dear. And if Sir Dedric's mind runs aught like mine did when I met you, then I would do well to drag him away now."

Elizabeth chuckled as she remembered the early days of their marriage. They were undoubtedly attracted to one another, but neither was sure whether they liked one another. Elizabeth knew her husband had loved his first wife, and his grief was a reason why he waited six years to remarry despite having a young daughter in need of a mother.

"Do you believe he's been sent to spy?"

"Most certainly."

"Do you think he will change his mind as I did?" Elizabeth spoke of a part of their past that neither liked, but there was little that could change the fact that her father, in agreement with King Edward, arranged her marriage to Robert the Bruce in the hopes that she would spy for them. Instead, she chose to make the most of her marriage, and when King Edward held her under house arrest, she resolved to never aid the man who tore her family apart, sending her stepdaughter to a nunnery and placing her sister-by-marriage and Isabella Duff in cages that he ordered suspended outside the castles where the women were held hostage. She was her husband's staunchest supporter and would have gladly cut King Edward's heart out with her own dirk if given a chance.

"I don't know. I met with him this afternoon, and the bitterness he feels toward Edward is genuine. I remember the raid on the MacLellans that killed his mother. It was led by a mon who had once been his father's friend. The fiend raped Hartley's mother and then turned the boy over to Edward. It would have been the same time as when Edward had you."

"That is as good a reason as I can imagine."

"Perhaps I'm not the one who will change his mind, but I will benefit if he does. He spent his life in Edward's court. Beyond battlefield strategy, there must be plenty he is privy to."

"Then I shall just make sure that Lady Isabella has an opportunity to become better acquainted with the lad. But Edward, I won't do more than that. We have been embroiled in far too many mangled love affairs of late. Deirdre and Magnus and your brother and Elizabeth still haunt me."

"You and me both, my love. We shall give them the opportunity, but if they do not want it, then I shall not force a match."

The music trailed off, and the musicians rose to take a break after the long set. Ric and Isa had managed to remain partnered for the entire set since none of the songs after the first one required partner changes. They had danced three in a row, including the first one. They knew they were pushing the limits before they sparked gossip, but neither was eager to let go. The Great Hall was stifling, so Ric led them to a space near a window and summoned a serving woman who carried a tray with mugs of ale. He lifted two off the tray and handed one to Isa. She sipped, but he could tell she wanted to take an unladylike swallow.

"Go ahead. It's hot, and we're both thirsty. I won't tell." Ric chuckled as Isa paused before grinning over the rim of her mug. She finished her drink in three long swallows and suppressed the hiccup that wanted to escape. Ric finished his just as quickly and waved another servant over to replace the drinks they consumed. They each sipped these.

"What were you doing in the scriptorium? You never did say." Ric asked.

"I was there to gather the last few illuminations that I finished. They had been drying, and I wanted to be sure that I secured them before they sprouted feet and walked off."

"They're quite valuable, and you were right. You could sell them for far more if you had your own stall."

Isa shrugged as she looked around before returning her gaze to Ric's. "I could, and I would like to, but it's impossible. Besides, I use the illuminations to give to the poor and to pay for the project that really interests me."

"Not the art? From what I caught a glance of, you're very talented."

"Well trained, not talented. A monk spent several years at the abbey near my home. My father and mother wanted me educated, and I fell in love with the process of creating the images. The monk taught me how along with the other things I needed, such as reading and sums."

"If that isn't what you want to be doing, then what is?"

Isa pulled her lips in and looked around once more, noticing that more than one of the other ladies was watching them. "I like history. My clan are descendants of the Picts. I am working on a history of my clan all the way back to its formation. I use a few pieces of parchment each month to create the illuminations, but I save most for my real passion."

Isa caught the flicker in Ric's eyes as she mentioned her passion, and she found herself swaying closer to him. Neither said anything, but their eyes spoke volumes.

"Will you show me your work someday?" Ric murmured.

"Yes. I'd like that. I–" Isa was interrupted when the gathering shifted, and the ladies-in-waiting moved toward the dais. The queen had risen, signaling it was time for the young women to retire. "I must go."

"I know. I recognize the signal. I will look for you tomorrow."

"Goodnight, Ric."

"Sleep well, Isa."

Ric watched as Isa followed the queen from the Great Hall and was ready to retire now that the only company he sought had left.

"She's very pretty but a bit naïve for a man of your tastes." Bella spoke from behind Ric's shoulder. "Do you think she can gain you the information you need? You should be looking to one of the more worldly women, who understands how the court game is played."

Ric did not turn to speak to Bella but kept his eye on Isa until she finally disappeared. He then shifted his gaze to the king who watched him with a calculated gleam. Ric stepped away from Bella and pretended as though he had not heard her behind him. He returned to the table where he had eaten; a few men remained. They had not been openly hostile, but they had made Ric feel unwanted. He welcomed their attitude, as it kept him away from Bella. The fact that she suggested he bed older, more experienced women confirmed that her only interest in him was for a quick tumble and the information Edward expected him to find. He was relieved that she did not seem to be holding a grudge after the incident at the MacLellan keep. He kept Bella in the corner of his eye and watched as she left with a man he did not know, but who looked quite important.

"Looks like the Earl of Atholl has a new mistress," one of the men mused as he lifted his mug in the direction of Bella and her escort.

"She is a beautiful woman, but something aboot her tells me she isn't worth the tupping for all the trouble she will bring." Another man spoke as he shook his head, and Ric wished he could speak up and confirm the man's guess. The other courtiers continued to discuss Bella before moving on to other women they wished they could bed.

"Lady Isabella looked particularly fetching tonight."

Ric ground his molars and gripped his mug, but he refused to show how the discussion's unexpected turn toward the woman he wanted bothered him.

"English, you danced with her. Does she feel as good as she looks? Are her tits as big as they look or is it the lacing lying to us men?"

Ric looked at the man who spoke, and he longed to drive his fist into the other man's face. "Perhaps it is the English knight in me or the Scottish honor my mother taught me, but I don't discuss innocents as though they're little more than tavern whores. You're talking about one of the queen's ladies. Show some respect."

Ric rose from his seat and slammed his mug onto the table before turning toward the entrance. He weaved through the crowd but did not make it to the door before the one voice that could force him to stop reached his ears.

"What did they say aboot her?" Ric turned around and bowed to King Robert, but he did not respond, pretending to not understand. "Don't feign ignorance. I'm too tired, and it's too late in the night for games. What did they say?"

"It doesn't bear repeating, Your Majesty."

"It was enough to upset you and make you leave."

"I intended to leave anyway. As you said, it is very late."

"You seemed in no hurry to leave when you wanted to avoid that other woman."

"She did not interest me."

"But Lady Isabella does." It was a statement, not a question. Ric knew there was no way to get around it.

"She is intelligent and beautiful as well as kind-hearted. I saw her in the market today giving some coins to a family of orphaned children. She wiped the youngest's nose with her own handkerchief. I can't think of many ladies who would do that."

"That is true. She is as you describe her, and she seems to have taken an interest in you."

"She overheard me when I approached the children after she moved on. I ordered my squire to take them to the inn where I spent the previous night. I had him see if the children could be hired on. She was equally surprised at my interest in them. Your Majesty, I could very well have been like those orphans. Had I been turned out of King Edward's service while in England, I would have had no choice but to beg like those children. I realize that while my life has had its share of misfortune, there are some things that I can't be ungrateful for."

"That is true. Edward is not known for being magnanimous often, but he can be quite generous. He did retain you all the way through your tenure." Ric remained silent once again, knowing the king had not said anything that necessitated his response. Ric understood this was not a conversation so much as another opportunity for Robert to form an opinion and pass judgment. "My wife and I stroll through the gardens midmorning each day that the sun is out. She has her attendants with her in case I am summoned away. She enjoys the company." Robert watched as Ric did not react. "It would not do you any harm to happen to be there as well."

Ric nodded before bowing to the king and retreating to his chamber.

SEVEN

R ic and Robbie were already within the chapel when Robert and Elizabeth along with the ladies-in-waiting arrived. The royal couple took their places at their *prie-dieu* and the women slid into the pews. Ric bowed his head and kneeled as the service dictated, but the liturgy he had heard his entire life faded into the background once he was able to spot Isa. She sensed his stare and tilted her head to look back at him as unobtrusively as she could. She smiled shyly once, then turned her attention back to the priest. She did not look at Ric again, but she could sense his attention throughout the service. When everyone filed out of the chapel, Isa found herself penned in by the other ladies-in-waiting all the way to the Great Hall. She broke her fast seated in her usual position, but Ric was shown to a table that put them in each other's line of sight. She suspected the queen had a role in that. Isa had been sent back to change her gown that morning; Elizabeth said that the color she chose made her look pale.

Neither Ric nor Isa wanted to draw attention to themselves, so they kept their eyes everywhere but on each other, or at least they attempted not to look at each other. When the women left to gather their cloaks, Ric awaited his summons from the king. They walked to the gardens together, and Robert the Bruce took the opportunity to press Ric for more information about his intentions.

"You have arrived in Scotland with no plans to return to England, but neither do you have plans for what you will do here."

"I had hoped to earn a plot of land, perhaps with a home already built, but if not, I will build my own."

"You intend to build your own keep?"

Ric glanced at the king and saw that he was not jesting. "I had not thought to have something so large."

"You will have been a royal knight for two kings. Do you not think you will have earned a manor home at the least?"

"I don't know that there are too many Scots who would like to be employed by an English man."

"Half, as you noted."

"It always seems like the less-useful half is the only one people remember."

"So you planned to live as a hermit? What aboot when your squire is ready to move on? Will you live all alone on your humble plot?"

"If that is what the land offers, then I shall be happy to know I have a home."

"That seems rather unassuming for someone raised in Edward's court, one of his most trusted knights."

Ric felt the hairs on his neck stand up as he measured his words before he spoke. "I was raised in Edward's court, but by tutors and knights who cared little about an orphan who could not bring them a suitable placement after their service to the king was done. I don't know that he trusted me very much after the last battle against the Kerrs. He was decidedly unimpressed with my answer when asked why we lost."

"And what did you say?"

"That there were more of you than there were of us."

The Bruce waited for Ric to go on, and when he realized that what Ric said now was all the knight had told Longshanks, he roared with laughter. "I can see why he did not appreciate you pointing out the obvious. He would have rather someone taken the blame for the botched attack than admit he was outwitted by the heathenous Scots once again. The tale I heard was the lot of you scarpered off before the Kerrs and Elliots could chase you back across the border."

"That retreat was not my decision, but it was one I agreed with. The day was lost, and there was no need to lose more lives simply for someone's pride."

"I don't suppose you told Edward that, too."

"No, Your Majesty. I chose to keep that to myself and keep my head along with it."

"For the best, I'm sure."

The men came to stand near a topiary in the shape of a stag. The wind was cold, but the last of the snow had made its appearance in the Lowlands several weeks earlier. Ric imagined what the garden would look like in spring, with the blossoms hiding the trunk and roots of the pruned bush. He knew he would not be there long enough to see the new growth and signs of new life. Before either man could speak again, the sound of women's laughter and voices floated to them. Queen Elizabeth and her entourage came into view, and Robert led Ric to be introduced to the queen.

"I believe we have both been guests of King Edward at the same time, but the duration of my stay was much shorter than yours." The queen's tone when she described them as guests was a firm reminder that neither of them had been given a choice when Edward decided they should be taken from their homes. The queen offered Ric a warm smile as he rose from his bended knee. He nodded and waited for her to continue. When she turned instead to Robert, Ric was left standing alone.

"Lady Isabella, would you be so kind as to guide Sir Dedric through the gardens? You know how easy it is for one to get lost in the maze. Sir Dedric, you might freeze in place, and we wouldn't find you until the final thaw." The queen tucked her arm through her husband's, and the couple led the way followed by the ladies-in-waiting who encircled Isa and Ric. Some were subtle in their attempt to eavesdrop on Isa and Ric, but others had no compunction about trying to listen.

"Are you warm enough, Lady Isabella?"

"Aye. I'm used to this climate, and it could be far worse. We could be in the Highlands, which are still blanketed in several feet of snow. Are you not accustomed to such long winters?"

"I am. I've spent most of my time in the north of England, so the weather is not much different. I simply wondered since your gown doesn't seem particularly thick." Ric made his final remark under his breath.

"My cloak is sealskin and lined with fur. It's far warmer than it looks, and I would say a far sight warmer than your own cloak. If you are going to remain in Scotland, you would do well to see a tailor aboot some properly made clothes." Isa slammed her mouth shut as she caught herself discussing a man's clothing with the man himself. She peeked at the other ladies who had grown bored with their conversation about the weather.

"I appreciate your concern, Isa. Is there a tailor you would recommend?" Ric kept his voice down.

"There is. Next market day I will take you, if you'd like." Isa looked straight ahead, but her cheeks pinkened with her presumptuousness.

"I would like that very much. Robbie can mend my clothes, but I don't trust him to tailor aught for me."

Isa covered her mouth to stifle her giggle. "You must have been a squire once. Do you not know how to sew? Have you considered making your own clothes?"

"I sew to mend, my lady, not to make." Ric grinned down at Isa, and her breath caught when she was certain his topaz eyes twinkled at her.

Isa was paying little attention to where she was stepping until she felt her feet slide out from under her on a patch of ice. Her arms flew up as she tried to keep her balance, but her feet were uncooperative. She clutched whatever she could reach, which happened to be Ric's surcoat and cloak. He came to a stop and pulled her against him. He kept her from slipping, but he brought them back to the position they had been in the day before when they kissed.

"Isa, are you all right?" he murmured, his warm breath smelling of mint as it misted around her lips. She could only nod her head while her heart continued to pound.

"Startled," she said at last.

"Did you roll your ankle?"

She shook her head, but she still felt unsteady on her feet.

"Lady Isabella!" The couple looked over as the queen hurried toward them. "I saw you slip. You are most fortunate that Sir Dedric was standing nearby. You might have taken a nasty fall." The queen stopped in front of them, and it was genuine concern etched in the lines of the older woman's face. "Are you hale, lass?" The queen inquired softly. The informality spoke to her worry.

"I am, Your Majesty. Startled and a wee shaken, but there is naught wrong with me."

"If you are certain." The queen sounded anything but. "Sir Dedric, do keep a tighter hold on her. The snow is gone, but clearly the ice is not. Lady Isabella is a slight thing. She would do well to have you tether her down lest she float away."

The queen and king, who had followed his wife to see what the commotion was about, moved on with their walk. However, several other ladies were not in the same rush.

"Bella, are you well? That looked frightful," Allyson Elliot gushed as she peered at Ric rather than Isa. Ric grimaced at the diminutive. He had not heard anyone call her Bella before, and he found he disliked it as much as he had when he heard Isa refer to herself as such.

"Is something wrong, Sir Dedric?" Cairren Kennedy purred as she eased closer to Ric.

"Naught is wrong, but I do think I shall take Lady Isabella to that bench I see just around the corner." Ric wrapped his arm around her waist and guided her to a bench that was blessedly only large enough for two.

"Are you certain you're well, Bella?" The soft-spoken Maude Sutherland seemed oblivious to the other women fawning over Ric.

"I'm truly fine, Maude, but thank you. I think I just need a moment to catch my breath."

Maude nodded before glaring at the other ladies, making it clear that they needed to catch up to the royal couple. Once Ric and Isa were alone, she sagged against him.

"Isa?"

"My chest hurts from my heart pounding so hard. It did give me a good scare. I'll admit that. Thank you for catching me." Isa looked up at Ric and was unprepared for the tenderness in the kiss he placed upon her nose, then forehead.

"You gave me a quite a fright."

"You and me both." Ric held her against his side, and she burrowed under his cloak which he draped around them both. They sat together in silence for several minutes. "We should rejoin the others," Isa murmured.

"We should." Neither of them moved, both enjoying the serenity of the garden and their embrace. "Tell me more of your research. I know little of these people you called Picts."

"They were the original people of Scotland descending from the Caledonii, inhabiting this land well before the Romans and Norse ever found our shores. They lived throughout Scotland until the Norse began to gain more strength and success with their raids. Their way of life slowly dwindled as the Norse and other Celts grew more dominant. However, there are lingering signs of their dominance all over Scotland. Standing stones with their art have been found in Lothian and Northumbria. There are records kept by the Romans and Britons that speak of fierce tribes that painted their faces white with ash or with blue woad and fought naked. They are much of the reason why the Romans failed to move much farther north than Hadrian's Wall."

Isa shrank into her cloak, embarrassed by how eager she had grown to talk about her interest. She knew few people who enjoyed history as much as she did. Cousins Deirdre and Elizabeth Fraser had both been scholars, but their interest lay in languages, whereas Isa longed to discover how their ancestors once lived.

"Tell me more," Ric encouraged.

"The land upon which my clan lives was given to my ancestors by the Picts when they won a battle against the Norse. The first keep was built on a rise overlooking the harbor. *Dun* means hill, so it became the hill of the Bar, the original surname of my ancestors. It eventually blended into one, and so my clan is now Dunbar. I come from the Dunbars of Mochum, near the southwest border. I wish I could travel to other places in Scotland where Pictish art still exists. There are many more in the Highlands, but there are even several in northern England."

Isa paused, having come close to the sensitive topic of the border. She still was not sure where Ric's loyalties lay on the matter. He may have left Edward of England's court for Robert of Scotland's, but that did not mean he agreed with either side's claims to the land.

"Are they tall rocks carved with swirls?"

"Yes. How did you know?"

"I've seen them in both Northumbria and Cumberland. They are as tall as a man standing upon another man's shoulders, and some would take three men forming a circle to wrap their arms around them. They are massive."

"That's exactly what I'm talking aboot."

Ric listened as Isa continued to explain different periods of Scottish history, especially that of the Lowlands. He gained a deeper understanding of why the land was so important to the Scots. While Edward wanted it to demonstrate his power and dominance, the Scots wanted it because they were bound to the earth. Their people had conquered the landscape and protected it from countless invaders over several centuries. Ric wondered if any of the Mac-Lellans knew half as much about the history of their land as Isa did about her clan's. Neither realized the amount of time that passed until the queen and her ladies returned with red noses and wind-chapped cheeks. Isa and Ric jumped apart like two scalded cats, moving to their own ends of the bench before anyone caught them snuggled together.

"I look forward to you telling me more," Ric whispered as he eased her back to her feet.

Isa stomped her feet as the blood began to circulate once more, and she nodded as the group returned to the warmth of the castle. Isa followed the queen, and Ric found his way to the lists. He released his pent-up need through his sword as he took on one Scottish warrior after another, demonstrating that he had earned the spurs he still wore.

Isa spent most of the day in the queen's solar as the women read aloud and embroidered. Isa sat at a loom and continued a tapestry she had been working on since before Hogmanay. The Lowlands had experienced fierce weather around Christmas, and days spent locked away inside had given Isa a chance to begin a tapestry that told the same story she had told Ric of how the Picts gave land to her ancestors. She hummed quietly to herself, but she nearly dropped the shuttle when she heard Ric's name.

"He is dreadfully handsome," Allyson Elliot commented conspiratorially. "I wouldn't mind passing the lists to see him train. I wonder if he'll still be here in spring."

"Why are you wondering aboot spring? I'm wondering aboot him now," Arabella Johnstone's whisper was meant for the entire chamber to hear.

"Because in spring, the men strip off their surcoats to train," Allyson shrugged as though her answer explained everything, and to Isa, it did. She tried to remain focused on her tapestry and not the jealousy that fluttered in her belly as she listened to the other women talk about seeing Ric half undressed. She realized that she very much wanted her eyes to be the only ones enjoying that feast.

"Allyson, you are horrible!" Cairren Kennedy giggled. "But you're not wrong. Perhaps we could take a stroll in a while. Just to check the weather."

Just to check the weather. Isa mimicked Cairren in her head. She attempted to keep her face neutral, but she could feel her neck beginning to get warm, and she wanted to squirm. She knew she had no claim on Ric. She had no way of knowing if he was already involved with someone at court, but she prayed that she was the only one he had been kissing. Dear God, what if he'd been doing far more than kissing since he arrived here? Isa began to feel ill at the idea that she had allowed herself to get so swept away the night before with a man she did not know, and then she remembered how she clung to him in front of the ladies just that morning. She had felt so comfortable leaning against him as they talked, but now she began to wonder if she was making a fool of herself. He was clearly older than she was, and she was not naïve enough to think they were both innocents. Her stomach dropped as she pictured Ric with one of the bored wives or widows.

"Lady Bella?" Queen Elizabeth broke into her thoughts. "You are looking markedly peaked. Are you still not recovered from your near-mishap this morning?"

Isa looked up, but it took her a moment to piece through the queen's words as the haze in her mind cleared. "I'm well, Your Majesty. I'm just planning what I'd like to do next with this tapestry."

"And that makes you pale? Perhaps you should retire until the evening meal."

Isa knew it was not a suggestion, so she deferred to the queen and stowed her yarns and threads before slipping from the chamber. As she wound through the labyrinth of passageways, she could not ease the tension between her shoulders as she wondered if she had made a fool of herself the night before. Even that day, she had sat pressed against him with his cloak draped around her shoulders. If anyone caught them, they could very well be on their way to the altar now. Isa was wise enough to not expect a future husband to be faithful, so she knew she had no right to wish for one who would be, but she did at least want to know her groom a little better than a passing stranger. A stranger who could very well be involved with any number of women at court despite having only just arrived. She had seen it before.

Isa told Ric her entire clan's history, but she knew almost nothing about him, and this only made her cheeks flame as she once again conjured a memory of their kiss. She did not regret it. It was the first real kiss she had ever experienced. She had been at court long enough for a few gentlemen to attempt stealing a kiss, but she never offered anything but a quickly turned cheek. There had not been anyone, until the night prior with Ric, who made her wonder if kissing could be as pleasurable as she had heard older women, even some ladies-in-waiting, describe. She had heard the descriptions of kisses being heart-stopping, world spinning, arousing exercises, but until she had done it herself, she could not appreciate how true the words had been.

A large window overlooking the courtyard and lists beyond drew her attention, and she did not bother attempting to discourage her curiosity. She peered through the glass, a rarity in most keeps but a more common luxury in a royal castle. She could see men moving about as they sparred and practiced archery. She wished she could be shooting her bow, but she rarely had a chance unless a hunt was organized and women were allowed to participate. Those had been few and far between in the years since she arrived at court.

"See aught of interest?"

Isa turned to see one of the most beautiful women she had ever laid eyes upon gliding toward her. "I was looking at the archery targets and wishing I could be practicing." It was a half-truth, which was better than a lie.

"Mmm. I would be looking at the men. They are quite the feast for the eyes, even covered up. Would that it could be spring." The woman grinned at Isa, and Isa was transfixed for a moment by the woman's appearance. She forced herself to look out the window before the other woman thought her rude for staring.

"I rather like that one," the unknown stranger pointed, and Isa followed her tapered finger and manicured nail until her eyes settled on Ric. She knew it was him even from this distance.

"He's English as well." Isa could not think of anything better to say, and the observation made her brow crinkle. What was an English woman doing at court? Isa's stomach soured as she knew there could only be one reason why an English man and an English woman would appear within a day when they were in the heart of where hatred for the English festered.

"Is he?" the woman tilted her head.

"Yes, I suspect you know that already." Isa curtsied and turned away from the window.

"And just how would I know him?" the woman called after Isa.

Isa paused and looked back over her shoulder. "I would think you recognize your lover."

Isa continued walking and did not pause until she arrived at her chamber. She entered and turned the lock before collapsing backwards onto her bed. As she lay looking up at the ceiling, she had never felt a greater fool than she did in that moment.

EIGHT

Ric had an uneasy feeling as he settled onto the bench in the Great Hall. He looked surreptitiously around him, and cringed when he saw Bella Fitz-Bigod standing among a group of young courtiers. He felt his temper spike as she flirted with one, then another, of the men. He was ready to throttle her. Ric's gaze shifted until he found Isa. He was prepared to offer her a warm smile, but her face was set in stone as she glanced at him then turned away. She looked directly at Bella, and Ric wanted to groan out loud. Isa's gaze shifted to the ladies surrounding her, and Ric knew he had been effectively dismissed. He spent the remainder of the meal sneaking glances at Isa while trying to avoid Bella and being ignored by everyone else at his table.

Once the tables were moved aside, Ric once more joined in the dancing, but he could not successfully position himself to partner with Isa. He was growing more and more impatient until Isa's current partner slid his hand far too low for Ric's taste and Isa's obvious comfort. He pushed away from the wall against which he had taken root and pressed his way to where the man was skillfully leading Isa to a less-crowded area, one that happened to be near the doors that led to the passageways. Ric's pace increased as he watched Isa come to a halt. She refused to budge, but the man whispered something in her ear that made her take a step back. It was a step toward the door. The man pushed it open and backed Isa through.

"My lord, I must return. I have not been excused for the evening. The queen will be most displeased with me if I disappear."

"Tell her you were finding a chamber pot."

"I will not. I will go back inside. Let go of me." Isa ripped her arm away from the man, but not before his other hand snaked around her waist. It was only a moment later that the man was doubled over in pain. Isa had kneed him in the bollocks, and she did not feel a moment's guilt for unmanning him. "I told you to let go."

She stepped around him and stepped into Ric's chest. She gasped as she feared another man had come to join the first. She balled her fist and raised her arm to strike. Ric pushed it aside before tucking her behind him.

"It's me, Isa," he whispered before turning to the man who was still doubled over. Ric grasped the man's surcoat and pushed him against the wall. "Do not ever touch her again. Come near her again, and I will kill you. I know what you intended to do, and I heard her tell you to let go. Know your death will come suddenly if you persist." Ric drove his fist into the man's stomach.

Isa watched as Ric came to her defense, and she knew she should be appreciative, but she was also angry that he had been watching her all night when he clearly had a mistress in tow. Ric turned toward Isa before looking around. He drew her to his side, and they walked silently to an alcove where Ric pushed aside the tapestry and nudged her within.

"Isa, are you all right?" Just enough light shone around the edges for Ric to find her jaw, which he cupped. A shiver ran through Isa at his touch, but she reminded herself that he was touching someone else just the same way, if not far more intimately.

"I'm well and must return to the Great Hall." She could not get around him in such a tight space, so she infused as much impatience and annoyance as she could into her voice.

"I'll take you back."

"No, thank you."

"Isa, you shouldn't be in the passageway alone."

"And going back in with you is safer? I think not. We are only just beyond the doors. I don't need your assistance, but I do thank you for coming to my rescue. You seem to have done that twice today. But please excuse me. I must return to the queen, and you should return to your friend." Isa could not think of a better term without bluntly admitting that she knew he brought his mistress.

"What friend? I would say you're my only friend here at court."

"I would prefer not to spell it out."

"I think you may need to. I don't know to whom you're referring."

"Your mistress," she murmured.

"My what?" It was not that Ric could not hear her, but it sent his mind reeling.

"The stunning woman with the English accent. Who else could she be?"

"Not mine, that's who she bloody well is," Ric barked. He cleared his throat and stretched his neck. "That is a woman I once knew, but I no longer tolerate her company. She most certainly is not my mistress."

Isa looked at him, but Ric could not read her expression. She seemed to be assessing him, and he felt determinedly lacking. It was not a feeling he cared for, though he was familiar with it. But coming from Isa, it hurt in a way he did not know was possible. He could not explain why her opinion mattered so greatly, but he was struck by how much he wanted Isa to think of him favorably. To think of him as she had while they kissed the night before.

"She's why you won't call me Bella." Isa's words cut through to Ric, who was shocked that she had deduced the truth. He looked away before turning his topaz gaze back to her.

"Yes."

It was a simple answer, but it sucked the wind from Isa's chest. She took a step back, nodded, and spun on her heel, and pushed the tapestry aside. She marched the few steps back to the Great Hall and yanked open the door. She weaved her way through the crowd, but she knew Ric was not far behind her. It took him longer to grasp her hand than she anticipated, but the warmth of his fingers entwining with her, hidden by the material of her kirtle, made her arm tingle.

"Don't run from me, Isa," he murmured. "Please."

The entreaty in his voice was so genuine that it gave her pause. She turned to look back at him, and she saw rejection and hurt flash in his eyes before the courtly mask fell back into place.

"I'm not running from you so much as I'm not running to you. What do you want from me, Ric? I certainly am not taking her place as your mistress."

"She's not, nor was she ever really, my mistress. She's someone I knew from a long time ago when I was young and impressionable. Barely a knight and hoping to make a name for myself that wasn't 'half English.'"

Isa looked past Ric's shoulder to where she could

tell Bella was attempting to watch them without being obvious. "Does she know that? She still seems very interested, even concerned, with you."

Ric wanted to rake his hands through his hair and groan. Isa was correct, but not for the right reasons. "I suppose because I'm the only other person she knows here."

"And that brings us back around to the question you never answered. Who is she and why is she here?"

"Lady Bella Fitz-Bigod, the illegitimate daughter of an English courtier. My guess would be she chased after the wrong married man one too many times and decided she would do well to set her sights elsewhere."

"And the Scottish court is where she wound up. Ric, I don't believe you. And rather than stand here while you lie or evade the truth, I would rather spend the rest of my evening with my friends." Isa pulled away, and this time Ric let her. He watched her rejoin the other ladies-in-waiting, a false smile of serenity plastered to her face, but he could see the smile was for appearance. She had the same haunted and saddened expression in her eyes that he was sure he wore, too.

It took Ric the better part of a week before he was able to speak to Isa again. She avoided him when she could and was distant when she could not. Ric continued to meet with the king in the mornings when the royal couple went for their stroll. The king and queen seemed determined to engineer opportunities for them to be alone, but Isa skittered away like a spooked doe. It was another near fall that finally forced Isa to confront Ric and her feelings.

"Thank you," she breathed as she covered her heart with her hand. "I seem to be making a habit of being clumsy. And of needing your assistance."

"I am relieved I was close enough to prevent your fall," Ric was cautious in how he approached their first conversation since they spoke of his previous relationship with Bella.

"You have taken a liking to walking with the king."

"I suppose one could say that. I've taken a liking to gardens and the beauty they behold."

Isa's eyes widened as Ric's meaning was clear. She nodded and looked around. They had been left behind by the others and were once more alone near the bench they had sat upon the first time Ric caught her.

"Ric," Isa looked around once more before continuing. "I shouldn't have been so rash to pass judgment upon you. I suppose I can't know what happens when I am not near, but I have seen how little interest you and Lady Bella seem to take in one another. Perhaps I was laboring under the wrong impression. I'm sorry."

Ric was surprised that Isa was offering him an apology when he had been trying to create an opportunity to offer his own apology. "You need not apologize, Isa. I can see how the situation would be confusing and appear unseemly. Please know that there is no one but one fair-haired maiden who holds my attention."

Isa's cheeks grew pink despite the brisk air. She smiled demurely and nodded before glancing away.

"I'd like to learn more of your history tales," Ric blurted.

"Really?" Isa was cautious about growing too excited. The last time she thought she could trust Ric she had been disappointed. But she reminded herself that it was her assumptions that placed distance between them. Not anything Ric actually did.

Their conversation was the beginning of many more within the gardens that spanned the next three weeks. Ric continued to join the king each morning, but he rarely spoke more than the necessary pleasantries to the king and queen. Later in the day, after he had trained and then bathed, he would slip into the scriptorium where Isa worked both on the illuminations that she sold at market and her research.

Ric even accompanied Isa to the market, and watched in awe as she warned the merchant that Ric would be acquiring the stall next to the mercer and would serve as her representative. They had laughed as they returned to the keep, enjoying a joke shared only between the two of them.

Throughout those weeks, by mutual and silent agreement, they did little more than walk with Isa's hand looped through his arm or dance after the evening meal. Other people at court began to notice the interest between the two, but they were cautious not to be too obvious. Ric sneaked a kiss to the back of her hand and even a peck on her cheek, nose, or forehead, but they did not repeat the tryst they had when they initially met. They used the time to become better acquainted, and both found they truly enjoyed the other's company.

Ric's summons to the Privy Council chamber came, and he was not looking forward to his conversation with the king. He was certain Robert had observed his interaction with Isa over the previous weeks. Ric had a sneaking suspicion that the Bruce was about to test him for the first time as one of the king's warriors. He had made a good impression on more than one man in the lists, proving that his spurs had been earned and not given. He was quick to learn and adapt to the Scottish method of fighting, having observed and fought against it for years before he was introduced to using it when he stayed with the MacLellans.

He made his way to the chamber to await his audience. He forced himself not to shuffle his feet, nervous about meeting with King Robert. He and Edward met countless times during Ric's tenure, but Ric had known the man since he was a child. He was well versed in how to manage his conversations with the temperamental regent. He was not at all familiar with Robert's disposition.

Once admitted, Ric made his way directly to where the king stood with four of his advisors. Ric did not know who any of the men were. But he did know enough about court life to realize that if they met with the king hours after the other courtiers who usually flocked around Robert had given up to pursue other activities, they held significance. He approached the group of men and bowed before waiting for the king's attention. He stood as patiently as he could, knowing that the Bruce was intentionally making him wait. The conversation would slow and nearly come to a lull before the king found another topic to discuss with the men who pretended as though he was not there. When the king could no longer delay addressing Ric, King Robert did little to keep their conversation private.

"We have had another skirmish along the border. This time it was with the Maxwells. The English are moving west. Did you know that the Maxwells border the MacLellans?"

Ric was aware, and his heart had already picked up its pace as he thought about his clan coming under attack. His heart skipped when he realized that he truly did think of the MacLellans as his family. They were no longer strangers distantly related to him, but rather people who had eventually welcomed him, reconnecting him to the family he lost.

"When do you expect them to reach the MacLellans?" The tension in Ric's voice made the king narrow his eyes.

"We don't know that they will."

"Your Majesty, if they're traveling west, it's because they know they can no longer gain victory over the Kerrs and Elliots. Edward has sent them to find a new way across the border." Ric's eyes shifted to the other men listening to their conversation. "Edward knows I returned to my mother's people. He has chosen them as his upcoming target, and I fear he has done so to punish me."

"You are not alone in that thinking. And that is why, Sir Dedric, you will be riding out with a contingent of warriors to meet the English." King Robert stroked his beard and once more narrowed his eyes. "You will undoubtedly come across men you know."

The king did not go any further, but the question was implicit. Ric knew the answer, his conviction true. "And I will kill any of them who threaten my clan."

The cynical laughter from the other men made Ric turn toward them. His voice was calm and smooth, but the determination brought the laughter to a sharp end.

"Were any of you stolen from your family? Or did your families send you to court to better their position? Did any of you grow up in a country you never wanted to belong to? I suspect not. The MacLellans are my clan, and they did acknowledge me. My mother and father died when I was too young to fight, but I'll be damned if another MacLellan dies now that I can fight." Ric turned back to the king. "Do I depart in the morning?"

"I had thought to give you a day to resolve aught

here at court." Once more, the Bruce did not say anything more, but the implication was not lost on Ric.

"I can be ready at dawn." Ric would find a way to see Isa if he could, but he would also avoid Bella like the pox.

"Very well. You will travel with two of my godsons who recently returned to court. They are none too pleased to be leaving their wives here, but they are among my most trusted warriors. They are Highlanders, but they will treat you fairly."

Ric knew what the qualification meant. The Lowlanders were fierce in their protection of their homes, but the Highlanders were unparalleled in their ability to fight, their loyalty to their land, and their unforgiving and unwelcoming character. Ric wanted to groan, but the king was not through.

"You will meet Tavish and Magnus in the morning. They are currently saying goodbye to their wives." This elicited guffaws from the men who had been smirking at Ric.

"If that's the case, no one is leaving until well after the nooning," one man offered.

"They won't be leaving for at least a fortnight," another chuckled.

"Not unless you send their wives home, and then you might not have them at all," a third chimed in. Ric looked at the men, then back at Robert.

"They are both newlywed couples, and both are love matches. Neither mon trusts anyone outside their clan to adequately protect their wives." Robert sobered for a moment. "Though they have fair reason to feel that way."

"May I ask why they brought their wives if they feel that way?"

"Both women were ladies-in-waiting to the queen and understand the inner workings far better than their impatient and straightforward husbands. They are also both very close to my sister-by-marriage, Elizabeth Fraser. There was an incident around Christmas, and Elizabeth and Edward left court to make their home in a nearby keep. Unfortunately, they have had to return here. The ladies came to visit with Elizabeth."

Ric watched as the humor Robert used to describe the two couples evaporated into a rigidity when he described his brother and sister-by-marriage. Ric could sense the swift change was not animosity toward his relatives, but a protectiveness and frustration at whatever happened that he could not control.

Robert reached out and unexpectedly clapped Ric on the shoulder before giving it a squeeze. "You are a leader, and I could see that in the lists today. But listen to Magnus and Tavish. They will keep you alive long enough to return and resolve things here."

Ric nodded as the king removed his hand. Ric wondered if the king meant earning a plot of land, determining what existed between him and Isa, or to die a spy. He was nearly certain Robert suspected him of such; he could not imagine how the king would not.

"Yes, Your Majesty." Ric bent at the waist and was prepared to depart. He needed to find Robbie and prepare the lad for their departure.

"She'll be in the scriptorium before sunrise." The words were barely audible, but Ric felt his chest expand. He nodded to King Robert and the courtiers before taking his leave.

NINE

R ic thought he would not be able to sleep when he returned to his chamber. He found Robbie with one of the maids and felt badly pulling the lad away when it seemed the younger man was making headway with the lass. Robbie gave the young woman a kiss that reminded Ric of the all-too-brief ones he shared with Isa. He was determined to find her before he left, if for no other reason than to say goodbye. He knew there was just as much chance, if not more, that he would die as there was a chance that he would return. He did not know the men he would travel with, and he was yet to meet the king's godsons. He was not naïve enough to believe that simply because King Robert sent him along, he would merit the aid and loyalty of the other Scots.

He and Robbie packed quickly, and both fell into a deep sleep with barely a word uttered once they extinguished the candles. Images of dancing with Isa and strolling through the gardens—with spring blooms offering them privacy as she regaled him with more of the knowledge she acquired during her years of studying history—filled his dreams. He could feel her in his arms as he slept, his mind progressing to images of stripping her bare, laying her down on the very bed in which he slept, and making love to her over and over.

Ric had not had such vivid dreams of a woman since he was enamored with Bella, and he realized now those dreams had all been physical. There had never been the prelude of seeking out Bella's company simply to be in her presence; he had never been fascinated by what she had to say. Bella had flattered his ego, but he understood now that he focused his attention on how she made him feel acceptable to his peers, not any genuine emotions of affection between them.

He felt a combination of emotions toward Isa, and they ranged from the merely friendly to the need to join his body with hers and claim her as his own. He awoke well before the sun was even considering making an appearance. He felt restless and aroused; neither feeling would dissipate by lying in a half-empty bed wishing he was tangled in the sheets with Isa. He had already informed Robbie that he would look for Isa before they departed, so he slipped from the bed while his squire snored softly on the trundle. He dressed in the dark and found a sprig of mint to chew on as he slipped from the chamber.

He found his way to the scriptorium and slipped inside just as he had done the night he discovered Isa within. This time he was sure he was alone. She had not arrived yet, and Ric prayed that she would come soon. He stood beside a window watching as the twinkling stars faded away, but the sun had not yet peeked over the horizon. He felt calm, which surprised him. He did not think he would feel this settled while waiting for Isa, and he almost never felt this way before riding off to the next battle. Ric was lost in thought as the sky welcomed splashes of pink and purple amid the yellow glow of the awakening sun. He heard the door click and the pause before it shut.

"Ric?"

Isa could not believe Ric stood alone in her sanctuary. While he had joined her there many other times, she had not expected to find anyone there, especially not Ric. He cast a handsome figure leaning against the window embrasure. His surcoat gleamed as light softly filtered through the glass. His dark hair and impressive physique gave him an air of danger, but Isa confessed to herself that she had only ever felt safe in his presence.

Ric turned when she whispered his name. He pushed away from the window and stepped toward her. "I leave in an hour," Ric did not have time to waste if he was to make any inroads with his goodbye.

"Where are you going?" Isa paused at Ric's unexpected declaration.

"Maxwell territory. There've been more skirmishes, and the English are moving toward my clan."

"And you're being sent to fight them?"

"Yes. I won't stand by while the people who welcomed me into their home face attack from those who have no claim on the land."

"You have changed your opinion of the Scots quite quickly for someone who has only been in the country such a short time."

"My opinion has never changed, but my ability to speak of it has." Ric stepped toward her, and she did not move away. "Isa, I came to say goodbye."

Isa swallowed before nodding. She understood he might not return, and the weight that settled upon her chest felt as though it would crush her. When he stepped close enough to pull her into his arms, she did not resist.

"I don't want you to say goodbye," she murmured. "Can we not say something else? Perhaps 'until later.'"

"Isa, you know that's what I would prefer. And I would kiss you, sharing with you a hint of what will have to wait 'until later.'"

Isa tipped her head back as her arm wound around Ric's neck. The feel of her fingers at his nape brought a rumbling growl from deep within. Ric's mouth descended to hers, and neither gave nor accepted quarter. The kiss was a conflagration of need and desire. Ric's hands roamed over Isa's body as much to remember the feel as to brand every inch as his. Her free hand slid over his chest and around to his back, as she seemed to need reassurance that he was truly within her embrace. Ric trailed kisses to behind her ear, and her whimpers of frustration voiced his own feelings.

"If I were not an innocent," Isa breathed.

Ric pulled his face away and looked into her eyes. "What are you saying, Isa?"

"You understand. If I were not a maiden, I would be able to offer you more. I could take more."

"Touch me." His meaning was clear, but he did not move, giving her the choice. Between being raised in a large keep and living at the royal court, she had seen and heard enough to understand how a man and a woman coupled, even the foreplay. Isa slid one hand down to the etched marble that was his backside. She explored the groove at his hip before her fingers wrapped about the perfect circle that his taut buttocks made. Her other hand slid to his waist before sliding lower.

"Kiss," was all Isa could say, and Ric happily obliged. As their tongues once more dueled, Isa slid her hand to cup his length. It was the first time she had ever felt one. She had felt his arousal press against her the first time they kissed, and it certainly pressed against her now, but she had never run her hand over one. "Are they all so long and hard?" she mused.

"Dear God, Isa. Say aught else like that, and I shall spend myself."

"Just from my words? Doesn't it need to be touched?" Her innocent question was accompanied by unsure strokes over his leggings. Ric grasped her wrist.

"This wasn't a good idea. I can't let you touch me. My thoughts are not ones that should be directed toward a virgin."

"How unfortunate for me then."

"Isa," he growled.

"Ric." Her purr was the perfect opposite to his guttural warning.

"I don't think you understand what you do to me."

"Then tell me." The tone was innocent, but the gleam of a seductress entered her eyes. It was a natural expression for Isa, not the practiced one of a courtier. She did not realize the power she possessed over Ric in that moment...in every moment, if he were to be honest.

"Isa, if I could, I would swipe that table clear of everything until I had space to lay you down and sink into you."

"You want to couple with me?"

Ric's head fell back with his eyes closed, and he took a deep breath. "More than I've ever wanted aught else."

"You're the only mon who has ever touched me like this, the only one to have ever spoken to me like this." Ric tried to pull away, ashamed to be taking advantage of her. "Don't." Her hushed tone matched the longing in her eyes. "I don't want to let go yet."

She slid the hand that rested as his waist over the ridges of his abdomen, over the hardened planes of his chest until once again her fingers entangled in the hair at his nape. She rose onto her toes as she pressed the full length of her tall body against his.

"Ric, I'm frightened you won't return. I don't want to let go of you yet." Isa prayed he understood the deeper meaning of her words, and she was rewarded with a deep kiss that was tender rather than needy. Ric's arms wrapped around her and pressed her against him, not in an act of arousal so much as a need to fuse them into one with nothing that could come between them.

"Isa, when I return, I shall ask the king to grant me permission to court you. I think we suit, and I would have us get to know one another better to see if it's true."

"Court me?"

"I intend to marry you, Isa." Isa's mouth dropped open in surprise, and Ric swooped in for another kiss. This one began with the tenderness that a pledge of marriage garnered, but once more need swept through them. "I don't know how long I shall be gone. It could be days. Or it could be weeks and months."

"I'm not going anywhere, Ric."

"But you're of an age when your father could announce a betrothal any day."

"Then ask the king before you go. Make your intentions known, and I will be sure the queen knows I welcome them."

"I don't want to leave you."

"And I can't come with you." They pressed their foreheads together before exchanging three more brief kisses. They both knew Ric could not linger, so they released each other. Neither was happy to let go. "I will walk to the bailey with you."

"Isa," his tone was a warning. "Do you know what people will think if they see us together this early in the morning?"

"Do you really wish to consider marrying me?"

"Of course, but–" Ric did not get to finish before Isa placed her slender finger over his lips.

"Then let them think what they like."

"And if the king denies me? If I don't return? Your reputation would be destroyed."

"If the king says no, would you not press the issue?" Isa ignored the possibility of his death.

"Of course I would. I will not be pushed aside so easily. I would find a way, regardless. I intend to ask merely as a courtesy."

"Then my reputation would not be ruined. We would simply be a betrothed couple saying adieu."

"Is that what you want? Do you not want more time to get to know me?"

"Part of me feels as if I've known you a lifetime already. More than one mon has approached me over the years since I arrived at court, but none has caught my interest. None have I considered pledging myself to."

"I feel the same. I don't understand it, but I feel as though I've found what I didn't know I lost. What I need."

The couple gazed at one another for another long moment before slipping back into one another's arms. Isa rested her head against Ric's shoulder as he stroked her back, and her arms wrapped around his waist.

"I'm scared you'll be hurt or won't come back. What if you're captured?"

"Isa, I am coming back to you. Now that I know

we have a chance, naught will keep me from you. Not Edward, not any of his men."

"Promise me you'll be as careful as a warrior can be in battle. Don't do aught foolish."

"Not when I have something, someone, so precious to return to."

They clung to each other a moment longer before they joined hands and left the scriptorium. They made their way to the bailey where they released each other before stepping outside. Horsemen and foot soldiers gathered as horses stomped their hooves and shook their bridles, creating a symphony of ringing metal. The buzz of voices made the inevitability of Ric's departure more real for both of them. Isa spotted Elizabeth and Deirdre Fraser and Ceit Comyn. The latter two were now Sinclairs, and they stood embraced by their massive Highlander husbands. Magnus Sinclair held Deirdre against his mountainous frame, her feet dangling in the air as she clung to him. Isa's heart went out to the couple. They had only been reunited for a few short months after being kept apart for seven years by Deirdre's ambitious parents. Ceit seemed to be giving her husband Tavish an earful before flinging herself into his arms. The kiss the couple exchanged had many people looking away. A slightly more reserved Elizabeth, now a Bruce, embraced her husband as the king's younger adopted brother, Edward, whispered in his wife's ear. She nodded before burying her face in his chest, but when she looked up, Isa could see the look of determination on her face that every woman married to a warrior wore when her man was about to ride off into the unknown. Isa followed Ric to where Robbie stood with their mounts. Using the horses as a shield, they tangled all four hands together.

"I believe the other ladies are friends of yours.

You shall have company beyond the ladies who serve the queen. I get the distinct impression that you are not fond of your companions."

"I'm not, but I'm not sure the Sinclair ladies or Elizabeth will welcome me. I allowed myself to be carried away with some rather unflattering, downright cruel, things that were said aboot Deirdre and Magnus. I'm rather ashamed of following the other ladies' lead."

"But you regret your actions?"

"Very much."

"Then apologize."

"It's not that simple at court."

"None of them are ladies at court anymore. It seems they have moved well past that. And I heard rumors that the challenges to Elizabeth and Edward's marriage have not been permanently laid to rest yet. I'm sure she would appreciate the added protection of a lady she can trust."

Isa looked in the direction of the others, but the horses blocked her view. She was not as confident as Ric that she would be forgiven for following along when the former ringleader of the ladies-in-waiting made disparaging remarks about Magnus and Deirdre. Ric lifted Isa's chin, and more was conveyed in the look they exchanged than the words they could express.

"I shall return to you, Isa. One way or another."

"Don't say that. I don't want it to be your body they bring back." Tears pricked behind her eyelids as she fought to control a sense of fear and grief she had never experienced before. She remembered when, as a child, she and her siblings watched with their mother as their father rode out. It had been a different type of feeling, watching her father versus the man she was considering marrying. She was not sure if her mother ever felt this way. Despite four children together, her parents were never warm to one another.

"I wish I could say don't worry about me, but I will admit that it feels more special than I imagined, having someone care whether I come back alive or not." Ric cupped both sides of her jaw, and Isa tilted her chin as their eyes once more locked. The need for one more kiss was evident. Their lips brushed together before pressing together firmly, Isa opening to accept Ric's tongue. He swept the satin of her cheek and velvety tongue as she leaned into the kiss, each with their hands fisted in the other's clothing. They were oblivious to the world around them until gasps and a new buzz of voices reached them. Neither noticed the horses had shifted and revealed them to everyone standing in the bailey. Ric pressed Isa behind him as his hands rested on his hips, dangerously close to the hilt of his sword and a knife. The Bruce approached, and Isa wanted to sink into the ground.

"Are felicitations in order?" The king's question was more of a demand.

"That is Lady Isa's choice, Your Majesty."

"Is there a choice when you've compromised the lady in the midst of my army and half the livery?"

"Yes." Ric's succinct answer made Robert's russet eyebrows nearly meet his hairline. The color began to rise in Robert's neck and cheeks.

"I don't believe the English rules of chivalry are all that different from the Scottish rules of honor. You've just been caught kissing a lady-in-waiting."

"Being caught implies a degree of guilt. I don't feel guilty for saying goodbye to the woman I'd intended to ask you if I might court, but I made my intentions clear to Isa before we stepped into the bailey. However, I will not take an unwilling bride. If Isa is not prepared to marry me or no longer wishes to, then I will take the fault for this. I will not force her to marry me."

Isa pushed past Ric and stepped in front of him. Even as tall as she was, she had to lean her head back to look up at the king. She did not bother curtsying as she felt pressed to speak up, knowing that their interlude and resulting conversation was delaying everyone.

"I welcome Sir Dedric's attentions, and I, too, am inclined to marry. We intended to have more time to determine if we suit, but that is not an option any longer." Isa looked back over her shoulder at Ric. "And I'm fairly certain we do."

The king looked between them before nodding. "Your father may not take this well. He's been in talks with the Maxwell chief, and I believe they were almost to the point of signing papers."

Ric wrapped his arm around Isa's waist and pulled her back against him. "If I keep his people alive, I believe bowing out is the least the man could do."

Robert grunted. "We shall see whether the laird and the lass's father agree so merrily."

Ric pushed against his horse's flank before spinning Isa around. He cupped her skull and paused long enough for Isa to nod just enough for his fingers to feel before his mouth covered hers. Their kiss rivaled Ceit and Tavish, who had made more than one person embarrassed, but at least they were already wed.

"Right. We understand your intentions Sir Dedric, and we are all aware that Lady Isabella accepts them. You are delaying everyone." The king's tone had a touch of jest, just enough to reassure Ric and Isa that King Robert would not begrudge them their decision.

"Come back to me," Isa whispered.

"No one is keeping me from you. Ever." Ric pulled away and mounted his horse. Before spurring his horse, he pulled his leather glove from his right hand and slid the signet ring from his finger. He leaned down to Isa, kissing the back of her hand before turning it over. He pressed the ring into her palm, once more giving her a choice. Isa closed her fingers around the ring before opening it and looking at the engraving. She would have to take a closer look once she was in her chamber. She held the ring above her fingers, and it was clear it would slide off any of them. She slid it onto her thumb and smiled as it easily spun but would not easily fall off.

Ric closed his hand around hers once more and gave it a brief squeeze before nudging his horse forward. Isa stood alone, watching the men depart. Ric looked back once before riding through the gate. The riders spurred into a canter as the foot soldiers followed, jogging behind them. Isa shivered as a sense of foreboding closed in on her. She tried to brush it off, but she was unsuccessful. She was unprepared when she found herself surrounded by three women she did not expect would approach her.

"It doesn't get easier, but you become accustomed," Deirdre Sinclair slid her arm through Isa's and gave it a squeeze.

"It helps to have friends," Ceit Sinclair offered. "You aren't alone. I was fortunate to have my sisters-by-marriage the first time Tavish rode out on a sortie. I tried not to cry in front of anyone, but then none of us wanted to. But once we each retired to our chambers, all of us sobbed. We arrived at the evening meals with puffy eyes and red noses. After that, we waited until our men rode out and then commiserated with one another."

"This is my first time, too," Elizabeth offered as she took Isa's other arm. Elizabeth had experienced her husband riding out to patrol, but never into battle. She leaned into Isa and whispered, "I'm terrified."

Isa looked toward her and nodded, unable to speak around the lump in her throat.

"Let's move inside before we draw attention," Elizabeth suggested

Isa swallowed and smiled. "I believe I've made that impossible."

The other ladies chuckled and led Isa to Elizabeth and Edward's chamber, the largest of all the couples' rooms by virtue of their status as the king's relatives.

TEN

The days stretched out for Isa as she tried to fill the time between waking and sleeping with her work. She retreated to the scriptorium or the library, where she could comb through the tomes that lined the shelves. She made her appearances at meals and as the queen dictated, but when she could escape, she did. She was surprised at how forgiving the queen was when Isa spent time staring at the door, wishing she could escape to solitude. The chatter of the other ladies was even more daunting than usual. While she preferred time spent alone, she had learned to navigate the world of court and the sociability expected of a lady-in-waiting. But as her mind floated to Ric, she found she was overwhelmed by the noise.

When she was forced to be in company, she gravitated toward the Sinclair women and Elizabeth Bruce. The women knew the ins and outs of being a lady-in-waiting, and they knew what it was to have their men go into battle. The other ladies-in-waiting were unmarried and unsympathetic. Many turned their noses up at Isa as word of her behavior with Ric became fodder for gossip. Isa's choice of a half-English man earned her snide remarks and snarky smiles. Those who did not look down upon her for her choice resented her for snagging the most handsome, and available, man at court. Isa did not miss that Lady Bella Fitz-Bigod disappeared as mysteriously as she appeared. Isa tried not to imagine the worst, as the woman's timing once again synchronized with Ric's.

As the days stretched into a month, Isa relied more and more upon the Sinclairs and Elizabeth Bruce. She counted her blessings as her fears grew. She had no way to know what was happening to Ric without Elizabeth's and Deirdre's fathers' connections. They reported to her what they knew. Some days the updates reassured her and brought her a sense of calm, but most days the lack of information only made her more anxious. She fell asleep each night remembering the kisses she shared with Ric.

Ric was fed up with being wet and muddy. He rode silently behind Magnus and Tavish Sinclair, who—after he and Tavish came to blows the second day away from the castle—had turned out to be more friendly than he anticipated.

The day after leaving for the west, Tavish and Ric had disagreed about where to stop for the night. Ric argued that they would be better suited to riding into the forest and making camp where they were less noticeable. Tavish asserted that they were too large a group for such an enclosed location and would only be caught with no way to spread out and fight if ambushed. He wanted to camp along the bank of the river, but Ric contended they were too exposed. Neither man could remember who took the first swing, as their fists seemed to connect to opposing faces at the same time. Their blows served to dissipate any rancor, and they were on good terms since both sported bruised faces and a smug sense of satisfaction that they had damaged the other just as badly as they had been injured.

Magnus had stood back and watched the two men as they rolled about on the ground and only shook his head when some men stepped forward to pull them apart. As one of four boys, Magnus was used to watching his brothers wrestle one another and fight others. For once, he had to admit to himself, he was not entirely sure his brother would win. Edward stood next to Magnus grinning. He remembered fighting with Robert and their other brother Edward, Robert's blood brother, just as Tavish and Ric did. There was more at stake than just pride. There was the other men's respect for their judgment and conviction. In the end, Magnus calmly pointed out that if they rode around the bend in the river, it appeared the tree line met the bank of the river. They could have the best of both.

As Ric plodded along, he kept his eyes roving over the landscape, aware that they were in an open expanse. It was a prime place for the English, who preferred open battlefields to maneuver into their formal positions, to attack. The hair on his neck stood up when he was certain he saw a glimmer in the distance.

"They're ahead to the right." Ric spoke loud enough for only Magnus, Tavish, and Edward, who rode in the lead, to hear.

"Are ye sure?" Tavish's voice floated back to him.

"I saw the gleam of metal. They will surely be positioned for an ambush. We should stop here. Force them to come to us and lose whatever advantage they believe they have. If we ride ahead, they will surely gain the upper hand."

"And what do we do to lure them out? If they believe they are positioned to win, why would they give up their location?"

"Because they are impatient." The other men were learning that Ric was a man of few words when it came to discussing strategy and outcomes. He was decisive and to the point when discussing business, while jovial when relaxed.

"And?" Magnus prompted.

"They will always believe they're superior to any enemy regardless of how many times they are beaten. The English will grow impatient at not being able to pummel us into defeat. They will come out on their own. Be prepared for them to charge. They will most likely try to sweep into the woods and then fan out to trap us between them and the riverbank. If we position ourselves in columns into the tree line, we use a closed formation to create a shield wall. We place archers in the trees and on their bellies along the riverbank. When they approach close enough, we move into a line formation for the shield wall to expand and strengthen. They will not be prepared for our numbers. I would wager they can only see those of us who are mounted.

"They will not be able to see the scores of foot soldiers behind us. If we send the archers into the trees and along the shore, they can begin to shoot before we even move from columns into lines. We have enough men to form two solid shield wall lines. If we spread our line far into the trees, they will abandon it because it will spread them too thin. They will want to re-form into a vee and hope to plow through our lines. When they do this, our men in the woods wrap around and use the encircling tactic the English are now hoping will work. We use their own strategy against them. The key is to keep the second line hidden as best we can, so they think they can break though and fight us from the front and rear."

"And if that doesnae work?" Tavish wondered.

"Then they learn that Lowlanders are formidable and Highlanders are the devil incarnate. Fight as you would amongst your own clans. If the shield wall breaks too soon, then we kill or unhorse as many as we can and fight them on foot. If that can be done, the superior strength and physical size of your men will overwhelm the English knights, who wear more than seven stones of armor. They aren't agile on their feet, and the average foot soldier doesn't have the protection that a knight does. Make them vulnerable, and you will defeat them."

"Do we ride or stand our ground?"

"I'll remain mounted, but the rest should be on foot."

"Why ye?" Tavish demanded.

Ric saw the skepticism in all the eyes of all the men who could hear him. "The earl can ride with me if he wishes. They will want to parlay before the attack begins. It gives them time to assess our numbers. I ride forward as though to speak and negotiate terms, so while the knights sit idle believing we follow the conventions of war, you begin your attack. It keeps them from being able to charge. I thought the earl would call the charge." Ric looked at Edward and shrugged. "If you are not confident that I will remain loyal to you, then ride forward yourself. You have fought the English in Scotland and Ireland. You know everything I've said is true, but if you would rather be the representative, then I defer to you. They will expect one of us, if not both. If I go alone, there will undoubtedly be time wasted belittling me and questioning my manhood for siding with you. This will distract them while they laugh at my expense. It is only to your benefit."

"And ye are willing to subject yerself to that?" Magnus interjected.

"What else would I hear? I suspect there will be several references to being half-heathen and how my father betrayed King Edward for a woman, so there will be questions about whether my cock does my thinking. The usual jabs and jibes in the hopes of unsettling me or guilting me into turning from you."

"And if they succeed?" Magnus pressed.

"If I intended to betray you, why would I have just described a strategy that will work? I could have simply said naught and when the ambush began, ridden to join them. Instead, I have stopped us to plan and put us in control."

"And if ye already had this planned with them?" Tavish demanded.

"Then I am as good as dead. If one of them doesn't kill me for believing I've turned on them, then one of you would kill me for turning on you. You may have noticed I have someone I intend to return to. I'm not in the mood to die before I marry Isa and live a long life with many children surrounding us." Ric sighed and lowered his voice. "I saw each of you with your wives. I want what you have, what my parents had. Even if I didn't like you, which I'm not sure I do, I wouldn't make widows out of your women. They are Isa's friends and innocent in this game Edward Longshanks insists upon playing."

The three men nodded as they acknowledged Ric's honor in thinking of their wives. None of them intended to die that day either, and it was the drive to return to their wives and families that pushed them to plan their tactics carefully.

"How much longer do you think we have?" Edward Bruce asked.

Ric shaded his eyes and searched the landscape ahead of them. Tiny specks flashed in the sun, warning Ric that the English were on the move. "Just long enough to get in formation. They are on the move."

"Bluidy hell," Magnus cursed.

Orders were given with hand signals and hushed voices. The men moved into the positions that Ric had indicated, and then they waited. It was as though Ric had written a script, the English movements were so well predicted. When he saw the man leading the enemy forces, he wanted to be ill. Lord Wingate—or Geoffrey, as Ric eventually earned the right to address him—was the baron from Northumbria that Ric had squired for.

Lord Wingate was also the man who presented Ric with his spurs when King Edward knighted him. Ric would be facing down his mentor. Geoffrey had been a rigid taskmaster, but it was his demand for excellence that guided Ric not only to knighthood, but to remain alive when many of his compatriots fell in battle. Now he would be utilizing the battle skills Geoffrey ingrained in him to potentially kill the closest person he had to a father figure. He had been thirteen when Geoffrey accepted him as a squire. While the man was only fifteen years his senior, he had felt far more like a father than even an older brother. The man had seemed old for his age, and it was several years into his service that Ric learned Geoffrey was closer in age than Ric ever imagined.

"Ric." Geoffrey nodded. "I wish I could say I was surprised to see you on the far side of the battle line, but King Edward warned me of your choice."

Dear God, that means Geoffrey knows I'm a spy. He will try to keep me alive, but I can't offer him the same protection. I'm loyal to him, but if I protect him, then the Scots will know I've double-crossed them. Then how do I serve Robert?

"You are not who I thought the king would send," Ric responded.

"He wanted to ensure the battle went as it should."

Ric wanted to groan. He knew what that meant as well.

Longshanks expects me to lead the Scots to their death while somehow remaining alive. Or perhaps he truly doesn't care whether I live through this to send any reports.

"Only God can ensure that." Ric forced himself to relax as his horse began to sway. He would not give away his discomfort through a horse that fidgeted.

Geoffrey's eyebrows rose as Ric's face set in stone. A look flashed from the older man's eyes as he understood Ric's meaning. "I take it the apple didn't fall far from the tree?"

"The apple never should have been taken from the tree."

"That is too far in the past to be changed. The apple should have grown into its own tree, with deep roots."

"It did. The roots of the new tree are entwined with the remaining roots of the original tree, which might be dead but still keeps the younger one grounded." Ric was tired of speaking in euphemisms, but he knew it was giving the others the time they needed.

"And what of the water and food given to the young tree to ensure it thrived?" Geoffrey persisted.

"There is no denying the tree benefited. It has grown strong and tall, but the roots have crept from the garden and found their way back."

Geoffrey nodded and rested his forearms on his pommel. He seemed to be assessing Ric, but the latter could not be certain what his former mentor looked for. There was little about Ric that Geoffrey did not already know. Ric could not imagine what Geoffrey might be looking for.

"Did you ever learn that Wingate was once part of Scotland? It was one of the smaller parcels of land that the Normans gained when King William attempted his invasion. The man should have known his limits."

Ric did know that piece of history, but he understood the subtext to Geoffrey's comments. He had often wondered how much of what Geoffrey did was simply duty, or true conviction to Edward's cause. Now, he had a sense that the man would rather not be fighting yet another skirmish for land that had passed hands for nearly two hundred years.

"Lady Marjorie will wish me to pass her regards." Geoffrey's abrupt change of subject to his own family disoriented Ric. Even when Ric lived among Geoffrey's household, Geoffrey spoke little about his own family. Ric knew the man was devoted to his wife and children, but it was not a topic he imagined they would discuss in preparation for a battle. "Dedric is nearly as tall as I am."

Ric felt his stomach go concave at the mention of his namesake. He and the boy shared the same difference in age as Ric did with Geoffrey. There had even been discussion that the younger Dedric would squire for the older, but the boy's mother was not ready for him to move so far away. "Is he squiring for Lord Havens?"

"He is. He is able to return for holidays, and we pay a visit when we can."

Ric nodded, wondering why the conversation was drawing on for so long. Geoffrey had not taken his eyes off Ric since the conversation started, but Ric was beginning to believe that Geoffrey drew out their talk to offer Ric's forces time to take their positions. Just as he came to that conclusion, Geoffrey nodded, and a call went forward from Edward Bruce. The Scottish archers began to fire in anticipation of the

English attack. Geoffrey nudged his horse forward, drawing his sword as he aimed for Ric. Ric drew his sword but spurred his horse away from Geoffrey's approach. He would not be the man to kill his mentor, and he was not going to die before returning to Isa.

The English responded to the Scottish war cry, taken off-guard by the commencement before Lord Wingate returned to their lines. The English surged forward, covering the distance between where they had waited and where the Scots moved from columns to a line, forming their shield wall. As English warriors came within range of the Scottish archers, screams of pain filled the air. Men and horses tumbled to the ground as the British charged toward the Scottish warriors.

Ric rode toward the trees and dismounted, slapping his horse's flank and trusting that the animal would find its way to where Robbie hid with the other horses. He watched English foot soldiers attempt to outflank the Scots, but the shield wall was too long. The English scrambled to re-form when they realized that they could not spread themselves so thin. Just as Ric predicted, they repositioned themselves into a vee. The mounted knights led the new battle formation but riding high upon their horses only made them easier targets for the archers.

The Lowland archers had experience with aiming through the English armor and knew where the susceptible points were located. They aimed for those points, and one man after another toppled from his horse. Those who managed to remain seated soon met the shield wall, their horses neighing and refusing to push through the wall as the Highlanders and Lowlanders beat the hilt of their swords against their targes. The horses' eyes rolled, and many reared. The knights tried to use this to their advantage to trample members of the shield wall.

Instead, it opened the horses to attack, and more knights were unseated.

Ric swung his sword over and over as countless English knights seemed to seek him out, making him their particular target. He cut them down, feeling little remorse for killing those who were his countrymen only a moon ago. It was his life or theirs and, as he had told the other men, he did not intend to die that day. He had discovered something, someone, to live for. He fought to return to Isa's side as much as he did to defend his true homeland.

From the corner of his eye, he caught glimpses of Magnus and Tavish, who fought at each other's back. The sight of the two nearly identical men moving in such unison caught more than one man's attention. It was impressive to watch either of them in the lists, but to watch how they moved as one inspired awe. However, Ric did not have the luxury of looking for long, or he would lose his head. He continued to cut through foot soldiers as he fought his way back to the head of the Scottish force.

The English broke through the first shield wall but were unprepared for the second one. The Scottish plan to outflank them was working. The Scots closed ranks and swept around them and crept inward from the trees. It was not long before the English were trapped in a noose of their own making. Ric stood breathing heavily as he watched impending defeat begin to register on the Englishmen's faces, though they continued to fight. He looked around to find Edward Bruce, who he had not seen since the beginning of the battle. He prayed Robert's brother had not become one of the victims of the Scottish king's feud with the English king.

Ric watched in horror as Edward and Geoffrey thrust and parried, and it appeared that Edward was gaining the upper hand. Ric crept around them and approached from Geoffrey's back where he drove the hilt of his sword between Geoffrey's shoulder blades and shoved him aside. Ric swept the older man's legs from under him as he lost his balance from the unexpected attack at his back. As Geoffrey staggered away from Edward, Ric brought the hilt of his sword down on Geoffrey's head. He intended to knock the man out, not kill him. When the older man crumpled at his feet, he looked up to see Edward watching him.

"He was the closest man to a father I had. I was his squire before he presented me with my spurs. We send him home in defeat to his wife and children." Ric's tone brooked no disagreement, so Edward nodded, acknowledging Ric's honorable demand.

With Lord Wingate laying sprawled on the ground and his second-in-command dead, the battle dwindled to a few remaining pairs. Magnus and Tavish wiped sweat and grime from their faces and brows. Magnus looked at a gash on his arm that would need stitches, but was not life threatening. Tavish clutched his ribs when he attempted to bend over to catch his breath.

"Getting soft, little brother?" Magnus taunted. Even though Tavish was older, he was the shortest of the four brothers. By a hair. But it was an ongoing jest, and not one Tavish found funny.

"Still more brawn than brains, I see. I'm fine." Tavish smirked as he pointed to Magnus's arm. "I'm afraid ma embroidery skills aren't what Deirdre's are. I willna be fawning over ye and yer looks like yer wee bride."

"And I'm more likely to squeeze the life from ye when I bind yer ribs than kiss them better. I canna imagine why Ceit bothers."

"Because she enjoys being thanked," Tavish grinned. The brothers embraced, unashamed to show their affection for one another. Both were relieved they had survived another battle. The brothers walked toward Ric and Edward, their arms resting on each other's shoulders. They looked down at the man who lay on the ground before Ric and Edward.

"Is he dead? Who is he to ye?" Magnus asked.

"I lived in his household as his squire from being thirteen to twenty. He was as close to a father as I ever had. He made me into a man. He has a son named for me." Ric looked down at Geoffrey before bending over and rolling the man onto his back. The older man groaned as his eyes fluttered open. From his position on his back, the English knight looked at the four towering men looking down at him.

"I should have known Hell would be filled with Scots," Geoffrey grumbled as Ric reached out his hand and pulled his former mentor to his feet. The English knight looked around and found a few of his men sitting injured or standing looking dazed. He was surprised the Scots were not sweeping through the injured, finishing off any who still breathed.

"You're defeated, Geoff. These men won't be fighting again any time soon. Return to Lady Marjorie and give her my regards." Ric spoke quietly as he tried to keep his raw emotions from rising to the surface. He was relieved his friend survived, but he knew letting the man live would only mean meeting him on a battlefield again. He knew without a doubt that he would not return to King Edward's service. He could not serve as the brutal man's spy, and he would not kill the countrymen who welcomed him rather than ostracized him.

Ric whistled, and two horses trotted forward from two different directions. It was the whistle Geoffrey taught him and made him practice over and over as he trained his destrier from a colt. Ric caught the bridles and led the horses toward the riverbank. He released them, so they could drink. Geoffrey had followed him.

"You're not coming back, are you?" Ric looked back at the older man and shook his head. "I knew it was only a matter of time. You have the soul of Scot, no matter how Edward tried to hammer it from you. Your father was a better man for loving your mother."

Ric swallowed and nodded. "What will you tell Edward?"

"What was it you said? Ah yes, 'there was simply more of them than us.' I think that will suffice, especially since I can send it in a missive." Geoffrey chuckled but held his head. "Did you have to hit me so bloody hard? My head feels like it's been used as an anvil."

"I couldn't let the Bruce's brother kill you, but I couldn't bring myself to force you to surrender." Ric looked out over the river before turning to Geoffrey. "Who will the king send to kill me? Will it be you?" Ric was not sure he wanted the answer.

Geoffrey continued to stare at the river and shook his head. "It might be me. The first time. I won't do it, so the king will have to find someone else, and I don't know who it will be. It wouldn't surprise me if it's Lady Bella. It wouldn't be the first time for her."

"That woman hasn't had a first time for aught since she was knee high to a grasshopper."

Geoffrey chuckled again, this time coughing as a result. "That is true, but I understand she is already here. Or at least in Scotland, that is."

"She appeared at my clan's keep, and I threw her out. She appeared at the Bruce's court, but I did not see her before I left."

"Is there a woman?" Ric rubbed the back of his neck before nodding. "Keep Bella away from her."

The warning was clear, and Ric's stomach soured as she thought about the two women being together at court. "She won't still be at court. She's bound to be somewhere nearby awaiting a report from one of these men. Hopefully, her informant is laying here getting cold. She'll tell Edward of your role in my defeat. She's bound to learn of it. She sees and hears more than God himself."

"Only because she's the Devil."

"Ric, I wish you the happiness your father found with your mother, but I also wish you the long life I've had with Marjorie."

"Thank you, Geoff."

"One day, maybe within our lives, there will be peace long enough for me to meet your lady."

"I would like that. Lady Marjorie would adore Isa."

"Isa?" Ric felt a bolt of panic not having meant to share Isa's name with Geoffrey. He trusted the man, but he did not trust the walls in Geoffrey's keep.

"Don't fear. I won't ask her surname, and I'll only speak her name to Marjorie when I'm sure no one will hear."

Ric nodded, feeling the tension ease slightly within his belly. "Take care, Geoffrey."

Both men knew their conversation could not carry on much longer. Geoffrey's men were already collecting the wounded and putting them on wagons to take back to their camp. The Scots were doing the same, while men from both sides were digging graves for the fallen. There were too many to travel with, so their final resting place would have to be where they fell.

"I wish you the same. Ric, the MacLellans are next. Ride there now or it'll be too late. Hargate's been given orders to raze the land and burn the keep." The men embraced, and Geoffrey mounted before giving the signal to his men who were not burying the dead to retreat. Ric walked back to his newfound friends and compatriots.

"My clan is next. We ride to the MacLellans. There's an order to raze their fields and burn the castle. I must warn my cousin."

"Yer father was betrayed by his friend, but it would seem yers is ever loyal." Magnus nodded toward Geoffrey. Ric watched Geoffrey ride away without moving. When the man faded from sight, he looked at the others.

"Lord Wingate is a good man. He is the one who taught me that honor is the only thing a man can ever truly call his own. He will fight for Edward because fealty binds him, but his honor also knows that Edward's determination to be the Hammer of the Scots is wrong. He lives along the border, too. He's seen, and lives with, the damage this war is doing. He's lost friends and family just as the rest of us have. He has risked a great deal informing me of Edward's next target along with losing this battle. He may very well die for this battle, even if it's not on this field. Edward will not accept defeat with grace."

"Then there will be a marker on yer head for leading us to victory." Tavish watched him closely, and Ric did not respond. What Tavish said was true, and the only way to appease the easily offended king would be to send back information that would lead to an English victory. This was something he was unwilling to do. He would continue to supply Bella with half-truths and lies, but he would not compromise his honor any longer. He was, finally and firmly, in Robert the Bruce's camp.

ELEVEN

The ride to the MacLellan keep was made in pouring rain that made the horses slip and sucked the feet of the soldiers in the resulting bog. The men grumbled about sleeping on the sodden ground, puddles forming around them during the night. By the time they reached the border of the Maxwell and MacLellan territories, Ric was ready to sell his soul for a dry chamber, a hot meal, and a steaming bath. The rain lessened over the next two days as they rambled on to the keep where Ric's cousins welcomed them. His mother's cousin Emelyn was just as happy to see him this time as when he rode in unexpectedly several weeks earlier. His second cousin was less excited, especially when he clearly began calculating how much it would cost his clan to house and feed so many warriors. Malcolm's demeanor did not improve with having to share his home with Highlanders, but he begrudgingly thanked them for their arrival when the impending dire circumstances were explained. It was Edward Bruce who finally convinced Malcolm that the threat was imminent, and just as possibly horrifying, as the one what killed Ric's mother.

Edward Bruce was familiar with Lord Hargate, just as Ric was. Both men knew the baron could be reasonable and judicious, but only where England's interests lay. He was ruthless and vindictive when it came to squashing the Scottish aspirations for independence. It was these reasons that led Geoffrey to warn Ric of his next opponent.

Their first evening in the keep saw Ric, Edward, and the Sinclairs well fed and attended. The serving lasses tried to catch the attention of each man, but none of them paid them any mind. By the fourth course, the women were growing impatient and frustrated that none of them had managed to garner more than a half-hearted, distracted smile. When one of them tried to seat herself on Tavish's lap, he pushed back on his end of the bench like a scalded cat and nearly unseated Magnus. The latter found it hilariously funny until another woman's breasts practically tumbled into his face as she refilled his chalice. He pulled away so abruptly that wine spilled across the table and dribbled from the edge. The woman squealed and almost tumbled back into Ric. It was a comedic scene that had many of the people sitting at the lower tables laughing hysterically while the men shot daggers from their eyes at Malcolm. Eventually, Lady Emelyn stepped in and shooed the serving women away, explaining they had set their sights on happily married men and that they would do better with the other warriors.

By the time the meal ended, Ric struggled to keep his eyes open. Each of the men had the opportunity to bathe before the meal, and when he entered his chamber, he found Robbie had already laid out his belongings. He had released the squire to find his own entertainment with the other younger men of the clan, who were not quite as suspicious as the older members. Ric climbed into bed, and his eyes drifted shut. His breathing was just settling into a deeper pattern when he heard the door handle jiggle. He did not expect Robbie back so soon, so he grasped the dagger he had tucked under his pillow. He kept his eyes closed, pretending to sleep, until he heard the door close behind the intruder. The unwanted visitor wore a heavy cloak, obscuring any chance of being recognized. Ric opted not to wait to discover if the person was friend or foe, so he flung the knife toward the doorway, embedding it into the wood only inches from the person's head. The hood flew back, and a livid Bella rushed toward him.

"You could have killed me," the irate woman hissed.

"And you know I am not a man whose chamber you should be sneaking into. Once again, Bella, what the bloody hell are you doing here?" Ric sat up but tucked the bed covers around his naked body. He glared at the woman who was rapidly becoming the bane of his existence.

"You led a very successful defense—or was it really an offense—against Lord Wingate. I'm not sure the king will understand why."

"Because refusing to fight would only make the Scots suspicious. I can't learn aught of worth if I don't have access to them, or worse, I'm dead." Ric's tone made his impatience clear.

"Do not speak to me as though I'm a simpleton. I—"

"Then don't act as one. Bella, you seem to be the one who doesn't want the king to gain the information he demands. You keep endangering this mission with your unwillingness to wait. You keep making appearances in the most inopportune places, and you made people suspicious at Robert's court."

"Do you mean the woman who kept making doe eyes at you the entire time? Does she suspect you're there for motives other than making a new home?"

Ric would not answer that. He would not endanger Isa, and he did not want to consider whether Isa did not trust him as much as he hoped. Never mind the fact that he did not want to consider his own guilt and complicity in deceiving her. His feelings for her ran true and deep, but he could not overlook the fact that he was still bound to King Edward.

"Are you not listening to me?" Bella demanded.

"Not particularly. I'm exhausted and will have to ride out early in the morning. I would like to enjoy my sleep while it is in a bed and not a pond."

Bella glared at him as she inched closer, and Ric pulled the bedding tighter. "Oh, do stop. I am no more interested in bedding you than I am any other Scot. I am here on the king's behest. And so are you. You would do well to remember that."

"And you would do well to remember how to be subtle. You will land us both in a dungeon if you persist in seeking me out. If I didn't know better, I would think you are the one trying to sabotage this mission."

Bella sniffed and turned her nose up before spinning toward the door. "Very well. I shall return to Stirling and await your return. You had better return with news of Scottish defeat and humiliation. I don't know of aught else that will appease King Edward. His messengers are demanding more information than I have to offer. You are complicating both of our lives."

"Perhaps if you had been in a battle or two, you might understand that there is more to winning and losing than who limps away with the least number of wounds to lick. Gathering useful and accurate information about an enemy's strength and weaknesses is not as simple as facing them once. You wish to do your job, but you must let me do mine. Now leave before someone passes the door and hears voices. I've already thrown you out of this keep once. Spare yourself the ordeal of me doing it again. Be discreet as you leave. If anyone questions, or even suspects, that I was tupping you, I will kill you. King Edward's delegate or not. I won't be of any use if they all question my honor when they believe I'm pursuing someone with genuine intentions."

"And are those intentions genuine? Do you wish to marry that insipid little girl?"

"What matters is the perception. Leave, Bella, before I throw you out."

The woman slipped out through the door just as quietly as she entered. Ric fell back against the pillows and prayed Bella would leave him in peace before she ruined everything.

Morning brought a throbbing headache for Ric as he squeezed his eyes shut. Robbie's snores reassured him that his squire made it back to their chamber in one piece. He wondered if having Robbie present would have helped or worsened his conversation with Bella. No one had come pounding on his door with accusations, so he assumed no one was any the wiser about her visit. He prayed nothing would be said at the morning meal.

Ric nudged Robbie awake before dressing himself in fresh leggings and surcoat. He chewed a sprig of mint and ran his fingers through his hair before making his way belowstairs. He scanned the occupants of the Great Hall and then the dais. No glares or whispers came from the people who saw him. He allowed himself a sigh. He took his place at the dais and poured honey onto his porridge, but he had not taken his first bite before Malcolm began demanding answers.

"How many men will be arriving to attack my home and my people? Are they coming because of you? What are you going to do to keep them from even stepping foot on my land?"

Ric swallowed the lump of porridge that sat on his tongue as he decided how best to answer his cousin's questions. He attempted not to grimace." I cannot say for sure how many men but knowing Lord Hargate and the demands he will have received from King Edward, I would venture to say well over two hundred men, if not more. It will depend upon whether he has enlisted the aid of any other border barons. They are coming because they have failed to gain any footholds to the east. The fact that I am here will only make trying to kill me all the better revenge for Edward, but I am not the only reason for their arrival. We already have patrols set up to assist yours, and I intend to depart on a sortie this morning. I imagine Edward Bruce and the Sinclairs will do the same. We haven't spoken yet. Once we have news of Hargate's location and numbers, we can plan accordingly."

"And if they are already on my doorstep? If they are so close they can spit and hit us?"

"Then we would already know. Hargate likes his comforts. He will have a massive tent with furnishings along with all that is needed to feed and support two hundred warriors. He is not going anywhere quickly or quietly. We will find him before he finds us. Even a hundred scouts could return here before his lumbering army makes an appearance."

Malcolm appeared mollified by Ric's brisk answers. He nodded, clearly pleased that Ric had answers without having to mull over anything. "I'll ride out with you. My men will only wear their dark plaids, naught to give away our clan, assuming this Hargate lord hasn't already crossed the border to my land. We look for his scouts and harry them enough to send a message, but remember, dead men don't speak. Killing all of them won't serve our purpose. I intend to give Hargate the impression that he is facing a larger force than he assumes." Malcolm spoke with the authority only a laird possessed, and Ric had to agree with the man's plan.

Ric finished his bowl of porridge as Malcolm spoke and rose from his chair. He looked down the table to where Tavish, Magnus, and Edward now sat quickly shoveling their own porridge. He signaled Robbie and told him to relay the news to the men that they would be departing within the hour. The sun had barely touched the horizon.

His cousin's tracking skills impressed Ric. They undoubtedly surpassed even his own. Rain had washed away much of the path Ric and the others took to arrive at the MacLellan keep, but Malcolm quickly spotted the remnants and followed it several miles east toward the border the McLellans shared with the Maxwells. Malcolm called a halt when he noticed a new set of prints that belonged to more than one horse.

"I believe we've found the first traces of one of their scouting parties. The prints are fresh from this morning. They haven't ventured close enough to see the keep, if they only came this way, but they are far closer than I'm comfortable with."

Magnus slipped from his horse, having remained

silent for most of the ride. He was a superior tracker in his own right, but he had deferred to the laird. He followed the hoofprints until they seemed to disappear. He moved aside brush and found prints leading toward a meadow. The open expanse would either allow them to catch the scouts or lead them to an ambush.

"These are heavier than the others. They're galloping, but my guess is they heard us rather than saw us. They're racing to give their report. They assume they've covered their tracks."

"I'll ride ahead. Stay far enough back that if it's an ambush, you're not caught," Ric's words were not a suggestion, but several heads shook. "How are we going to catch them without alerting them? There are forty horsemen with us. Forty charging horses make quite a lot of noise." Everyone knew Ric's observation was an understatement, but none of the other leaders were in agreement with Ric's plan.

"Ten of us ride ahead. I doubt their scouting party is any larger than that, so we will have to ride hard to catch them before they can rejoin the rest of their men. By the time we're done chatting with them, our own men will have caught up," Tavish reasoned.

"And if it's an ambush, I'll be leading the king's brother right to his death," Ric's mouth firmed into a thin line.

"You speak as though I've haven't spent the past fifteen years of my life fighting. I suspect it will be saving your arse rather than the other way around." Edward Bruce's temper flared at the unintended insult.

Magnus mounted his horse and spurred it forward before tossing over his shoulder, "While ye squabble, they're gaining more of a lead. Follow if ye wish, but I ride on."

Tavish was quick to join his brother, leaving Ric, Edward, and Malcolm little choice but to follow. Malcolm called orders for his men to follow at a slower pace, then pulled ahead as the only one familiar with the land. It did not take them long to spot riders in the distance. They could tell the other men rode at a breakneck pace, and it would be difficult to overtake them.

"There is a faster way if we head to the left and follow a riverbed. The meadow wraps further ahead, and the riverbed follows it. We can cross it and be waiting for them." Malcolm steered the sortie party as they charged through the meadow that stood between them and their detour.

It was only fifteen minutes later that Ric and the others sat facing the approaching riders. They stood within a cluster of trees that grew along the riverbank. Magnus and Tavish had brought their bows and arrows. The first man to approach received Tavish's arrow to his thigh. His horse bucked, sending him flying to the ground. The seven other men looked toward the trees, trying to discern where the attack was coming from. Magnus and Tavish unleashed a volley of arrows that landed near the horses' hooves, agitating them and nearly unseating several more of the Englishmen. As they attempted to regain control of their mounts, Ric and the others surrounded the men. The surprise arrival of more horses only made the English ones nearly unmanageable. The Scots laughed as they waited for the horse to settle enough to begin their interrogation.

"Your surcoat insignia shows you are Lord Graystone's men. I take it Lord Hargate doesn't travel alone," Ric mused. The men looked at one another, but none spoke. Magnus and Tavish both drew dirks, and Edward and Malcolm followed suit. Ric crossed his arms over his pummel and leaned forward as though he would strike up a conversation with a friend. "I already know that Hargate has been tasked with attacking the MacLellans. What I would like to know is whether Graystone travels with Hargate or if King Edward doesn't trust Hargate to get the job done and has sent Graystone to finish the task." Ric looked at each of the men before looking at the Scots. "String them up and cut off their bollocks. Perhaps their screams will bring their compatriots to investigate. They may even be cut down before they bleed to death."

Ric sat up and appeared to be ready to turn his horse, but one of the men spoke up.

"I'd rather keep my twig and berries just as they are." The whiny voice brought a smile to more than one Scottish mouth. "Hargate and Graystone ride together. Hargate sought Graystone's assistance when he discovered you were on the way to the Mac-Lellans. We already know of Lord Wingate's defeat and disgrace."

Ric wanted to rail against the notion that Wingate was disgraced, but he knew the English would not see it any other way. Instead, he sat and waited along with the Scots. None of them would speak first, each having been taught to wait out silence until someone else was too uncomfortable and had to fill the void. They were not disappointed.

"Hargate couldn't raise enough men because most of his knights have already served their forty days, even though the new year is still young. He had to ask Graystone because King Edward didn't send any other knights or foot soldiers." The whiny man continued to speak as his terrified eyes darted around the group. "We're merely scouts."

"Scouts who intend to return to your barons and inform them of your findings. Findings I would very much like to know aboot." Edward Bruce spoke up.

"We found the tracks of your army that marched to the MacLellans. The size of the force, along with what we know of the MacLellans, made us turn around."

"And just what does that mean?" Edward continued to press.

"It means you are prepared to put up a mighty fight."

"Ye said Hargate could nae raise all forty knights. Assuming Graystone did, that would still be less than eighty mounted warriors. How many foot soldiers have they?" Tavish cut in.

"Between the two, just over a hundred and fifty."

The Scots looked at one another, and Ric tried to gauge the unspoken messages that seemed to flow easily among the four men. Tavish broke the silence when he nudged his horse forward and grabbed the man closest to him by the front of the man's surcoat. His fist landed squarely against the man's cheekbone, and the crack was audible. Magnus followed suit, driving his fist in a nearby man's nose. When Magnus pulled away, the nose was clearly twisted halfway across the man's cheek.

"Do any of you need convincing to send a message back to the barons?" Malcolm asked. Collectively the men shook their heads. Between Magnus and Tavish's punches and the dirks the four Scots continued to hold, none of them were interested in tempting further violence.

"Tell your lords that if they persist in their attack, they will find themselves outnumbered." Malcolm declared. "Not only do the MacLellans possess more men than you've described, we are now joined with King Robert's forces. There is no chance that they will be allowed to leave with dignity like Hartley allowed Wingate. We will slaughter each and every mon who steps foot on my land and deliver your entrails to your king." Malcolm held his knife up, catching the sunlight that shone against the razor-sharp blade. "Did you know that a knife thrust upwards behind the sternum will kill a mon even faster than a sword through the belly? Interesting notion."

The malevolent grin he offered the English men had them nodding. The circle opened for them as they spun around. Just before they were out of range, Malcolm flung his knife, catching one of the Englishmen in the neck. The man tumbled from his horse, dead before his body landed.

"Just to reinforce the message," Malcolm smirked.

Once they reunited with the larger group, Malcolm and Edward tasked men with extra patrols and scouting. Ric was deep in thought about Isa when Magnus's voice finally broke through.

"So what next?" Magnus asked.

"One of two things. English pride is not so different from Scottish pride, and it will be pricked. An attack will come within the next two days. If that doesn't happen, they will try to wait us out, capturing or attacking our party when we leave for Stirling."

"And which do ye think is more likely?" Tavish inquired.

"It all depends on how those men present the news. If they try to save their arses and don't relay the message exactly, then it will be a waiting game. If they are accurate, then Graystone's and Hargate's tempers will get the better of them. Both men posture and present themselves as far superior warriors than they are. Not only will they want to defend their pride against us, but it will make them want to prove themselves to each other. We wait and see."

Ric rued his words when the next fortnight passed at a remarkably slow pace. His mind drifted constantly to Isa and whether she would still feel the same way about him after so much time apart. He feared she would reflect upon their actions and decide she had made the wrong choice in becoming involved with him. He wished he had some method of sending her a message, but sending anyone out was too great a risk. He lay awake in bed listening to Robbie snore, wishing he was sharing his chamber with Isa. His cock would harden as he remembered the feel of her warm, supple body against his. He had not realized how much he enjoyed her height, not having to bend to kiss her, their bodies aligning perfectly when he pulled her against him. When he did sleep, his dreams were even more vivid. He awoke frustrated and irritable. It was only during his baths that he could ease the tension. He sent Robbie on an errand after the squire filled his tub, then he allowed himself to soak in the warm water as his hand acted as a poor substitute for what he knew Isa could offer.

As they moved into the third week of confinement at the MacLellan keep, scouts returned with news that the English force chose to return to the east. According to the scouts, the army began to move east when much of their camp washed away as the banks of the river upon which they camped swelled. The rushing water from the beginning of the spring thaw left the English with diminished food and shelter. The weather was still unpredictable enough to make living outdoors without adequate shelter life threatening. Without enough food, the two barons faced men deserting.

The Scots remained another four days to ensure the English were not moving on as a decoy for an intended attack. When another three patrols reported them continuing to move east, eventually crossing the border back into England, Ric and the others decided it was time to return to Stirling Castle. Ric had never been more relieved to return to a royal court than when they rode out of the MacLellan keep.

TWELVE

I sa felt listless and unsettled as the days slowed into weeks of waiting. She discovered even her research and illuminations no longer held the same fascination when she could not cease wondering how Ric fared. She thought of him throughout the day, finding things that reminded her of him despite only having known each other for a short time. She performed her duties as a lady-in-waiting, but she was more reserved, even withdrawn, than usual. Her only comfort came from her time spent with the Sinclair women and Elizabeth Bruce.

In the beginning, she feared the women would shun her after her less-than-noble comments about Deirdre and Magnus, but a sincere apology remedied the past. Then she feared they would believe she was an interloper who did not belong with their family, especially after making her attraction to an English knight so obvious. In her own mind, she considered Ric to be Scottish, but she also knew not everyone shared that sentiment. She heard it at every meal and often when the other ladies whispered about her behind their hands or fans. If Deirdre, Elizabeth, and Ceit had not taken her under their wings, she was not sure how she would have endured without slipping into despondency.

Isa tried to reason with herself that her extreme shift in mood was unreasonable for how briefly she had known Ric, but try as she might, her mind could not convince her heart to cease feeling Ric's absence everywhere she went.

As time dragged on, she wondered if she was equipped to be a warrior's wife. She was not convinced that she could be as brave as the other ladies if she had to watch Ric routinely ride out to battle. She questioned whether she would make a suitable wife for a man like Ric, and while she wanted to believe she would, she doubted herself. She did not want to fail him, but she also could not imagine finding a man she desired more for a husband. The conflict waged on in her mind as she attempted to research the standing stones left across Scotland and northern England. She still found the information fascinating, but she caught herself wishing she could share her discoveries with Ric. It soured the time spent in the scriptorium and castle library and only made her feel more isolated. It was moments like that when she sought out the company of the other women.

"Isa, what did you write aboot today?" Deirdre asked as she looked up from her own parchment and quill. Isa had not realized how much she missed being in the presence of the only two other women who were as enraptured by ancient texts as she was. She had never been great friends with Deirdre or Elizabeth, but she had shared the scriptorium and the library with them many times. It was now lonely without them there.

"I have found accounts from the Romans of the standing stones near Carlisle, and I am attempting to reproduce the designs using only the Romans' written descriptions. I have to admit that my Latin is not serving me as well as I need."

Deidre came to stand next to her, and Isa pointed to the lines she was attempting to translate and then recreate as an image. "*Lapidibus instar gigantum pertingat ad caelum ferre. Titanas venias maris magni stare inter arbores.*" Deirdre read aloud. "The stones bear a resemblance to giants reaching toward the heavens. The great titans of the seas come to stand among men and trees."

"The Romans could certainly be poetic, even when conquering all of known civilization," Elizabeth chimed in.

Deirdre squinted as she mouthed the next lines before reading them aloud. "*Runs in similibus arcubus noctem stellas caeli movent. Helices infra lunam egestas ornare petra vultus amo.* The swirls and arcs resemble the stars as they move through the night sky. Spirals decorate the rock faces like women dancing beneath the moon."

"Quite poetic but I haven't a clue how to draw any of that," Isa grumbled as she ran her finger along the grooves between her brows. "I can't know what direction these—"

Ceit burst through the doorway, interrupting Isa, with flushed cheeks and a wide smile. "They're home! The guards have spotted them. They'll be within the walls in less than half an hour." Ceit spun toward the door before pausing and looking back. "The guards counted all four of them on horseback!"

Parchment and books forgotten, Elizabeth, Isa, and Deidre followed Ceit out of the library. The four women wound through the passageways until they reached the enormous double doors that led to the bailey. They stood with their arms wrapped around each other's waists as they waited for the riders to approach the portcullis. The clatter of horse hooves and bridles along with the scores of foot soldiers following the horses was nearly deafening, but Isa was not distracted from watching Ric ride through the gate. His gaze found hers the moment she became visible to him, and the smile that brightened his exhausted face made her heart thud painfully against her ribs. She caught herself before she lurched forward, refusing to make another scene like when the men departed. As the men reined in and began to dismount, the wives ran to greet their husbands, but Isa was unsure of her role as neither a wife nor a formally betrothed woman. She twirled the ring that she wore on her thumb. She had only taken it off to bathe, and that was only because it slipped off her wet hand. She waited nervously for some type of cue.

Ric watched as Isa stood upon the bailey steps, and he could read the uncertainty in her eyes. She looked as though she wanted to step forward, but she remained in place. When his horse came to a stop, Ric dismounted in a hurry and threw the reins to Robbie. He was across the bailey and standing at the bottom of the steps in what felt like only a handful of paces. He looked up at Isa, waiting for her to decide on how they would reunite. When she swayed but did not step forward, Ric turned his palms to her and raised his arms toward his hips. It was the invitation Isa sought. She flew down the steps, leaping into Ric's arms, never doubting he would catch her. She buried her nose in the crook of his neck and absorbed the heat and strength that radiated from him. They stood silently clinging to one another as the scores of men and horses carried on around them. They were blind to the people continuing their daily chores as they moved about the bailey. Isa and Ric only had thoughts for one another.

Isa ran her hands over his head and shoulders as if checking that he had returned in one piece while Ric's hands itched to cup her backside and carry her off to the nearest flat surface where he could make love to her. He knew none of that fantasy was possible, so he reveled in the feel of her pressed against him, holding on just as tightly as he did.

"I'm hale, Isa. I'm back in one piece, with nary a scratch to tell the tale," Ric whispered against her hair.

"Thank Michael and all the angels. God's greatest knight watched over you and returned you to m—here." Isa caught herself before she presumed too much. Despite being in Ric's arms, she was not sure what his thoughts were after being apart for so long.

"I returned to you, Isa. Don't doubt that." Ric lowered her to her feet but cupped her jaw as he lowered his mouth to hers. Before brushing his lips against hers, he inhaled her fresh scent of heather and honeysuckle. "I'm going to kiss you, Isa."

And with that pronouncement, Ric fused his lips to Isa's, and she returned his ardor with her own. She fisted his surcoat as she pulled him against her lithe frame, then slid her hands up to his shoulders before tangling her fingers in his hair. The kiss was one that rivaled the ones the other ladies shared with their husbands.

"I see you have returned. And not a moment too soon," Robert's voice once more boomed entirely too close to Ric and Isa.

The couple pulled apart, and Ric did not miss the Bruce watching them from the corner of his eye, though his attention appeared to be directed toward his army. Ric kept one arm wrapped around Isa as he tucked her against his side. He could not bear the idea of not being in contact with her after dreaming of her the entire time they were apart.

"I'm going to ask the king to notify your father that I intend to ask for your hand." Ric's warm breath tickled Isa's ear as she attempted to look as though she was listening to the king.

"Are you certain? Do you not want to spend more time getting to know one another?" Isa bit her bottom lip as she prepared herself for Ric's answer. She would offer him the opportunity to retract his offer.

"Regardless of the inevitable assumption that we will be married, I want to marry you. I had days, weeks really, to consider this. I never imagined I would marry. I never wanted to until I met you. I find that I have all sorts of notions that I never dreamed of before meeting you. My only question is whether you can overlook me being a landless knight."

"I don't want to spend my life at court, but if this is your new home, then it is where I wish to stay."

"And if I am not invited to remain?"

"Did you lose?"

Ric chuckled at Isa's practical approach. Her earnest expression told him that she was already assessing their options. "No, we did not lose. We have not returned in disgrace, even if it was rather anticlimactic."

Isa's eyebrows shot up as her lips pursed in dismay. Ric had never seen an expression of both shock and disdain that was as adorable as Isa's. He chuckled again, but Isa dug her elbow into his rib.

"It's not funny. Anticlimactic means you came home in one piece. I like anticlimactic."

"I know, my sweet, but after days of slogging

about in the rain and mud, it was rather frustrating to have done so with naught to show for it."

"Did you not succeed in defeating the English? You said you didn't lose."

"I don't know that defeat is the word. We chased them off."

"Isn't that the best thing that could happen? Lives saved and the English gone."

"Unfortunately, no. It just means they live another day to harry the Scots or to build their armies."

"So you didn't fight at all?" Isa wished she had let the matter drop when she saw a cloud cross Ric's face, and he seemed to withdraw before her eyes. She placed her hand over his heart, concern on her face. Ric covered her hand before bringing it to his lips. He kissed the back before placing it over his heart and pressing it against his chest.

"We did fight once. I faced off against my mentor, the man who presented me with my spurs. He was more like a father to me than any other man since my actual father died."

"Ric," Isa's voice was little more than the puff of air that escaped.

"I didn't kill him. I couldn't, and I wouldn't allow anyone else to. We spared him, and I sent him home. But I wonder now if that was still a death sentence. One that will be far crueler than dying in battle. Edward will cry foul and cast Geoffrey out in disgrace. My former friend may lose his lands, if not his life. His heir could be stripped of his inheritance and left with naught. I fear for him, but I could not kill him."

"Ric, I'm sorry." Isa rested her head against his shoulder as they stood together, once more forgetting that anyone else existed but them. Ric kissed her forehead and welcomed the moral support that he realized only Isa could offer.

"I think we had better talk," King Robert's presence forced them apart once more. "I believe there are papers that will need to be drafted and banns read sharpish." Robert clapped his hand on Ric's shoulder and squeezed to the point where Ric wanted to wince, but ground his teeth instead.

"Until the evening meal, my lady," Ric bowed and followed the king into the keep.

Isa looked around, once more alone as the families of the warriors gathered to greet their returning heroes. Her friends were engrossed with their husbands, and each couple made their way back into the keep. Isa was certain of their destinations. She felt out of place yet again, so she decided to return to the library where she could work until it was time to prepare for the evening meal.

The king summoned Isa to his solar chamber before the evening meal, and she felt her hands grow clammy as the doors were opened for her to pass through. Her skirts had barely cleared the entry when the door slammed shut behind her. Her gaze riveted to Ric, who wore a fresh surcoat and leggings, and she was positive she saw water droplets on the ends of his hair. Ric moved toward her, ignoring the king's throat clearing and the tsks of several of the king's advisors. He offered her his arm, and they approached the king together.

"I understand you already possess Sir Dedric's signet ring. He was unable to finish signing the betrothal documents without it."

Isa swallowed as she listened to the king announce her impending marriage. She looked toward a table that had various parchments scattered across it, and she wondered if any of them were the documents that would bind them just as tightly as a church service.

"I do, Your Majesty," she responded when she was convinced her voice would not betray her nervousness. She slid the ring from her thumb and held it up before handing it to Ric.

"Then I believe everything is in order for you to sign. You can be wed in the morning."

Isa coughed before turning a concerning shade of red. Ric swept her off her feet and growled at several courtiers who did not leap to offer their seats on a bench to them. He settled Isa on his lap with complete disregard once again to propriety.

"Are you well?" Ric's voice barely hid the panic that struck as he watched Isa's face and neck flush. He had hoped to tell Isa about the king's demand that they marry immediately, but he had not been given the opportunity.

"Tomorrow?" she squeaked. She cleared her throat before attempting to speak again. "How can we marry so soon? The banns haven't even been read once."

Ric tucked hair behind Isa's ear as he prepared himself for what he anticipated would be a displeased reaction. "The king decided to forego the church's requirement and order our marriage to happen posthaste. In exchange for your hand, he has granted me the title to land within your clan's territory. I will serve the king as one of his border lords, protecting your clan and mine from the English."

Isa sat and listened to Ric as he explained that the king had already informed her father, having sent a missive the moment Ric and the others left. Her father had already responded and signed the betrothal documents. The banns had already been read twice, but the king would absolve them of waiting until they had been read thrice. She closed her eyes as she listened to her life take a drastic turn with decisions already made for her. She was not surprised that her marriage had been arranged with no say from her; however, she was surprised at the speed with which things were progressing. By sundown the next day, she would be wedded and possibly even bedded. The last thought made her lip twitch with a smile that attempted to break through.

"What's making you smile after all this?" Ric wondered.

"Naught. Go on. When will we leave?"

"Before the end of the week. The king has agreed to grant us a few days here after the wedding to prepare for our new positions and home."

Positions? Home? Bluidy hell. He's right. That means I'm going to be the lady of a keep where I may not know a soul beyond sharing the same surname.

Isa's mind began to tick with lists and plans in preparation for their departure.

"Slow down, my sweet. You don't have to plan our entire attack right this moment." Ric kissed her cheek. "You can make your lists and plan in a couple of days. The keep we shall move to will not tumble down between now and then."

"How did you know?"

"Because your mind works much the same as mine, and I have already planned the next six months of improvements, and I haven't even seen the land yet." Ric kissed her forehead once again. "Isa, this is moving very fast. What do you want?"

"You." Isa gasped at her frank and thoughtless response, but Ric pulled her closer to whisper in her ear.

"And you shall have me. Over and over and then over again. But not until you are ready. I will not rush you or push you to do aught you don't want or don't feel ready for."

Isa felt a rock settle in her stomach. "Do you not want to marry me? Or do you want a marriage in name only?"

Ric's flabbergasted expression made Isa relax, but she still did not understand his sudden reversal. "Isa, we most certainly will not have a marriage in name only. I don't know that I could survive it. I want you to feel comfortable and safe with me, and I don't want you to feel rushed. Your desires matter to me, and if you do not desire making love, I will never force you. Once we are wed, we have a lifetime together."

Isa would not allow herself to read too much into him referring to their coupling as making love. She knew it would only break her heart later.

"Except for the bedding ceremony," she responded.

Ric's mouth set into a thin, hard line. Isa felt the muscles in his thighs contract underneath her backside. His hands clamped onto her waist. "There is not a man alive who will see you without your clothing unless that man is me. And I will not have anyone watch me make love to my wife. Ever."

"What of other women seeing you without clothing?"

"Why would they?" Ric appeared truly baffled.

"I'm sure you've had ladies of the castle bathe you. What aboot after we are wed and you travel without me?" Isa held her breath knowing that she was overstepping her bounds questioning her future husband about his intentions to be faithful.

"Where would I travel without you? If I'm not riding out to fight, why would I go anywhere without you? And why would I have a woman bathe me when I have a squire to ensure I have everything I need or better yet, you?"

"You mean you don't have women assist you with your bath now?"

"Not since I was seven."

Isa's mouth formed a perfect circle as she realized he meant that no woman had bathed him since his mother died. Ric looked at Isa's raspberry lips and could not keep his mind from picturing those same lips wrapped around his cock. He had managed to keep his manhood only semi-aroused while she sat on his lap, but now his rod screamed for attention.

"Isa, stop making that face," his hoarse whisper scratched his throat. At her look of confusion, he shut his eyes before speaking again. "You are making me picture things, things between us, that I have no right to."

"No right? But aren't we to be wed tomorrow? Then won't you have all the right?"

Ric groaned as she shifted to look at him more closely. "The things I'm thinking of are not fit for a lady."

"Then I think that's exactly what I'd like to learn to do."

"Isa," he hissed. He could not believe his ears.

"If what you're imagining is something you would like, then I would rather it be with me than someone else." Her final comment was a bucket of cold water over Ric's head.

"Isa, there will never be a someone else." Ric entwined their fingers together. "I will always be faithful to you. I will not stray. Ever. My honor would not allow it, and I don't think my heart would either."

Before Isa could respond, the queen swept into the chamber and marched directly to the couple. "Lady Isabella, I understand you are to be wed to this young mon tomorrow, but you are not wed yet. Do you realize you are seated on the mon's lap and in front of half the king's solar? Come along."

The queen spun around and glided back to the door where she waited without looking back. Isa scrambled off Ric's legs but not before giving him a peck on the cheek.

"Tonight," she whispered, leaving Ric to nod and wonder what his plucky bride meant.

THIRTEEN

Isa sat through one poem after another in the queen's salon, but her mind drifted, just as it had for the past few weeks. This time, she dreamed of the wedding that would take place the next day. Her practical nature kept her from imagining anything lavish, but she hoped that Ric would find her pretty and be as happy about the nuptials as she found herself. She imagined herself as the lady of a keep. She had been raised to know that one day she would marry, and her position as a laird's daughter ensured she would marry a man of similar stature. Her mother had trained her for years to manage and run a large household, and she knew she was prepared to do so, but to imagine her own keep was exciting and nerve-wracking enough to give her butterflies in her stomach. She would not admit to anyone else, but she was picturing the wedding night as well. She viewed it with equal parts curiosity and trepidation. She understood the mechanics and had overheard, even overseen, couples to know that it could be highly enjoyable for both people. Isa just was not certain if she would enjoy it.

She knew she desired Ric, her body aching for him whenever they were apart and practically going up in flames whenever he was near, but she wondered if she would find the actual act pleasurable. She also worried about whether she would please Ric. She believed his pledge that he intended to be faithful, but the image of the beautiful Englishwoman niggled in the back of her mind. If it was not the woman from Ric's past, then she worried about the women in the future, even at court. Isa was not blind to the reaction Ric created in women, and while she wanted to gloat that he chose her, she was not confident that it would remain that way always. Isa was not so sheltered as to believe wedding vows were a vow of fidelity. She knew plenty of lairds who kept lemans, and there were hordes of mistresses at court. She wondered how soon they could leave for their own keep.

"Lady Isabella, are you lost in thought aboot your handsome groom?" Isa had not seen Queen Elizabeth approach until she stood beside Isa's seat. Isa rose and demurely nodded. "I can understand why. Your knight is a handsome and brave mon, but be that as it may, he is a blessed mon to have found such a special bride."

Isa's head shot up as she looked in the queen's eyes. She had never received such a compliment from the woman, and she was not certain what prompted it.

"Isa," Queen Elizabeth dropped her voice. "You were raised along the border, so you know the challenges you will face. Being the lady of the keep, even if it is a smaller one, during a raid will require determination and levelheadedness that most of my young ladies-in-waiting do not possess. Watching your husband ride out on a mission or to battle never gets any easier, but you have the constitution to carry on even during the most trying of times. Don't underestimate yourself. The king would not have approved the mar-

riage, nor given Sir Dedric the land, if he did not believe you both were up to the task."

"Thank you, Your Majesty." Isa dipped into a
curtsy as the older woman took her hand and gave it
a gentle squeeze.

"Marriage in these trying times is no easy feat,
but I know that you can stay the course, no matter
the obstacle."

Isa prayed the queen was right. She knew life
along the border would not be easy, and while she
missed living among her clan, she did not miss the
ever-present threat and danger. As the ladies followed
the queen to the evening meal, Isa wondered if she
would even see Ric that evening. She had questions
she hoped to ask about their travel and their destination. She was yet to learn which of the keeps the king
had granted Ric, and it made her curious whether it
was one her father would willingly relinquish, even if
it was to his daughter and her husband.

As they arrived at the Great Hall, Isa spotted Ric
waiting against one of the walls in the passageway.
He pushed away when he saw her and offered his
arm as she approached. They entered the Great Hall
together, but Isa was prepared to release him and
follow the other ladies to their table.

"Not any longer," he murmured. When Isa
looked up at him, he shook his head and steered her
toward a table with other married courtiers. She
wanted to cringe until she looked further down and
noticed the Sinclairs and the Bruces. She relaxed
when she realized that she could once more sit with
Elizabeth, Deirdre, and Ceit. Isa watched as the couples defied custom with husband and wife sitting next
to one another rather than across. As they settled
onto the benches, Isa blushed as the husbands
wrapped their arms around their wives, and the
wives slipped their hands along their husbands'

thighs. Isa knew she could not be that brazen without being married first, but she looked forward to when she could.

The meal began soon after they were seated, and Ric took her hand beneath the table. They shared a trencher and a chalice, and Ric ensured the best selection was placed on Isa's portion of the trencher before his was filled. He offered her the first sip every time their chalice was refilled.

"The wedding will be during the noon Mass, with a feast to follow," Ric's soft tone carried only to Isa's ears. She nearly choked to hear that she would be married during the midafternoon service. She had not expected it to be held so early in the day. "I would marry you at Vespers if permitted. I wouldn't wait until tomorrow."

Isa tilted her head to look at Ric, and his irrepressible grin sent a shiver through her. As his shoulder brushed against hers, her gaze swept around the room to see if anyone watched them. She saw a few glances their way, but no one appeared to be paying them any extra attention. She released the hand she held and slid her palm along Ric's thigh. She bit her lip as she tested Ric's response and her own brazenness. She surprised herself, but then she remembered how she had welcomed Ric's kiss when she barely knew who he was. They were to marry after knowing each other only a handful of weeks. She had thrown caution to the wind already, so she saw little reason to suddenly grow shy.

"I would marry you then too, but I wouldn't want a feast immediately after."

Isa watched a wolfish glint enter Ric's eyes as his own hand rested high on her inner thigh. "I know precisely what I would feast upon, and no, it would not be in here."

Isa had no idea how to respond beyond a slight

nod, but she found herself gripping his leg with fingers like a vise. She relaxed them and thought to pull them away, but Ric's hand covered hers. "It is the sweetest torture," he murmured.

They were not given the opportunity to continue their hushed conversation as Magnus, Tavish, and Edward drew Ric into the conversation while the wives gave her a sympathetic smile. Soon after, the tables were pushed aside, and the musicians tuned their instruments. Ric looked forward to holding Isa in his arms, but he loathed the idea of seeing her dance with another man. He felt his ire rise as he realized she had undoubtedly danced with any number of other men while he was away.

"I only did what was expected of me. I would have much rather waited for you." Isa looked into Ric's topaz eyes, and he was surprised that she could read his thoughts. She laughed softly before continuing. "Your feelings are written across your face. But I am not eager to see other women maneuver their way into being your partner."

Ric scanned the crowd as he guided Isa toward the door, and once through them, he led her to the room where they had first found one another. This time there was no one to overhear, and the chamber was cast in darkness. Ric locked the door and pocketed the key before spinning Isa around and pressing her against the wood. Her arms snaked around his neck with no prompting. Their mouths collided with no finesse as they finally satiated the hunger that had gnawed at them both since their all-too-brief reunion in the bailey. When neither could go another moment without drawing air into their lungs, Ric kissed the satiny skin behind her ear as Isa's head fell back against the door.

"Ric," she breathed, unsure of what else to say, unsure that she could say anything else.

"Do you understand what we shall do tomorrow eve?" Isa nodded, too distracted by the scorching ache that burned low in her belly.

"I don't know that I can wait until tomorrow," she confessed. "I don't know what to do aboot how I feel. I ache, and it's as if my body knows something is missing."

Ric leaned his forehead against hers, forcing himself to slow their tryst before he hoisted her skirts and then thrust into her innocent body. His heart and body screamed for him to claim her, to make her his forever, but the last shreds of decency and honor demanded he stop. He would not welcome his bride into the pleasure of the flesh before they were wed, and certainly not against a door.

"We are meant to join together, Isa, and we will. Our bodies know what our minds and our hearts are just figuring out. But I won't take your maidenhead until you are truly mine. I don't have the right to claim such a privilege."

"And if it's mine to give away? What if I know that you are the only mon I want to touch me? We are to be wed in less than a day, and you've promised me no bedding ceremony."

Ric stood up straight and grimaced. "But I didn't promise you that we wouldn't have to fly the sheet."

Isa opened her mouth then snapped it shut. She could not disagree with him, even if the idea of everyone witnessing the proof of her virginity was humiliating.

"I would spare you the embarrassment if I could, my sweet, but neither of us is in a position to refuse. My position as a member of Robert's court and as the new lord requires I conform, and there can be no doubt you are my wife in name and deed." Ric brushed his lips across hers, and she lifted her chin to meet him. "I will do everything in my power to protect you, Isa. Always."

Isa melted into Ric's embrace once more, and they stood together for a long moment before they both accepted that they would have to return to their separate chambers. Ric walked her to the passageway that led to the ladies' chambers and waited until he saw her slip into her room.

***

Isa awoke to a knocking at her door. She rubbed the sleep from her eyes and pushed her hair away from her face. She pulled on a robe as she approached the door.

"Who is it?"

"It's us," Ceit's excited voice carried through the door. Isa pulled it open, and Deirdre, Ceit, and Elizabeth surged forward.

"What will you wear today?" Elizabeth's excitement was contagious, and Isa broke into a grin.

"Hopefully, not much." Isa's eyes grew to the size of saucers as she clapped her hand over her mouth. She could not believe she had let her most private thought slip out.

"Good lass," Deirdre chuckled. "But before that, we can't have you walking aboot the keep in naught but your skin. I don't think Sir Dedric would appreciate that. I'm fairly certain he would be like Magnus and gouge out the eyes of any mon who dared breathe in your direction."

"You might be right. He was very adamant that there wouldn't be a bedding ceremony." Isa looked around at the other three women and hoped they would be able to offer her some reassurance that a crowd of people would not force their way into her matrimonial chamber to observe the loss of her virginity.

"None of us can speak to that. We, uh, all hand-fasted before we went to the kirk." Elizabeth spoke softly. "There wasn't much use in a bedding ceremony once we were wed in the church."

Isa looked at the three women in front of her, and not one of them had a look of remorse. "You're fortunate to be Highlanders," she grumbled.

The others laughed before Ceit embraced her. "You're wishing you'd thought of that last eve, aren't you? We saw you slip off with Sir Dedric."

Isa had no idea what to say. She had grown close to the other women, and she had listened as they spoke about some of the more private aspects of being married, but they had respected the fact that she was a maiden and not spoken too vividly. She had questions she wanted to ask but was far too embarrassed to bring up.

"You shall wonder how you two will ever fit, but you will." Ceit grinned, and Isa nearly choked. "I'm assuming you haven't seen a mon's, well, manhood before. You will wonder how your bodies could ever come together. After all, Sir Dedric is rather larger than you."

Isa swallowed before nodding. "I think if we're going to have this conversation, you should call him Ric. It seems rather stiff to use his title." As soon as the words came out of her mouth, she flushed a bright red.

"I should rather hope it's stiff," Deirdre chimed in. "Isa, what do you know of the marriage bed?"

"I know the mechanics, but I will confess that I worry aboot how it will happen. I know it can be enjoyable for both the mon and the woman, but I don't know how to make it enjoyable for either of us." Isa could not bring herself to look at the other ladies, but they swallowed her into their embrace.

"Do you fear that because he is already experienced and you're not that you won't live up to his expectations?" Ceit asked softly, and when Isa nodded, Ceit stroked her hair. "You don't know of my husband's reputation then. I'm not sure how you could have missed it, but he was not a celibate mon when I met him. Or at least he hadn't been until he learned of our betrothal. I felt like he had a list that could go on for a month of Sundays to compare me against. But he admitted the first time we made love that it was different with me because he loves me. I'd hazard a guess that Ric will feel the same way."

"But you and Tavish were a love match. I mean, I remember hearing you were betrothed before you knew each other, but you married because you love each other. We aren't a love match so much as a lust match. That can't last forever."

"Don't some of the greatest unions grow out of fierce attraction? Don't you think that's what first brought us together with our husbands?" Elizabeth grinned before looking back at Deirdre. "Well, maybe for Ceit and me. Deirdre fell in love with Magnus because he carried her books and vellums back when she dropped them in the dirt."

"And I was thirteen then. By the time we handfasted a few years later, I was more than aware that I had the brawest mon in all of Scotland wanting to marry me. But before that, I knew I was not the first woman Magnus was with. He explained it to me very clearly, and I know he told me the truth. He had coupled with a few other women before we began courting, he even said he'd tupped them, but I was the only woman he has ever made love to. I don't think our men use that term lightly. Has he said it to you? Have you talked aboot this?"

"He has. Twice, but we haven't had much of a chance to talk aboot bed sport. He said he wouldn't rush me and that there wouldn't be anyone watching us, but he would have to show the bedsheet. It's not an easy topic of conversation." Isa watched as Cheshire cat grins spread across the married women's faces. "At least not yet, it isn't."

"Look at it this way," Elizabeth offered her a soft smile. "At least one of you needs to know what to do."

Isa's mind yet again conjured the image of the stunning Englishwoman. She knew it was because the woman was the only one from Ric's past that she knew about, but it was a reminder that her soon-to-be husband had far more experience than she did.

"Let Ric introduce you to passion. There is a pride that he will take in knowing no other mon has touched what he claims as his, but you should also take pride in knowing he chose you. He did not marry any of the women from his past. If he did not want you as his wife, he never would have made his interest so public. You have claimed something no other woman can: his future and his heart," Deirdre reassured. Isa nodded, not convinced that she truly had the latter, and she could only pray that God would grant her the former.

FOURTEEN

The women went to Terce together in the chapel, but they knew the men had been called into the king's council chamber for an unexpected meeting. It was rare that the Bruce missed attending the morning Mass with his wife, so each of the women was slightly on edge. When the Mass ended and the ladies found their husbands waiting, the tension eased for them, but Isa could not find Ric.

"He went to his chamber to prepare, lass," Tavish explained then succumbed to laughter. "He's demanded the king move yer wedding forward. He refuses to wait till midafternoon. Ye'll be wed before the midday Mass."

Isa looked at the other women and then to Edward, Magnus, and Tavish.

"A mon after ma own heart," Magnus grinned. "He was vera adamant that he wasna going to wait any longer than the next service to call ye his wife."

Isa had no idea what to make of Tavish and Magnus's news. She felt excitement grow as she considered Ric's impatience, but trepidation took root too as she wondered why Ric insisted on moving the wedding forward even a few hours.

"We had better return to your chamber and help

ready you," Ceit spoke softly but glared at her husband. Tavish's laughter ended abruptly, and Isa wondered if there was something Ceit knew that she did not. She knew Ceit had once been a spy for King Robert, and now Isa felt a prick of unease that Ceit might be aware of something that would affect both her and Ric's future. Ceit looked back at Isa before continuing. "My husband is being an arse. He was just as eager for us to wed as your groom is. He conveniently forgets that I'm the one who needed convincing."

Tavish pulled his wife into his arms and once again they shared a kiss that was indecent. He tapped her on the backside as they drew apart. "I believe ye're convinced," Tavish's laughter rumbled through his words.

"Lucky for you," Ceit danced away and linked arms with Isa before the women left the men watching them leave.

————

Ric stood in his chamber as he ran a comb through his damp hair. His stomach was in knots in equal parts anticipation and dread. He was eager to join Isa at the kirk and pledge himself in marriage, but he dreaded telling her that Robert had ordered him to the border, and they were to leave after the nooning. It was not the wedding day he had planned for Isa to have, but he had refused to leave without her and refused to delay the ceremony. The king's only compromise was to have the ceremony earlier in the day, then allow them to celebrate at the midday meal before departing for Dunbar territory.

He cursed Graystone and Hargate for their ongoing insurgence into the Lowlands, and he doubly cursed King Edward for his pride and merciless pursuit to live up to the moniker the Hammer of the Scots. He dreaded taking Isa anywhere near danger and wished he could journey to the Highlands with the Sinclairs. He even considered sending Isa with the Sinclairs when they returned north rather than bringing her to the border, but selfishly, he could not bear the idea of being apart from her again. Ric walked to the window embrasure and stared out at the sunny day, looking beyond the castle wall to the rolling hills and river just beyond.

At least it's a better day for travel than any of the ones I had before. Let it remain like this, so Isa doesn't have to suffer any sooner for the folly of two kings. I pray we make it to the safety of our home without Isa being put in danger. Now that I've found her, I don't know that I could go another day without her. It makes no sense. I know we are still virtual strangers to one another, but there is something that draws me to her in a way no one ever has. There is a sense of rightness and completion that has been missing all my life. I finally feel set-tled when I am with her. What is it my heart knows what my mind still hasn't figured out? How can I be so certain?

Ric's thoughts were interrupted when Robbie pushed open the door just enough to peer around it. "You have a visitor," Robbie whispered. The squire stepped aside, and Bella pushed past. Ric wanted to vomit.

"What're you doing here?" Ric hissed. "You can't be in the keep, and you can't be in my chamber. Not any day, but most definitely not today."

"Worried your bride will hear you've been with your mistress again?"

Ric lunged forward and grasped Bella's arm, giving her a little shake. "If Isa hears aught of you being my mistress, I will know it came from your lips. If anyone sees us together, I will turn you over to Robert as a spy. Ruin this day for Isa, and I may very well throttle you."

"You care about your little bride. How very quaint. Just make sure you remember where your true alliances lie." Bella's gaze hardened like shards of ice. "Your body may lie with that insipid little girl, but your alliances lie with King Edward."

Ric flung open the door, making Robbie jump, and looked both ways down the corridor. He pushed Bella out into the passageway before turning his temper on Robbie. "I don't know why you thought I would want to see her. I will deal with that later. But you will remove Lady Bella from this keep, and if she falls into the river along the way, all the better for us all."

Ric slammed the door shut, knowing Bella would leave in a huff and Robbie would stand quaking in his boots, but he was too furious to think straight. Bella's visit reminded him that she would remain a thorn no matter where he went, and he feared how she would most certainly interfere in his marriage. She also reminded him that King Edward still believed his loyalty lay with the English, but Ric's mind was clear on where his loyalties lay, and it was with the country of his birth and the home he would make with Isa. Ric left his chamber and made his way to the chapel where he found the king already waiting. The queen was nowhere in sight and neither were the ladies-in-waiting.

"What will you tell your wife?" Robert the Bruce inquired.

"The truth. You have offered me the land and the keep in exchange for my fealty to both you and Laird Dunbar.

"Is that all?"

"For now. Until I can see the situation for myself, I'm not going to frighten Isa unnecessarily."

"And the woman who visited your chamber?"

Ric wanted to shrivel into the ground. He had

hoped the news would not be carried on the wind and he could avoid it until after the wedding. "As you know, Lady Bella is an informant for King Edward. She came to remind me of my duties to him. And to taunt me. I'm certain that while she no longer sees any benefit to pursuing me, she has no qualms about destroying my relationship with Isa."

In exchange for the land, Ric had been pressed into explaining his original intention for arriving at the royal court. Robert told him that he already knew as much, having caught one of Bella's messengers, but he had waited to see whether Ric would confess. Pleased that it had not taken much for Ric to be forthcoming and after his service along the border, this time to Robert, the king offered Ric a bargain: the land and marriage for his agreement to a public pledge of his fealty and to serve as a double-agent of sorts. The king required him to appear a neutral border lord during the day, but to harry the English at night, stealing from them and ambushing their camps. He was to continue to provide Bella with false information, but report to Robert the truth. Isa's hand in marriage was the incentive. Ric had offered to marry Isa regardless of the land, but Robert had not been so quick to give away one of his wife's ladies. Without his agreement to sabotage the English, Robert would not let him marry Isa and swore to marry her off underneath Ric's nose.

"Then for your sake, you had better find a way to keep the woman away from her. Lady Isabella does not strike me as the type who will forgive you if you break your oath to her."

"I have no intention of breaking any oaths made to my wife. I mean what I say, and I will before the priest. There is no one else for me. If I could go back in time, there would never have been anyone else for me."

"How are you so certain? You've spent mere weeks with the lass, and yet you speak as though you're in love."

"I've asked myself that same question countless times, and I'm not sure that I have devised an articulate answer other than, I just know."

"That was the way of it with my own Isabella. Perhaps it is something in the name." The Bruce rarely referred to his first wife, who he married when they were both still very young and lost shortly after delivering his daughter Marjorie. Robert waited six years before remarrying, and the union was originally a political match, though the king and queen were a loving couple now. Their conversation was cut off when the queen and the other ladies-in-waiting arrived.

"Sir Dedric, I believe it is time you entered the chapel. You cannot have your bride milling aboot in the passageway." Queen Elizabeth's voice was lowered in deference to the chapel, but the command was evident.

Ric nodded his head and attempted to see past the queen, but the other ladies blocked any peek he might have caught. He walked down the center aisle and took his place at the rail and before the priest. The man cast him a severe look, then seemed to forget Ric stood before him. The rest of the court filed in, and Ric felt his palms grow clammy as he waited for Isa's turn to enter. The seconds dragged into minutes, and a buzz began in the congregation. Ric's throat went dry with fear that Isa had fled. Just as he was prepared to search for her, the chapel doors opened, and he caught the scowl she cast the guard. He had no way of knowing what she said, but it was clear she was displeased. She stepped through the doorway and looked to Ric. He watched as the frown eased into a radiant smile that shone so brilliantly no one could doubt Isa was a willing participant in the ceremony. She made her way down the aisle, her gaze never straying from Ric, and when she met him at the rail, he kissed the back of her hand.

"Bluidy guard didn't want me marrying an Englishman. As though he had a say. I made sure he understood he didn't." Isa spoke from the side of her mouth, trying to keep her words only for Ric, especially once she realized she had sworn within the house of the Lord. Ric could not keep from returning her smile and entwined his fingers with hers, eliciting another scowl from the priest.

Ric and Isa floated through the ceremony, standing and kneeling at the appropriate times, intoning the vows while looking into one another's eyes. Isa felt the depth of Ric's sincerity, and she found her mind finally settled after a day of anxious energy. They held hands even during parts of the service when they were expected to clasp their own hands in prayer. When the ceremony was finally over and the priest announced them married, Ric pulled Isa in for a kiss. He cupped her jaw as he smiled down at her and her eyes filled with happy tears. His thumb caught one, and he was in no rush to hurry through their first kiss as a married couple. He brushed his lips against hers twice before they sealed their fate with a kiss that had Isa melting against Ric's larger frame. He held her as though she were something precious and delicate, and to him, she was. It was only when they both sensed people milling about near them that they pulled apart. Isa's close friends pulled her in for an embrace while the Sinclair men and Edward Bruce pounded Ric on the back and made jokes Isa did not understand but made Ric's face go up in flames. Isa realized she had never seen Ric blush before, and she found his discomfort rather charming.

Ric had just extricated his bride from her friends when he caught sight of the king's taut expression. He nodded before looking down at Isa, who was watching him. A frown marred her forehead for a moment before it disappeared. He knew she was astute and already understood something was afoot that she was not aware of. He lifted her hand and brought it to his lips.

"Let us adjourn to the Great Hall, and I will explain everything." *Or at least most of it.*

Isa nodded and leaned into Ric's embrace as they left the chapel with his arm wrapped around her waist. She held her head high as she walked past people who pretended to offer sincere felicitations. Some barely hid their disgust that an Englishman was allowed a place within the Scottish king's court, content to disregard Ric's Scottish heritage. Others, mainly women, glared at them, specifically Isa. They did little to veil their animosity since Ric had eyes for no one but Isa. They were unaccustomed to any man ignoring them, let alone one they deemed still an eligible catch. Isa knew that if they stayed long at court, one, if not all of them, would offer to be Ric's mistress.

Ric led them to the where the king and queen were about to be seated on the dais. Isa dipped into a low curtsy that afforded Ric an unprecedented view of her ample cleavage as he bowed before the royal couple. Ric felt his cock hardening, and he was grateful for the long surcoat that covered the growing bulge in his leggings. He wished for the plaids Magnus and Tavish favored.

"Sir Dedric and Lady Isabella, we offer our congratulations and best wishes. I shall be sad to bid you goodbye, Bella. The meal shall be all too brief, and then you shall be on your way."

Ric winced at both the use of the other diminutive for Isa's name and the fact that the queen announced their departure before Ric had a chance. The look on Isa's face made the queen cover her mouth.

"Might I have the use of your antechamber for a moment, Your Majesty?" Ric asked softly.

"I think that would be for the best," Robert glared at Ric before offering the fatherliest expression she had ever seen the man bestow. She found the entire conversation disconcerting.

Ric led Isa behind a tapestry that separated the king's antechamber from the Great Hall. He looked around to be sure they were alone before pulling Isa into his arms. She stood rigid before relenting and returning his embrace.

"I did not intend for you to learn of the king's newest plan from anyone but me." Ric cupped her shoulders, and she nodded. "I was summoned to his Privy Council chamber this morning, and that is why I missed Terce. The king has learned that Hargate and Graystone have turned back and intend to raze as many farms along the western border as they can. King Robert has ordered me back to the border and to our new keep. Isa, I couldn't bear the thought of leaving you here, of leaving without calling you my wife. It's selfish, but I want you by my side. I didn't want aught that might disrupt the wedding, so I didn't seek you out like I should have."

"Did you worry I wouldn't marry you?"

"Perhaps not today. And I didn't want to wait."

"Wasn't the intention all along for you to gain a piece of land in Scotland? I read the betrothal papers that granted a parcel and keep to you as part of my dowry. Why wouldn't I come with you?"

"I feared something would interfere, and if I rode out without you, then I wouldn't know when I might see you next. Without being my wife, you couldn't come with me."

"Is that why you demanded the ceremony be moved?"

"Yes." Ric slid his hand over her shoulder until he could cup the bare flesh of her nape and tangle his fingers in the wisps that rested against the neckline of her kirtle. "I also don't want to make love to my wife for the first time on the ground with all and sundry around to hear us. I don't know that we will be able to stay at an inn each night. There may be some spent under the stars. I don't want the hard ground to be your introduction to the marriage bed."

Isa stood listening as she absorbed this information. She wished someone had thought to share the news with her sooner, but she understood that women were not generally consulted on such matters. It was not hers to reason why. She looked back over her shoulder in the direction of the Great Hall before looking at Ric. She bit her lip as she weighed her options.

Do we forego consummating the marriage until we reach Dunbar land? Do we wait and hope for an inn? What aboot what Ric said, making love surrounded by his men? The thought of staring up at the stars is rather nice, but not if others know what we've been doing. Can't we escape now and get this out of the way? No! That's not how I want to think of being with Ric for the first time, but is that how he thinks of it? He said "make love" again, but does he really just mean wedded and bedded?

Isa's thoughts were running away with her, and Ric saw the uncertainty that clouded her eyes as she looked at his shoulder rather than his face.

"Isa, we don't have to do aught you don't want. We can also do things any way that you want to," Ric's hushed tones brought Isa back to the present, but just as quickly, his final words created a lurid image of them tangled together flash before her eyes.

"Do we have to attend the feast? Wouldn't the king understand why we might want to retire before a journey where I shall be the only woman?" Isa stepped back. "I will be the only woman, won't I?"

"Unfortunately, yes." Isa pushed away from Ric as he tried to understand the rapid shift in Isa's mood. One moment he was sure she was alluding to them consummating their marriage and the next she was pushing him away. When understanding dawned on Ric, he could have kicked himself. "Isa, I meant it's unfortunate because there will be no one to help you, and I'm not sure you will enjoy the company of gruff and grizzled men. I find it most fortunate since I shall have to serve as your lady's maid, and I am quite looking forward to being at your service."

Isa nodded as she forced herself to be more rational as her mind scrambled to put together all the moving parts. "Ric, I'm not sure I understand everything. The king ordered you back to the border, and since you already have the land granted to you as part of my dowry, that's where he will send you for now. You didn't want to leave me behind, so rather than tell me that we're to leave today, you moved the ceremony forward, presumably to give us more time together, but now you say that we don't have to do aught that I don't want. Are you assuming I don't want you?" Isa shook her head. "The first time we spoke of marriage, you said you wouldn't rush me. The last time we spoke of it, you seemed eager to make our marriage more than just a signed document, and now you're back to putting distance between us. I just don't understand. It makes me question whether I should be feeling the way I do. I'm ashamed of myself."

"Ashamed? What could you be ashamed of?"

"Of my curiosity. Of my anticipation. Perhaps I am not a lady but in name."

Ric opened and shut his mouth several times before he yanked Isa against him. His mouth crushed hers as his tongue swept across her lips. She parted them, and he pressed his tongue past her teeth. His kiss was gentler than she prepared for, but the heat and need were evident. She returned his ardor as her hands roamed over his back and chest. There was a door on the far side that led away from the Great Hall. He grasped Isa's hand and tugged her behind him until they entered the passageway.

"My chamber is closer," Isa offered before taking the lead. It was her turn to tug him. She lifted her skirts above her ankles as they raced through the passageways. They arrived at her door winded and laughing, but their humor stilled as Isa once more cradled Ric's jaw and pressed herself against him, using the door behind her to hold her up when she was sure her knees would give way. Their need coalesced into impatience as Isa fumbled with the door, eventually having to turn away from Ric to unlock it. Once inside her chamber, Ric quickly turned the key and dropped the bar. He refused to risk anyone interrupting them until they were ready to leave. Isa unfastened the belt to her kirtle as she kicked off the slippers that matched her gown.

"How much do you like this gown?" Ric growled as he spun her around and began pulling on her laces.

"I've never worn it before, but it's my favorite."

Ric groaned before kissing her nape. "Could you replace the ribbons and laces if need be?"

"I suppose." Those were the last words Isa spoke before she felt a snap then a cool breeze across her back. She looked down when she heard a clatter. She gasped when she realized Ric had used a dirk to slice open her gown, but he was already pushing it down her arms. She snapped her attention back to him and turned to face him. His expression was a purely predatory one, and she licked her lips as she unfastened the empty sword belt, letting it drop to the floor next to the knife. She pushed the surcoat up as far as she could reach before Ric whipped it over his head. In the brief moment his face was covered, Isa slipped free of her gown. Ric tossed the garment aside before pausing to take his first look at Isa standing in only her chemise. The thin shift teased him as he made out the curves of her body. As riveted as he was, her eyes lingered on the swelling bulge in his leggings. The longer she looked, the more painful his arousal became.

"Isa, there will be some pain this first time, but all I will ever intend to do is bring you pleasure. I want you to enjoy our coupling. Each time we join together, it makes us one in a way even our vows before God could not do."

Isa nodded slowly before taking a small step closer. "May I touch you?" her voice so low Ric almost missed what she asked.

"You need never ask. Isa, I'm your husband as much as you are my wife. You are entitled to seek your release with me just as a man does with his wife."

"Release?"

Ric paused as the reminder that his bride was truly an innocent slammed into him. "That's one way to describe the physical enjoyment that should come when a man and woman couple."

"Does it always happen?"

"I shall do everything within my power to make sure that it does. Isa, I know you've heard and seen couples in various stages, but have you never heard the crescendo of moans and groans even grunts?"

"Yes. It seemed to be when the couples were most passionate."

"That is because they were striving for and reaching a climax. Their release."

Isa's fingernails scraped along the ridges of Ric's belly before pausing at his waist. She waited until he nodded before continuing her progress until her fingers trailed over his rod. The look of bliss that swept across Ric's face amazed Isa, and they had not even finished disrobing.

"Do you have any idea what you do to me, my sweet? How close you drive me to the brink of losing control?"

"Would that be so bad?" Coming from any other woman, Ric would have believed those were the words of an experienced coquette, but his bride appeared mystified.

"Perhaps after your first time," Ric choked out as he guided Isa's hand to stroke him. His eyes drifted closed, and Isa watched the cords in his neck jump each time her hand slid over him. Ric slipped his hands to the hem of Isa's chemise and inched it up to her hips as he spied his first glance of the thatch of curls at the juncture of her thighs. As the fabric crept higher, Ric exposed a trim waist, then full breasts that he knew would fit his palm as though God had placed them there himself. Isa raised her arms, and Ric whipped the gown over her head.

Isa stood still, unsure of what to do as she stood before her husband with no clothes and he was still half dressed. She wanted to see him, too, but she was not sure how to proceed. Her eyes darted to her bed, which she now realized would be far too narrow for them.

"We will fit, Isa, since I have no intention of letting go of you." Isa nodded before her gaze dropped to the outline of Ric's shaft that pressed against his leggings. "We will fit, Isa." Ric reassured as he pictured what his bride's vivid imagination must have wondered.

"Can we—now?"

"Yes, my sweet one. Do you wish to get into bed, and I'll cover the windows before I finish undressing?"

Isa shook her head slowly then she moved faster. "Can I not see you, too? I've wondered. I mean, I had hoped. I—I—" she trailed off unsure of how to state her curiosity without coming across as even more brazen than she already had.

"You don't have to fear telling me aught, and certainly not when we are alone. I didn't want to frighten you or embarrass you."

"Embarrass me? I think we're well past that. I'm standing in front of you completely bare, and you have the security of still being covered up."

Ric tipped Isa's chin up and whispered a kiss against her lips. "Don't be embarrassed. You are the most beautiful woman I have ever seen, and it is the barrier of clothing that has kept me from mauling you already. Once I am undressed too, I will make love to you. I will become your husband in truth."

"And I your wife," Isa murmured. "Please, Ric. No more waiting." Isa hooked her fingers into the waist of Ric's leggings and began to push them down. "Can I touch you again?"

"I sincerely hope you will. And quickly." Ric kicked his legs free as he fisted his cock and stroked.

"I'd like to do that," Isa offered.

She reached out, and Ric guided her hand until she wrapped her fingers around his length. Once more, Ric's eyes drifted shut as the feel of Isa's skin against his nearly pushed him over the edge. Ric smattered kisses along the side of her neck until he reached her collarbone. He kissed her shoulder as his hands kneaded her plump breasts. Their mouths found one another, and the kiss erupted. He ripped the coverlet back before easing them onto the bed. He was careful to not press his full weight against Isa, fearing he would crush her. While she was tall, she was also willowy, and Ric was certain his body would smother her if he was not careful. Isa's hands explored the ridges and troughs of the muscles that twitched in his back as her touch spurred on his need to claim her. Her feather-soft fingertips ran along his spine, making him shiver with anticipation.

"Ric, I ache for something that I don't know, but my body screams for you. I don't know what I want you to touch first, but please, more."

"I will give you aught you wish." Ric slid his tongue along Isa's collarbone and made a course for her breast, where he circled her nipple with the tip of his tongue. He flicked the hardening nub as Isa arched her back, silently begging for more. Ric's teeth rasped over the puckered skin before he drew her nipple into his mouth. He suckled as his cock twitched when Isa moaned, and her nails raked over his shoulders. He sought the other breast and lavished equal attention upon it. As Isa pressed upward, offering him more, Ric increased the pressure as his fingers trailed along the inside of her thigh.

Too focused on the sensations and newfound heaviness of her breasts, Isa didn't notice Ric's exploring fingers until she felt them brush apart the swollen lips at her entrance. She gasped as the tip of one dipped within her folds. Ric lifted his head to watch Isa as he eased his finger further into her sheath.

"More?" Isa asked.

"So much more. But I will go slowly. I do not want to hurt you, nor do I want to rush us. I would savor every moment with you."

"I want that too."

Ric swept his finger along the satin skin of her sheath, adding a second and hooking them to rub a spot he prayed would excite Isa to match his own need. When her hips undulated against his hand, he knew she was drawing closer to her first climax. His thumb sought her pearl and circled it. Isa's sharp inhalation told him what his fingers soon discovered.

"Ric? Dear saints and angels. I—" Isa couldn't finish as the simmering ache in her belly finally released in a wave of pleasure that warmed her entire body, spreading out to her limbs. She watched as Ric shifted his weight as he fisted his cock. She reached for him, silently asking him to release his length so she could work his rod. She stroked slowly, praying she was doing it right. She couldn't imagine what else to do, but it matched what she'd seen him do when he kicked off his leggings. When a tiny pearl leaked from the tip, her eyes locked with Ric's, and she guided him to her sheath.

"I want you with a ferocity I'm scared I can't control, Isa. If I'm too rough, tell me. I never want to hurt you."

"I know you don't, Ric. I trust you." Isa's three words made Ric's chest feel like it would explode, but his conscience prickled when he recalled how he'd withheld the full story of their departure. He eased himself further into her core as they exchanged a tender kiss that belied the need raging between them.

The time for waiting had come and gone; they claimed one another with an explosive passion and joined as one. Ric rocked his hips until he pressed against Isa's barrier. She sucked in a breath but tried to relax her body, remembering the advice from her friends. Ric's hand found hers, and he brought it beside her head, entwining their fingers. Their clasped hands signified their partnership as much as their joined bodies. Ric closed his eyes as he surged forth, unable to watch the moment of pain on Isa's face.

Isa's nails dug into the back of Ric's hand before her fingers flexed. His eyes snapped open to see hers scrunched closed. He brushed back hair from her damp neck. The backs of his fingers grazed along her cheek as he waited. His cock throbbed, demanding that he satisfy his own need, but he couldn't bring himself to move if it would cause Isa more pain. When her eyes fluttered open, he saw tenderness, then confusion. She glanced down between them, her brow furrowing before she looked up.

"Yes. There's more," he confirmed with a smile. "But I would be certain you're all right."

"I am. It stung, and it stole my breath for a moment. But it wasn't nearly as bad as they say. I think matrons terrify virgins to keep them from discovering that after the pain, it feels quite nice." Isa shifted as her knees fell wide. Her hips tilted before she moaned.

"Quite nice? I shall endeavor to show you it can be far more than quite nice," Ric grinned. He inched his way further into her sheath until there was no more to give her. He rocked his hips as he waited for Isa to become acquainted with the feeling of their bodies being one. When her free hand grazed over his back, then grasped his backside, he withdrew halfway and thrust back into her, testing what she could endure and what she enjoyed.

"Yes," Isa moaned. Ric began to move, and it was only a moment later that Isa caught onto the rhythm, her hips rising and falling in time with each surge of Ric's cock. They moved together, alternating speeds as Ric fought not to end their first time as quickly as his bollocks begged. Sweat slid between his shoulder blades as he moved with Isa, drawing out their coupling until their groans shifted from pleasure to frustrated need.

With his arm wrapped around Isa's waist, Ric rolled them until he laid on his back, grasping Isa's hips. She looked at him in surprise, but she soon discovered that she had control of the speed and motion with which they moved. She rocked against Ric as her sheath clenched around his cock. In silent communication, they moved faster, with more demand in each thrust and pull. When Ric noticed Isa's furrowed brow, he realized that she sought the release she'd found earlier but didn't know how to reach it. Wrapping his arm around her once more, he rolled them over, so he was once more on top. He ground his pubis along her button until their bodies froze and euphoria flooded their senses, their bodies pressed together until their muscles relaxed, bliss replacing hunger.

As they floated back to earth, Ric attempted to roll onto his side. "I don't want to crush you."

"You're not. I just–" Isa looked up at Ric, emotions swirling within her that she feared confessing. She was sure that the occasion had not been anywhere near as momentous for him as it had been for her.

"What is it, Isa?" Ric brushed hair from her damp temple. "You can tell me aught. Tell me what you want, and I shall endeavor to give it to you."

Isa searched for something within his eyes that Ric could not guess, but when she cupped his cheeks and strained to reach his lips, he was lost all over again as his kiss poured forth equal parts tenderness and need. He rolled them so she rested across his chest.

"I don't want this to end. I would make this moment stretch on before we must return to reality, return to our duties and responsibilities. I would like to just savor this one time together."

"One time? Never doubt how much I crave you, Isabella. I will never get enough of you."

"Good, because I suspect I shall be a very demanding wife."

It did not escape Isa's attention that Ric used her full name. He had not done that since they met. His seriousness made her wonder if his feelings might run deeper than mere attraction. Isa pushed her mind away from those wonderings, sure that the deeper feelings were still just forms of lust. Pounding at the door shattered their bliss and brought them crashing back to reality. Ric placed a finger against her lips and shook his head.

"Don't move," he mouthed.

Isa's brow furrowed, but she nodded her head. She did not realize it, but her arms tightened around Ric as though she feared being ripped away from him. The pounding continued, and they could hear muffled voices beyond the door. After two more rounds of knocking, silence returned. Neither dared move for several long moments. Ric's arm tightened around her waist while the other hand rested possessively over her backside.

"We're not leaving this chamber until morning," Ric glared at the door.

"But I thought the king expected us to leave after the midday meal. We were to have that then depart."

"He's a fool if he thinks any newlywed man would make his bride ride out on the day of their wedding."

"I can think of plenty of men who have done just that when they've married other ladies-in-waiting."

"Then they weren't enamored with their brides, nor desired them more than their next breath," Ric grumbled. "I'm not letting you out of my reach nor am I going to force you to ride a horse today after what we just did. It would be cruel."

"Ric, I'm fine. I've been riding my entire life. I'd rather not anger the king." Isa watched as a wolfish grin spread across Ric's face.

"I can tell you like to ride." He pinched her backside, and Isa's eyes widened before she ducked her head. "Don't hide from me, my sweet. I enjoyed every second of it, and I shall gladly be your stallion."

Isa grinned up at Ric before adding her own risqué comment, "Hmmm. A stud I would gladly mount. I–"

Isa did not get to finish before Ric's fingers tangled in her hair, and he brought their mouths together. The kiss was languid as they explored and found more of what each enjoyed. They discovered what made them sigh and what made them shift restlessly. When they finally broke apart, Ric's wolfish grin was back in place.

"Have you always had such a cheeky sense of humor?" He gave her backside a light smack.

Isa shook her head. "I've never said a thing like that before in my life. I may have jested with some of the ladies aboot some of the more handsome men, but I have never said aught so lewd."

"Then I shall be your first for yet another thing."

When a cloud passed over Isa's face and all she did was nod, Ric could have kicked himself. There he was lying in bed with his bride still draped over him, having just experienced the most mind-rattling, earth-shattering climax of his life, and he had to point out that only one of them was experiencing it for the first time.

"Isa?" She nodded but would not look up. "Isa, that was insensitive of me. I'm sorry."

"It's fine," her voice was muffled as she leaned against his chest.

"No, it's not. Isa, please look at me." Isa lifted her head but looked at the pillow behind Ric's head rather than at him. She tried to make her face neutral, but she feared it showed everything. "Isabella." A note of warning made her gaze snap to his.

"That's the third time today that you've used my full name. You never do that."

"Because each time I wanted you to know how serious I am. Isa, ever since I met you, I wish I could go back and erase the time before I met you. While it's not the same, this has been a first for me, too." Isa's eyes narrowed, and Ric realized he had better explain carefully.

"I never considered marrying before I met you; I never wanted to. And I knew what it was like to grow up without a father. I was very careful about not siring any bastards, which meant never finding the release that I did with you." Ric watched Isa to be sure she understood him. "You're the only woman I have ever wanted to marry, and the only woman I have ever imagined having children with. Do you understand what I'm saying?"

"No." Isa's succinct answer made Ric smile even when he wanted to groan. He was not looking forward to spelling this out.

"Do you know how a couple conceives a child?"

"Of course. That's the reason for what we did."

Ric nearly bit the tip of his tongue off when her words registered. "Isa, what we just did may result in a child, but getting you pregnant was not why we made love." Isa tried not to read too much into that phrase he used yet again. "I have always pulled out before finding my release because I never wanted to risk siring a bastard. I didn't pull out with you because I want to make a family with you one day. But it was more than that. I didn't pull out because I couldn't bring myself to end the connection I feel with you. You're my wife because I want you and no other. I hope I'm your husband for the same reason."

Isa caught the note of uncertainty at the end. She stretched and kissed Ric's nose. "There's no one else I want. I wasn't ready to marry until I met you." A sensation in his heart that Ric had begun to feel only around Isa took hold once again. He did not know if it was the beginning of love, but he knew he wanted it to grow. They settled against one another, and it was not long before they drifted off to sleep.

FIFTEEN

A knocking at the door awoke Isa and Ric, but this time it was lighter and less demanding than the one that came hours earlier.

"Isa, it's Deirdre." Isa looked at Ric while biting her lip. He pulled it loose and gave her a quick kiss. "Isa, I've brought a tub and steaming water. I think you may appreciate it."

Isa's longing look prompted Ric to lift her off him and lower her to her feet beside the bed. She furrowed her brow, but at his nod, she dashed to put on her robe. Ric enjoyed the view of his wife's swinging hips and breasts. He snatched the covers and drew them to his chest before everyone knew just how much he enjoyed it.

Isa opened the door just wide enough to see Deirdre and the crew of servants who waited behind her. She stepped back and pulled the door wide, allowing the servants to enter. She caught more than one of the women looking past her at Ric. She glanced over her shoulder and saw that he had pulled the blanket to his chin, but his relaxed pose of being propped up in bed with one arm tucked behind his head only made him more attractive. She breathed a silent sigh when she realized that his eyes were riveted on her, and none of the movement distracted his attention.

She glanced back at Deirdre to thank her for the thoughtfulness, but her friend disappeared. Isa waited until the servants left before once more locking and barring the door. She was unprepared for Ric to spring from the bed and catch her around the waist. Her body slammed against his, and she was sure hitting a wall made of marble would feel the same way, except her body reacted with arousal rather than pain. Before she knew what was happening, Ric stripped the robe from her and spun her around, pressing her at arm's length toward the tub. She tried to see over her shoulder, but the position was too awkward. When she looked forward, she caught sight of them in her looking glass. Ric's gaze was on her backside as she continued to walk.

"I'm going to bathe you, and then we are going to slip back into bed. To sleep. I am not going to hurt you by overdoing it your first time."

"It really wasn't that bad. Nowhere near what I feared. Could we not—?"

"You'll feel differently in the morning when you can barely walk let alone ride," Ric shook his head.

"Then we shouldn't let the water cool anymore. A soak will do me good. Then can we please find something to eat? I'm ravenous."

"Ravishing," Ric muttered.

"What's that?"

"You're ravishing, and that's the whole problem. Let's get you in the bath while the water is still hot." Ric held her hand and helped her into the tub. Isa slid to the back of the tub and patted the water in front of her. Ric shook his head, so she flicked water at him.

"Dip your head under, and I will attempt to wash

your hair." Ric offered, but this time Isa shook her head before patting the water again.

"If you wait until I'm done, the water will be too cold."

"That may be just what I need," Ric grumbled, but when Isa pouted and flicked water at him again, he relented. He found he could not deny his bonny bride anything.

Ric eased into the tub, and Isa turned to rest her back against his chest. They sat like that, the water lapping around them, for a long time. Their fingers entwined as they enjoyed the quiet and affection. Ric pressed kisses against her temple from time to time, and Isa drew his arms around her more tightly. It was only when the water did begin to chill that they lathered two linens and ran them over each other. Ric marveled at the feel of Isa's white-blonde tresses as he scrubbed her scalp, then poured clean water over her. With her hair slicked back, he had a chance to appreciate just how perfectly formed her features were. He knew other men found her attractive, but he was certain none had ever seen her look more beautiful.

"Why are you staring at me?" Isa wondered softly.

"You take my breath away."

Isa was unprepared for such an honest response, and she felt her cheeks heat. "Thank you," she whispered. She looked away, suddenly embarrassed and feeling more naked than she had even when they coupled. Her eyes alighted on the bed, and she furrowed her brow and bit her top lip.

"What're you thinking about?" Ric slid a wet lock of hair behind her shoulder.

"I was very comfortable earlier when I dozed, but that was because you're huge and made a wonderful pillow. But you couldn't have been very comfortable on such a narrow bed."

"You think I'm huge?" Ric waggled his eyebrows.

"Yes. In just the ways I like." She waggled her own eyebrows in response.

"What have I unleashed?" Ric pulled her onto his lap and slid forward in the tub, giving her room to wrap her legs around him. The water sloshed around Isa's breasts, and he could see the faint outline of her nipple just below the surface. Bathing with her, and now holding her once again, was the singularly most erotic experience of his life.

"You've allowed me to be myself in a way I only want to share with you. In a way I never imagined." They filled their kiss with tenderness and promises neither were ready to speak aloud. A pounding at the door, along with an announcement that the king summoned them both, made it impossible for them to carry on. Ric groaned as Isa whimpered softly. Isa tried to keep the petulance from her voice, but she knew it was there. "I don't want to go."

"Neither do I, my sweet. Stay here and rest while I answer to the king."

"No. I played a part in our truancy, and I won't let you take the blame alone."

"Isa, every man in the Privy Council will know what we've been about. I won't embarrass you by having them smirk at you."

"Both of our names were said. We're both expected there."

Ric's lips thinned, but he nodded. He helped Isa out of the tub then rubbed her dry with one of the linens. She ran a comb through her hair and quickly braided it while Ric dried himself. He assisted her with a fresh kirtle but took forever with her laces. She wondered if it was intentional until he admitted he was not sure how to fasten her gown. She walked him through it, and then once he was dressed, Isa and Ric left her chamber. They walked with Isa's arm threaded through Ric's, her hand resting on his forearm. The couple did not pass many people in the passageway, but the few that they did gave them knowing looks. Isa attempted to ignore the appreciative looks women gave her husband, but Ric was not so tolerant of the men who ogled Isa. His hand went to the hilt of the knife sheathed at his waist.

"I shall have to get one of those to carry around, too. It seems quite a deterrent," Isa remarked.

"A deterrent for what?"

"All the women, of course."

"What women?"

Isa assumed he was being purposely obtuse until she realized Ric did not seem to notice any of the women they passed. Each time she looked up at him, he was watching her. "If you don't look where we're going, you're liable to walk into a wall."

"I trust you to steer me away. You're far prettier than any of the walls. I'd rather look at you."

"You're turning into quite the romantic bard."

"What I'm turning into is a husband with a wife more beautiful than he could have ever imagined and who would gladly follow her anywhere like a loyal hound."

"Shall I scratch you behind the ears?"

"My sweet, you may scratch me anywhere you please, hopefully while we are making love," Ric lowered his voice for the last words as they approached the doors to the Privy Council. He looked around and pulled Isa into an alcove before they reached the guards. "Isa, no matter what is said in there, I'm not going anywhere without you, and if you don't feel well enough to travel today, tell me now, and we will not leave until you are. Don't say what you believe the king or I want to hear. Tell me the truth."

"I don't want to leave today, but I am well enough to do it."

"I will argue that there is little sunlight left for us to depart now. It would be safer for everyone to leave in the morning. It's true, and it will give you a chance to sleep. I told you before, I don't know if we'll be able to stay at any inns. We may have to make camp most nights."

"Ric, I've made more than one journey where I've slept on the ground. I will manage. I just don't want to end the time we've had as just the two of us."

Ric kissed her softly. "Neither do I."

"Let's get this done with, and then hopefully we can return to our chamber."

"Our chamber shall be the one I occupied. It has a larger bed. If only I had more time to chase you across it, but it will ensure you get a better night's sleep."

"Is it so large I won't be able to reach you?"

"No," Ric drew out the word as he wondered if that was how she would rather sleep.

"Good, because I don't want to lose you in the middle of the night. I found sleeping on you is the most comfortable I've ever been."

"Keep saying things like that, and I shall abscond with you to the Highlands, where no one will find us."

"Do you promise?"

"I wish that I could."

"Let's be done with this."

SIXTEEN

R ic led them from the alcove and wrapped his arm around Isa as sentries admitted them to the king's meeting chamber. Advisors and scribes filled the room. Isa had never been within the chamber but had heard it described more than once. They approached the king, and while Ric bowed, Isa curtsied.

"I see we were able to find you after all. I began to wonder if you'd slipped away." Robert's tone held only traces of humor. "I assume the deed is done, and you are truly wed now."

Ric felt Isa stiffen, and he saw the leers several of the men gave her even if the king had not deigned to look at either of them yet. Ric pulled Isa more tightly against his side, and she welcomed the sense of protection, even if did not stop the looks or whispered comments. "Your Majesty, my wife is present. I'd rather she not be spoken of in such a way before others."

Ric's defense made Robert's head jerk up, and the king glowered at the knight. The russet-haired king did not bother to hide the flush that rose from his neck as his temper boiled.

"I'm aware of where your wife is, and where she

191

has been." The king flicked his wrist, and a man appeared from a corner carrying a bedsheet. Isa gasped when she noticed the red streak and understood where the sheet came from. She turned into Ric's chest, mortified that proof of her virginity was on display. "You shall take this with you and fly it from the laird's chamber window. You will use it as proof that you have a claim to the land Laird Dunbar exchanged for your protection."

Isa looked up at Ric as she understood that she was the proof. The fact that she was wedded and bedded gave Ric the right to hold the land the king had ceded to him and that her father had always intended to be part of her dowry. She grew up thinking it was her dower lands in case she one day had daughters who would need a home if her husband died without sons. Now she understood that they had bartered her between her husband and her father. They had each gotten what they wanted, and she had been the payment that exchanged hands.

"That is why you wished for the wedding to be sooner. Not so that we could have time together before being surrounded by others. It was so you could ensure you had a sheet to prove you'd bedded me," Isa hissed in Ric's ear.

"Isabella," Ric warned. She turned to face the king, no longer willing to cower against a man she thought had her best interests in mind, but truly was just as ambitious and manipulative as any other man at court. She lifted her chin as her eyes scanned the crowd, daring any of the men to make another comment or offer her another lascivious glance.

"You were to leave more than an hour past. You seem to have a rather short memory."

"Your Majesty, as you so plainly pointed out, my wife and I had matters to attend to." A muscle in

Ric's jaw twitched. "As such, it is too late to set out today. We shall be ready to depart at sunrise."

"I think not. If your wife is unable to leave today, then she may follow at some other time."

"Your Majesty," Ric's voice took on a tone that bordered on insolence. "My wife is under my care now. I already told you I would not leave without her, and I will not endanger her life, on our wedding day or any other, by making her ride in the dark. You are just as aware as I am of the highwaymen who frequent the roads just outside of Stirling. I will not make her prey to them. We leave with the sun."

Ric pressed Isa behind him and stood with his hand on his hip where the hilt of his sword normally would have rested. He looked about the chamber, a dark and brooding scowl on his face that warned away anyone who might test his commitment to his wife's safety.

"Very well," the king relented far too easily. "You shall ride out in the morning. And Sir Dedric, you'd do well to remember in the days to come just how readily you came to your wife's defense. She is one of my wife's favorites."

Ric breathed a sigh of relief to realize that the king had only been testing him and that he had passed. He turned back to reach for Isa's hand, but the glare she fixed upon him was as though she had discovered a rat before her, rather than the man she had spent hours making passionate love to only a short while ago. She spun on her heel and marched toward the chamber door and passed through it without looking back. She turned in the direction that would take her back to her own chamber, but Ric caught her arm.

"The chamber I used is in the other direction."

"Then I shall bid you adieu until morning. Sleep

well." Isa attempted to take a step, but Ric's hand was like an anchor that kept her in place.

"Adieu? Sleep well? Isa, where are you going?"

"To my chamber, just as you are going to yours."

"We do not have his and her chambers, we have ours. And I thought we agreed to the one with the larger bed."

"Why? Wasn't the sheet from mine big enough? It won't make a difference since, as the king pointed out, I'm already wedded and bedded. There won't be another sheet to fly from your chamber window."

"I warned you that no matter what was said, I would protect you. You must have realized the king was testing me."

"With the truth. You married me to get the plot of land you came here for. You needed to prove your entitlement to it by showing all and sundry that my dowry is now rightfully yours. You've done that. You have no need of me until it is time to ride out tomorrow. Do as you please. Wherever and with whomever you please."

Ric scooped Isa into his arms and growled when she opened her mouth to complain. "Do not speak until we reach our chamber."

Isa was left with few options but to wrap her arms around Ric's neck to keep from feeling like she would fall. She knew he would never drop her, but she felt safer holding onto him, and for that, she wanted to kick herself. When they arrived at his door, he pushed the handle then kicked it open. Robbie sprung to his feet from where he was polishing Ric's armor.

"Out," Ric barked, and Robbie scrambled past them without looking at either of them.

"Isabella—"

"I don't think I like it when you use my full name," she interrupted.

Ric took a deep breath to calm his temper. "Isa, would you like to hear the truth of my negotiations with the king or would you rather let what he insinuated ruin what we created today?"

"He didn't insinuate aught, Ric. He made it very clear to me and everyone else that my father bartered me for the land and in return received a well-trained knight."

"No. That may be the outcome, but that is not how it came to be. Isa, please listen to me." Ric had placed her on her feet, and the moment they touched the floor, she fled to the window embrasure where she looked out over the town of Stirling. "The king offered me a piece of land after it became obvious that I intended to marry you. The king made it contingent upon my willingness to serve your father, which I gladly agreed to. Isa, I don't care about the land, but I do care that he wouldn't have let me marry you without swearing fealty to your father and to him, which I did without hesitation. If you don't want to live at that keep, if you'd rather return to your parents' home, then I will relinquish any claim to the land. But it means I will be apart from you much longer and more often. I still have to patrol the border where the land the king gave me lies. That is what I was trying to avoid. I refused to leave without you, and that is why I insisted the ceremony be moved forward. I knew Robert wanted me to leave before the sun set today, and I was not going to risk running out of time to marry you."

"Yes, because you needed proof before you arrived on my clan's land. And you would have no authority without first being married to me."

"Bloody hell, Isa. No."

She spun around, irritated at the exasperation in Ric's voice, but his expression was drawn. "I wish someone, you in particular, had told me of this arrangement before we married. It doesn't paint you in a good light."

"I only found out this morning. That's why I missed Terce. The king was making his demands, and I was doing everything I could to ensure I didn't have to leave you behind."

"Why does me joining you matter so much? Plenty of couples live apart when they are courtiers for a king."

"I am no courtier. Not for Robert or any king. I may have been a knight for Edward and now a warrior for Robert, but I will never accept a court lifestyle, and I will never accept living apart from you. My wife. And how Robert, after the separation from Elizabeth that he was forced to endure, could consider I would voluntarily do the same is beyond me. I think I've made it clear from the beginning what my intentions were."

"Yes. To serve Robert until you earned land on which you could retire."

Ric stalked across the room and lifted Isa's left hand. He twirled his signet ring around on her thumb. "And how many days after I arrived did I make it clear that I would marry you? I gave you my ring. The one you still wear along with the one I placed on your finger today. I did that well before Robert ever spoke of land to me."

He lifted her hand so the light shone on the bright emerald that sat in the band of gold on her ring finger, as well as on the thick band of the ring on her thumb. After they had signed the betrothal papers, Isa slipped the ring back onto her thumb without thinking about it. Ric had liked the look of her wearing something that bore his coat of arms so much that he had not asked for the ring back. She wore it to their wedding and still wore it now.

"It's not aboot the land?" she whispered.

"It stopped being about land and started being about a home the moment I met you. Isa, my home is wherever you are. After years of drifting, at the end of the day and at the end of the battle, I want to go home. To you. Everything with you is different, better than aught else I have ever experienced." Ric's voice caught and there was a rawness about his confession that humbled Isa. She was sure he had never spoken that way to anyone before. She opened her arms to him, and he buried his head in her neck.

"It just hurt so much to hear the king speak of me as though I meant naught more than a means to getting what you really wanted."

Ric wished he could confess everything to Isa, so she would understand what Robert's test really meant, but he would not risk her life by sharing anything an enemy might use against either of them. He was committed to protecting her, and if he was willing to admit it, he was devoted to her as well.

They spent the rest of the night tucked away. Ceit knocked once and announced she had arranged for servants to deliver trays. When the next knock came, Ceit was nowhere in sight, but four footmen carried trays overflowing with enough food to feed them for several days. They undressed and sat before the fire to eat. Isa told him more about her years at court, and Ric shared what he dared about his time at Edward's court. Isa did not bring up either of their childhoods, not wanting to share stories that Ric could not match. When they were both full, they moved to the bed where they made love again once more, this time without haste. Ric continued to worry about Isa having to ride the next day, but his bride was too alluring to ignore. They dozed off and on as they awoke to make love twice more before dropping into a deep sleep, Isa draped across Ric's chest, one leg tucked between his two as his arms held her in place.

———

Isa was certain she awoke before Ric, but she laid motionless as she luxuriated in the feel of being pressed against her mighty husband's body. The covers had fallen to their waists, and she took the time to let her eyes travel over his muscular arm, the ridges next to his ribs, down to the outline of his thigh. She tentatively ran a finger over his shoulder, and when he did not stir, she felt more brazen. She swept feathery caresses over his chest, mesmerized at the heat Ric generated along with the feel of solid rock beneath smooth skin. She tilted her head to look up at him as she ran her fingers along his jaw. She gasped when she realized he was watching her. She attempted to pull her hand away, but Ric captured it with a gentleness she now knew she should antici- pate. He brought her fingers to his lips and kissed each one before replacing her hand on his jaw.

"Don't stop," he whispered. She continued to ex- plore his cheekbones and patrician nose before brushing her first two fingers across his lips. Ric rolled to his side so he could kiss Isa. "Am I dream- ing?" he wondered.

"No, my heart," Isa returned his whisper, trying out an endearment for the first time.

"Say it again," he pleaded.

"My heart," Isa murmured beside his ear.

He had no willpower to deny himself the plea- sure of her affection. In the first day of his marriage, he had realized several things about himself and his wife. He had no idea that he longed for affection until she offered it. He had no idea how much better coupling was with someone he cared about until he joined with Isa. And he had no idea how he would keep his secret from her. It would destroy the tender bud that was their relationship when all he wanted was to nurture it. He knew he was falling in love with Isa, and he prayed she would one day return his feelings. But if the truth came out that he was a spy for Edward who was forced into spying for Robert, she would never trust him again.

SEVENTEEN

I sa and Ric rose when there was no longer a way to avoid the inevitable departure and long journey ahead of them. They slipped back to her chamber before anyone else in the castle stirred. How quickly Isa could prepare for the unexpected move impressed Ric. She packed two satchels with the most essential clothing and toiletries and dressed just as quickly as Ric had. She shrugged when Ric asked her about leaving the rest of her belongings behind.

"They'll be sent along behind us, I'm sure. They're mostly gowns I would only wear at court anyway. They aren't fitting for life among my clan."

They returned to Ric's chamber just before Robbie arrived, having been summarily dismissed the day before, to assist Ric with his full armor, but the knight refused to wear it. He had put on his gambeson, a padded doublet, and only accepted Robbie's aid in putting on his hauberk, a knee-length chain metal tunic, before adding his surcoat over the top. Ric had watched Isa dress and worried silently that she did not have any protection for her body should there be an attack. He would insist she ride in the middle of the group of warriors King Robert was assigning to Ric.

"Shall we make our way to the bailey?" Ric held out his arm to Isa, and she gladly slid her hand through until it rested on his forearm.

"I suppose we haven't much choice. I don't think the king will allow us another day alone."

"I don't believe he would. But the sooner we set off, the sooner we can arrive at our new home."

Home. A word that brought both excitement and trepidation to both of them. Isa was looking forward to returning to her clan's land after so many years at court. Her father, though a distant cousin to King Robert, had sided with the English early in the Scottish struggle for independence. Laird Dunbar had done what he thought would keep his people safe, but he had not chosen the victorious side. He and the king eventually reconciled when Dunbar pledged his fealty to Robert, and he had remained loyal ever since.

But part of the price of reconciliation had been Isa's service to the queen's court. She had been only fourteen when she arrived eight years earlier and had not had many opportunities to visit her family on their land. She traveled extensively with the royal household, but it was rare for them to visit the western Lowlands. She was eager to assume her role as lady of the keep, realizing she wanted to make Ric proud of her. However, she was nervous about arriving with a husband who sounded so English, and worried about how her people would receive them. The Scots were not a trusting lot, and those living on the border understood that trust given to the wrong person could be deadly.

Ric had never lived anywhere he considered home. He was not even sure he understood the concept of living somewhere for the rest of his life, somewhere welcoming and permanent. He had endured his service at King Edward's various castles, and he had endured his training with Sir Geoffrey, but neither place had felt like home. He had longed for somewhere that he would look forward to returning to and where he could finally find a sense of peace after moving so often. He wanted to create a life with Isa where they could be happy together, but he was nervous about proving himself to both Isa and her clan.

They arrived in the bailey to see many of the warriors had already arrived, but the horses were still being readied. Ric had learned that the keep he would inherit already had a strong standing defense, and the Bruce intended the men who would travel with them to be ones who rode on patrol with Ric. He had not yet identified which ones were Robert's personal spies. He knew the only reason Robert would insist on such an arrangement was to ensure that someone was present to send missives back to the king to report on Ric's progress. He knew because he had served in the same capacity to Edward Longshanks more than once.

Isa watched the hive of activity in the bailey as the horses stood awaiting their riders. She smiled when she saw her own pure brown gelding brought out. He rivaled the size of some battle-trained horses, and she knew he would be faster as she was a lighter mount. She was about to walk down the steps to greet Bridei with an apple she had saved from the previous night's feast when women's voices stopped her.

"You didn't have to come out so early," she smiled as Deirdre, Ceit, and Elizabeth opened their arms to embrace her. While the women were smiling, none of their husbands looked pleased to be dragged from their beds.

"We wanted to see you off. We're going to miss your company," Elizabeth admitted. "I wish you didn't have to leave so soon."

"I agree. It won't be the same without you. I've grown very fond of you." Ceit Comyn Sinclair had arrived at the royal court in much the same manner as Isa, with a family in disgrace. She had kept mostly to herself, and Isa now knew it was because the Bruce had enlisted her to spy on her traitorous uncle, who led the force opposed to Robert's kingship. Her marriage to Tavish had relieved her of those duties, and she felt free to make friends.

"I am sure we will return to court from time to time," Isa reassured them.

"But we will not, at least not if Magnus can help it," Deirdre frowned. "I can't blame him. I wouldn't have come back if it weren't to aid Elizabeth."

Elizabeth had suffered a coach accident just before Christmas, and it was determined that it was intentional. They had yet to resolve the situation, so the king summoned his two godsons as trusted investigators, but their time spent riding out with Ric had kept them from their original duties.

"And I'm eager to return to Culcreuch where Edward doesn't have a score of guards following me everywhere." Elizabeth looked at her husband with a serene smile that belied her grumbling.

"You shall have to come visit us in Dunbeath," Ceit offered. "I've come to appreciate the beauty of the northern Highlands after so long in the Lowlands."

"I would like that. And I think the Highlands would suit Ric."

"I recognize that look in your eyes," Deirdre grinned, and at Isa's puzzled expression, the other ladies giggled. "You're rather more than just smitten with your husband."

"I'd say so, too," Elizabeth chimed in.

Deirdre took pity on Isa's confusion and wrapped her arm around her. "I think you're falling in love with your husband, lass."

Isa looked down at the ground and swallowed several times trying to keep tears from forming. She nodded but could not bring herself to look up yet lest she embarrass herself further.

"What is it?" Ceit asked softly. The mood among the friends had shifted. "Oh Isa, are you afraid he doesn't feel the same way?"

Isa finally looked up and nodded. She welcomed the second embrace from her friends and wished it did not have to end.

"Isa, it's clear to anyone that Ric cares aboot you, and I would venture to say he is falling in love with you, too," Ceit whispered.

"I can only hope so, or it will be a long and lonely life." Isa pushed her shoulders back and lifted her chin as she took a deep breath to compose herself. "A life that shall begin in moments. It looks like the men are ready to ride."

The women embraced a final time before returning to their husbands, who looked mollified after chatting with Ric. He turned to find Isa and caught the expression she wore before she put on a brave face. He wondered if her regrets were for leaving the court or for leaving with him. He took her hand and assisted her down the steps, having noticed that the skirts to her kirtle were longer than usual.

"I shall miss them, but I am excited for this new adventure." Isa looked up at Ric, and the softness in her eyes and smile reassured Ric that she was not dreading the journey as he had feared.

Ric looked around for Isa's mare and was just about to send Robbie to find the horse when he saw Isa walk up to a giant chestnut gelding and take the reins from a stable boy. She was in the saddle before Ric could warn her away from the beast. She mounted astride and settled her long skirts around her to keep her legs covered. He understood now why the kirtle was cut the way it was, and he observed Isa sat like an experienced horsewoman. He walked over and checked Isa's saddle despite her already being on the horse.

"I never would have guessed that your horse would be nearly as big as mine," Ric grinned.

"Bridei and I have been together since he was a colt. I had no idea he would grow to be so large, but he is a gentle giant. Unless provoked. Is your horse polite?" Isa returned Ric's smile.

"Rarely," Ric snorted. "Bridei?"

"He was a Pictish king not long after the Christian conversion."

Ric nodded and thought to himself that he should have known it would be a Pict name. But he grew serious as he finished checking the girth and stirrups. "Isa, next time, please wait for me to check your saddle and horse before you mount."

"Why? I've been riding since I was five. I know how to saddle my own horse, and I know what to look for when someone else has saddled one for me."

"Because you're now the wife of a border lord who lives in Scotland but sounds English. I didn't see you check aught on the saddle."

Isa felt like reminding Ric that she had also been the daughter of a border laird her entire life, but instead she nodded.

"If you wish." She reached down and patted the hand Ric did not realize rested on her calf. "Thank you for caring," she finished in a whisper.

"Careful or I will lift you off that beast and kiss you squarely in front of everyone."

"We do seem to have a habit of that."

"Isa," he warned, but his smile softened his tone.

Ric mounted and the other warriors followed suit. While Isa spoke with her friends, Ric had given his captain of the guard the order that Isa was to ride in the center, surrounded by warriors, and if there was an attack, the men's purpose was to protect her rather than pursue. They clattered out of the gate and through the town of Stirling until they left the city gates. As the road widened, the men took their formation, and the riders separated Isa from Ric, who rode in the lead. She was about to call out to him, but his rigid body and hand on his sword hilt made her bite her tongue.

They rode until the sun was well overhead, and Isa was hot and uncomfortable. She realized she should have heeded Ric's warning the night before, but she did not regret the time spent with her husband. However, now, she found it was impossible to find a position that did not anger her sore body. Ric had looked back at her several times, and she had smiled before he turned back to watch the road. He had not invited her to move forward nor fallen back to ride with her. She felt cut off and alone, even though she knew Ric had given the order to protect her. She refused to complain and easily kept up with the other riders, even if she wanted to cry out in pain whenever Bridei's gait jarred her, which was often on the rutted road. She gritted her teeth and breathed through her nose.

At midday, they stopped to let the horses rest and for everyone to stretch their legs. Isa dismounted before Ric could help her, but he was there to catch her when her legs did not want to bear her weight.

"Thank you," she whispered.

"Are you well?" Isa could hear the concern in Ric's voice. He turned her to face him and noticed the teeth marks in her lip. He brushed his thumb over it but pulled away when she gasped. "Isa, what's the matter?"

"Naught."

Ric shook his head, then his eyes opened wide. "Are you too sore to ride?" he murmured.

"No."

"Isa, you don't have to tell me what you think I want to hear. Tell me the truth."

"I am. I'm well enough to ride."

"And if you continue, will you be able to walk by this evening? Will you be able to ride tomorrow?"

"You're whittling."

"I'm concerned for my wife." Ric knew what the problem was, and he was angry with himself while growing frustrated with Isa.

Isa stifled her groan and stretched to kiss Ric's jaw, which she could see ticking. He caught her around the waist and gave her a punishing and passionate kiss. She returned it with equal measure until they both knew Ric's men would be watching soon. They pulled apart, and Ric kissed her nose.

"You're riding with me." Ric spun on his heel and yelled orders for one of the men to tie Bridei to his saddle after the man took the horse to drink. Isa was left staring at her husband's back as she tried to comprehend his highhandedness. She knew he was trying to look after her, but she did not appreciate being given an order, then abandoned. She looked around and noticed a few of the men watched them, but most were busy with their own steeds. Isa spotted a tree with a broad trunk and bushes surrounding it and decided she would make use of the privacy.

Ric looked back to see if Isa was following him, but she was not standing where he had just seen her.

He scanned the group, but she was nowhere to be seen. His heart raced as his fear alternated between thinking someone had nabbed her and that she had run off. He was about to bellow orders to search for her when she emerged from the trees brushing out her skirts. His rational mind told him she had sought out privacy, but his emotions were on high alert, making him fear the worst. He marched over to Isa and stood before her. Her smile faded when she saw his scowl.

"Don't wander off like that."

Isa's chin drew back, and the look of indignation made Ric realize he had gone too far. "I didn't wander off. We may be married, but I don't need your company while I relieve myself. I've been able to do that on my own for quite some time." Isa pushed past him and made her way to the riverbank but paused before bending down. "Would you like to be my nursemaid and make sure I don't fall in? Do you trust me to rinse my hands and face, or do you think I can't do that alone either?"

Isa knew she was being testy, and while she tried to keep her voice down, she knew she was drawing stares. She was in pain and irritated that Ric was embarrassing her in front of men she would have to travel and live with for the next several days. Ric marched over to her and put his hands on his hips.

"Isabella."

"Stop that. I'm not a child in leading strings. I detest when you use my full name because it's only ever when I've annoyed you, Dedric." Isa crossed her arms and tapped her toe before arching an eyebrow. Ric dropped his arms, unable to deny she was right. Except there had been one time when he had used her name, and he was most certainly not frustrated with her. He pulled her against him and was thankful that the hauberk and surcoat hid his arousal.

"I can think of twice that I used your full name, and I was aught but annoyed. Do you not remember the first time we made love?"

Isa's breath caught as she caught a whiff of Ric's fresh scent. They had used the pitcher of water in their chamber left there earlier in the day to complete their morning ablutions. Ric's soap had smelled of pine and sandalwood. She could smell it now as he filled her senses and her mind jumped back to the night before.

"Of course, I do. It was only hours ago." Her voice was a breathless whisper.

"Then you'll recall that I used it to be sure you understood how serious I was."

"But it felt very different from when you use it to scold me."

Ric paused as he looked at the hurt in his wife's emerald eyes. While they were apart, he had often thought of how they matched the grass after a heavy rainstorm. "I worry about you, whether it's within that viperous court or out here where we are exposed. I would protect you at all costs, and sometimes that means I need to warn you."

"I'm not a child, Dedric. I can make my own decisions, and I haven't done aught to endanger myself at court or here. I stepped around the tree closest to the twenty-odd men you have with us. If aught, I was in danger of one of them spying me with my skirts lifted rather than someone making off with me. And I navigated court life for eight years before I met you. I'm not a novice."

Ric had not known Isa lived at court for so long. He had to admit there was much about his bride that he still did not know. He was allowing his fear and overprotectiveness to get the better of him, and it was about to drive a wedge between them. "Isa, you know my mother died living near the border because of who she married. I fear the same might happen to you."

Isa watched the chords in Ric's neck strain as he swallowed. She had not thought about his family, and so it never crossed her mind that bringing her with him might be upsetting. "Should I have stayed at court where I wouldn't be a distraction?" she asked softly. "I don't want to be in your way."

"No. Absolutely not. I was not leaving without you. You're not in the way, and you're not a distraction. I never want you to feel that way. You mean a great deal to me, and I worry about you."

Isa wrapped her arms around Ric's waist and leaned her ear against his chest. "I don't like this armor," she muttered.

"Why?"

"Because I can't hear your heart. I realized last night that I find it soothing," she admitted. Ric used his finger to lift her chin and pressed a gentle kiss against her lips.

"It shall be sweet torture, but will you ride with me, please?" Isa nodded and tightened her hold on him. " I should have asked instead of ordered, shouldn't I have?"

Isa nodded once again. " Ric, I can still ride. You're right that I'm sore, but I'd much rather be in your arms than alone again."

"Alone? Men have surrounded you the entire morning."

"You're right." She let go of Ric and was ready to walk to his horse, but he held onto her waist.

"You meant because I rode ahead and left you with men you've never met. Isa, I'm sorry. Once again, my need to protect you made me insensitive."

"I know you mean well. It just reminded me of when my father sent me to court for the first time. My father had barely mended the rift with the king and didn't dare show his face. I was sent with a contingent of guards and a maid. No one spoke to me for nearly the entire journey. Only the maid did, and that was more often to grumble aboot the ride than to help me. If I hadn't been a lass, I wouldn't have had her as a chaperone."

"No one from your family presented you at court? You were just delivered to the queen?" Ric was aghast.

"Who was going to present me? I told you my father was not in Robert's good graces at the time, so he could not go himself and he refused to send my mother to travel back and forth. I wore leggings and a long tunic, so I looked more like a lad. My mother would have stood out. It was safer for everyone the way it was."

Ric could not believe what he was hearing. Once more, he realized he had much to learn about Isa, but his anger was growing as he heard more about the man he had pledged fealty to through his marriage.

"I don't feel the same way as your father. Perhaps it is because you're a beautiful woman any man would covet. If we're attacked, you will be the first person they will try to reach. Whether to keep you or to ransom you. I wish there was another way to reach our keep, but there isn't."

"I know. I do appreciate your concern; I just don't care for being ordered aboot like a wean."

"Wean?"

"A young child. You shall have to learn some more phrases if you're to understand our people."

Our people. Ric had not thought of the men, women, and children who would be at the keep as his people, but he supposed he was part of the Dunbar clan now, and as the lord, they were his people. Isa took Ric's hand and led him to his horse.

"Isa, meet MacLellan. MacLellan, this is my bonny bride. You shall treat her well while she rides with me."

Isa covered her mouth to hide her giggle as she listened to her mountain of a husband coo at his horse. "You named him after your mother's people? That must not have gone over well with the English."

"I rarely needed to use his name in public, so few people knew. When I was given him, he was still a colt, too. I was to become a squire and angry about being sent away from court to yet another place where I knew no one. I suppose I was being rebellious, but in the end, I liked feeling like I had at least some connection to my family, even if it was only my horse's name."

Isa ran her hand along the horse's neck and smiled when it turned its giant head to see her. The destrier was pure black and a striking contrast to her entirely chestnut gelding. MacLellan had a wider girth than Bridei, but they stood the same height. Isa pulled herself up but found herself lifted into midair by two strong hands that gently lowered her to sit sideways. Ric mounted behind her and helped her arrange her skirts. She sat bracketed by Ric's powerful thighs, and when he wrapped an arm around her middle, she gladly sank into the wall of muscle that seemed to cocoon her.

"I feel safer here than I did with all your men around me," she whispered.

Ric looked down and realized that despite her height, her willowy body made her appear petite compared to him. His heart pinched as he felt her huddle against him, trusting him to protect her, while her eyes were closed, and she attempted to stifle a yawn. "Rest, little one. We still have several hours of travel. I will hold you while you sleep."

"I'd like that," she managed around another yawn.

Ric spurred his horse forward and gave an order for the men to surround him now as he held his precious cargo. Isa was already asleep, having relaxed once his arm went around her. He wondered if she might be developing feelings for him just as he was sure he was falling in love with her. He corrected himself. He was fairly certain he was already in love with her.

EIGHTEEN

I sa dozed for much of the afternoon, but when they stopped again to water the horses, she insisted she was well enough to ride on her own. She took a few faltering steps on her own before Ric swept her into his arms and carried her to some bushes where he kept watch while she made use of them. Then he carried her to the bank of the small loch and set her down before making use of the bush himself. She felt better after splashing water on her face, but she longed to be able to pull her skirts up and wade into the cold water. She was sure it would soothe her inflamed flesh. When Ric returned to her side, she gazed past his shoulder to Bridei, who stood nodding his head at the horse standing next to him, almost as though they were having a conversation, then she looked back at Ric.

"I think I'd rather ride with you again," she confessed.

"Are you still that uncomfortable?"

"I am still sore, but I'm—" She trailed off as she felt the heat rising in her cheeks. She did not want Ric to think her too meek to handle the trip, but she was embarrassed to admit that she was enjoying the feel of being held by Ric.

"I'd gladly have you ride with me any time you'd like. I enjoy the feel of you, too." Ric winked as he once again swept her into his arms.

This time, Isa stayed awake for the rest of the day, and she and Ric chatted about their different impressions of arriving at court as a child of seven as opposed to a young woman of fourteen. They found that many of their experiences had been similar despite the difference in ages. Isa discovered that Ric's time as a squire-in-training was close to her own as a lady-in-waiting. It just had not consisted of the physical trials Ric was put through, unless she counted the hours spent kneeling in prayer alongside the pious queen. They shared their happier memories of growing up in royal service.

By the time they stopped for the night, Isa felt more connected to Ric than she ever had outside of the chambers they shared the day before, and Ric enjoyed finding someone who understood how he felt for much of his life. Isa did her part to help prepare the evening meal by skinning more than one rabbit. It shocked Ric that she knew how, but when asked, she only shrugged and said she had not spent her entire life at court. Isa and Ric sat together to eat, listening to the men chatter rather than talking much. As the evening wore on, Isa found herself getting sleepy again. She was unsure of whether she should dare, but she leaned against Ric's shoulder. He immediately wrapped his arm around her and pulled her closer.

"Don't fall asleep yet, lass." Isa smiled at Ric's attempt to sound a bit more Scottish. She nodded and enjoyed the heat Ric generated. The air was still cold, and there was frost on the ground most mornings. She had not said anything to Ric, but she dreaded sleeping outdoors in this time of limbo between the dead of winter and the early days of spring.

Isa and Ric sat together as the first watch posted and the men began to settle in for the night. Ric stood and pulled something from his saddlebag before he took her hand. He led her away from the camp and toward the bank of the loch where they had stopped for the night. He murmured something to the guard they passed, but Isa could not hear. The man nodded and disappeared, but he was back only moments later, now standing with his back to the loch and them. Ric stooped near the water and dipped what Isa noticed was a drying linen into the cold water.

"The men won't look. I thought you might appreciate being able to use the cold compress."

Isa's cheeks burned as she looked at the back of the man standing nearest them before nodding. She turned her own back to Ric before lifting her skirts and placing the wet linen between her legs. The cold immediately soothed her flesh, and she wanted to moan in relief. As she stood with the cloth pressed against her, she considered how cold it was. It was not nearly as bad as she had imagined, and she could see there was no ice left in the water. An idea formed in her mind that she knew would infuriate Ric, but once she had thought it, her body demanded she follow through. She bent over and unlaced her riding boots. She carefully toed them off, her long skirts hiding her feet from Ric, who still stood behind her.

Once she had her shoes off, she dropped the linen and rolled down her stockings. She glanced back at Ric and the guard before gathering her skirts and hoisting them to her knees and dashing toward the water. She threw the skirts over her shoulder and wrapped them around her as she waded in until she was mid-thigh deep. She lowered herself until she submerged her backside and allowed herself a moan of pleasure.

Ric was unprepared to catch a glimpse of his wife's perfectly shaped bottom as she flung her skirts out of her way. He was also unprepared for her wading into the freezing water. He followed her until the water lapped at the toes of his boots.

"Isa, come out," he hissed. "You'll catch your death. That water has barely thawed."

"And it feels marvelous. I won't be long. Even I know it's cold." Isa could feel the pinpricks beginning as most of her skin rejected the ice water. She allowed herself a few more moments before she stood and walked out of the water.

"Stay there. Stay right there and don't move. Keep your skirts away from your legs but lower." Ric ran back to the camp, leaving Isa bewildered. He was back before she could figure out why he had run off. She could see a surcoat in his hands, but she did not understand why. When he was before her again, he lifted her skirts before lowering to his knee. He used his surcoat to dry Isa's legs and backside but kept the rougher material away from where she had put an end to the pain. He picked her up and carried her to a nearby rock before fetching her stockings and boots. He dried her feet and put her stockings and boots back on her.

"I wish you'd warned me that was what you were about," Ric whispered.

"So you could refuse me?"

"No. I would have joined you. I could have held your skirts out of the way."

Isa grinned. "I rather doubt that. I think you would have stopped me."

"Do you feel better?" Ric's voice softened, and Isa heard the concern and guilt.

She pulled at the front of his surcoat, and when

he leaned forward, she cupped her hand around his ear. "There's only one thing that would make me feel better, but I don't think we'll have a chance for that until we arrive at our destination."

Ric groaned. He had stepped between her legs so she could reach his ear, and now his rod pressed against her sheath even with layers of clothing in the way. "You were just in that freezing loch because of your discomfort. Now, you're thinking of the very thing that drove you into it."

"Yes, and now that the skin is a bit numb, I rather wish we could."

"Numb? You wouldn't feel aught."

"I most certainly would." It was Isa's turn for a wolfish grin. She still had a hand fisted in Ric's surcoat as she leaned back on her elbows. Ric followed her, and his body stretched over the top of her. He had taken his surcoat and hauberk off before they ate and now only had his leggings, a tunic, and his gambeson on. Isa savored the feel of his larger body pressed against hers. Ric could tell Isa was mulling something over, but he could not imagine what she was thinking.

"Is it true?" Her eyes flashed up to his before looking at the center of his chest.

"Is what true?"

"What you said earlier, after we saw the king, aboot a difference."

Ric scooped Isa off the rock and shifted so she was in his lap as he perched on it. "In ways I never imagined possible."

"I can't imagine. I mean I can see how people would enjoy coupling, regardless of whether they cared aboot their partner, but I can't imagine how it would feel different." Ric was not sure he liked the idea of Isa picturing coupling with a man she did not care about, a man other than him. She tapped his chest, and Ric kissed her cheek. "I didn't mean me."

"It's completely different. It's—it's, well, it's more complex. It's not just about finding a physical release anymore. The pleasure during and after is unlike aught I've ever known or imagined, Isa. And I know it's because it's you. I could never go back after what I've shared with you."

"Is that your way of telling me you'll be faithful?"

"One of them. I've told you before, but I want you to understand why."

"Because of how it feels."

Ric flinched and prayed Isa could not see in the dark. He wanted to tell her it was more than just the physical feeling, but he was not ready to confess his deeper emotions in case she did not return them. He knew she cared for him, and he could tell from her voice that she wished he would say more, but he also knew that did not mean she felt more, too. He had been down that path before.

Even though Isa was nothing like Bella, the latter had tried to manipulate him into confessing sentiments he now understood were only infatuation. He was certain his feelings for Isa went far deeper than that, but he lacked the courage to admit it. So instead, he poured his heart into the kiss he offered. It was slow and tender. Now he simply wanted her to know they were more than just two people who enjoyed coupling with one another.

Ric eased Isa from his lap and took her hand before leading her back into camp, where they had placed their bedrolls next to one another. When they laid down, Ric pulled Isa's back against his chest. They both fell asleep quickly, but each had thoughts that weighed heavily on their mind.

———

The remainder of their journey was uneventful. They sneaked off when they could, and Ric even arranged for them to spend a night at an inn, but both avoided any conversations that brought up feelings. They did discuss the situation near the border, or rather, Ric took several opportunities to warn Isa about the danger and to insist that she never ride out of the keep's wall without him or at least ten men. Isa had to wonder if he simply forgot that they were moving to live on her clan's land where she grew up, or if he did not remember enough of his own childhood and assumed she did not either. She had suspected he would be gone much of the time just as her father had been, but they were less than a day away before he admitted that the king expected Ric to ride on patrol more than remain at the keep. She had taken a deep breath and plastered her courtly serene smile on her face. She worried about his safety, too, but she feared sounding like a nag if she told him too often.

NINETEEN

They paused at the top of the rise as they looked down at Barsalloch Point, their new home. Isa had not seen the keep since she was a child. She had traveled with her parents when they left Druchtag Motte to travel to the Stewarts. Both castles dated to before the Normans, but the Dunbars of Morchum had inhabited them for several generations.

Isa was once more atop Bridei, having reverted to riding her own horse five days into the journey when she felt well enough and she and Ric silently agreed that riding together was too much torment for them both. She leaned forward as she saw something flap against the castle tower's wall. She shielded her eyes and was sure she saw a pennant.

"My parents," she murmured. "Mama."

Ric looked to her and frowned.

"My father is in residence, and I pray that my mother is too."

Isa spurred her horse forward, and Ric was unprepared for her to lean low over her horse's withers as she galloped over the landscape, taking jumps that made his heart lurch into his throat. MacLellan easily kept up with Isa and Bridei. When Isa whistled loudly, Ric saw the portcullis open and several men on the battlement waved. Ric's men followed them as they clattered into the bailey. Ric noticed an older man and woman at the top of the steps to the tower. The woman had a look similar to Isa's, but the man wore a deep scowl and looked unhappy to see them riding into the castle. Ric reined in beside Isa, but she was already throwing her leg over the saddle and slipping to the ground. She lifted her skirts to her ankles and ran toward the steps. The woman raced down the steps, meeting Isa in an embrace that nearly knocked them both over.

"Mama," Isa cried.

"Oh, Bella," the older woman sighed. "I am so happy to see you, lass."

"Me too. But Mama, I want to introduce you to my husband."

Isa pulled away and found Ric standing not far from her. He offered her space to reunite with her family, but she could tell he was on edge as his eyes scanned everywhere within range. She reached out her hand and stepped toward Ric. He did not hesitate to take it, and this time it was Isa who pulled Ric to her side. Isa looked up at her father and sobered. Ric saw the smile slip from Isa's face, and he realized he desperately wanted to find a way to make it return. She had been so excited to see her mother, but her father appeared distant and disinterested in Isa and more concerned with Ric.

"Mama, Father, I would like to present my husband, Sir Dedric Hartley." Isa dipped into a curtsy as Ric bowed.

"Welcome to Barsalloch Point, Sir Dedric. We welcome you as the new lord of this keep and chieftain of this sept of our clan." Laird Dunbar seemed anything but welcoming.

"Thank you, Laird Dunbar."

Laird Dunbar flinched at Ric's accent. Isa knew

it was an uncomfortable irony for her father, who once sided with the English to protect his land, to hand over one of his holdings to an English knight who represented his former enemy, the Scottish king.

"Please do come inside. I'm sure you are in need of refreshment," Lady Dunbar intervened. Isa held onto Ric's hand as they entered the Great Hall. They only released one another when Ric pulled back Isa's chair then seated himself beside her.

"Thank you," she smiled at Ric.

"What would you like, Isa? Something to eat or something to drink? Both?" Ric asked.

"Who's Isa? Do you not know your own wife's name? It's Bella," Laird Dunbar barked, and it was Isa's turn to flinch.

"Father, I prefer Isa. There were other Isabellas, Arabellas and Bellas at court. Ric, I mean Sir Dedric, suggested Isa, and I find I'd rather be called that."

"Very well, Isabella."

Isa plastered her courtly serene smile as she cringed at her father's inhospitable attitude. No one spoke until after they had filled the chalices and brought a platter of cheeses and cold chicken with a heel of bread out for the couple. They kept the conversation neutral and revolved around benign pleas-antries. Isa grew tired, and the wine made her head feel heavy.

"Isa, would you like to retire until the evening meal? You look exhausted, my sweet." Ric spoke softly.

"I think I would, but I don't want to leave you with my parents."

"I must speak with your father in private sooner rather than later. I'll see you to our chamber, then return to seek an audience with your father."

Isa nodded and looked to her mother. "Mama, I

think I would like to rest for a while. I find I'm rather tired."

"Of course, Isa." Her mother looked as though she was trying a new food, one she was not sure she liked, as she tested Isa's preferred diminutive. "Your chambers are on the second floor. The laird's and lady's chambers will be available once we depart."

Isa looked at Ric before blushing and looking back at her mother. "Chamber," she said softly. Her mother nodded, but her father's florid face flushed so brightly, Isa feared he would be ill.

"I beg your pardon."

"My lady wife requested a single chamber. We share." Ric's tone made it clear their decision was made.

"Absolutely not," Laird Dunbar bellowed, disregarding both Isa and Ric.

Isa stood and placed a hand on Ric's shoulder before he could stand, too. "Father, you may occupy the laird's chamber in my home, but you can no longer dictate where I sleep. That is for my husband to decide, and I have made my wishes clear. He agreed and decided to grant them. We are only in need of a single chamber."

Isa held her head high and glared at her father, tempting him to argue with her in front of the clan, who silently watched the battle between father and daughter despite not being able to hear.

"You have been at court too long, lass. You are not who I raised," her father grumbled.

"Before Christmas, I might have agreed with you aboot being at court too long, but now I find I was there exactly the right amount of time." Isa turned to her mother. "Is it the chamber I used as a child?"

Her mother shook her head before finding her tongue. "I'd planned for you to use that chamber, but it will not suit your husband. You shall use the one just before it."

"Thank you, Mama."

Ric eased her chair back, so she could walk past the table and offered her his arm as they moved off the dais. When they reached the stairs, Isa leaned into Ric, making it difficult to keep his arm between them. Instinctively, he wrapped his arm around her waist. She sighed, and Ric knew it was both in contentment and relief.

Once Ric had helped Isa out of her gown and then helped her into bed with only a minimum of delays and distractions, he made his way below stairs and sought his father-by-marriage. The man was where they had left him, and Lady Dunbar sat near the fire sewing.

"My laird, may I have a word?" Ric swallowed the distaste in his mouth as he attempted to keep his face neutral as Laird Dunbar glared at him.

"I suppose. Agnes," he called to his wife. "You may as well come too since you will pester me until I tell you everything that is said."

They entered the laird's solar, and Ric could tell it had been some time since it had been in use. The room was clean, but it looked as though nothing had been touched or moved in years. He slipped past the older couple and made his way directly to the desk that sat before a window. He brushed his hand over it, ensuring Laird Dunbar saw him claim the space. He looked to see if there was a decanter of whisky, and he found a full one that looked like the only new thing in the chamber.

"Would you care for a dram, my laird, my lady?"

"I believe I shall need it," Lady Agnes muttered. "Patrick, I believe you'd benefit from one, too."

Ric poured whisky into three mugs and handed two to the couple before making his way to the head of the table. He tried not to rush, but he was determined to be seated there before his father-by-marriage claimed it. He made it in the nick of time, and he believed he heard the older man growl as Ric pulled out the chair.

"I don't see any need to dilly-dally with pleasantries. The king expects you to fight against your own people, and for that you received my land and my daughter."

"They are not my 'own people' as I never considered myself English. I was a Scot stolen from his home and raised in England."

"By Edward."

"In Edward's court until I was sent to squire."

Patrick Dunbar assessed Ric as he would a piece of livestock he considered trading. Ric knew of the Dunbar's past; the man had originally sided with Edward. Isa had said it was to protect their people, but the Dunbar had sought his own claim to the throne, and Lady Agnes was originally a Comyn, which he believed only strengthened his claim. Ric was old enough to remember when Patrick Dunbar was King Edward's ally. He had not understood much as he was just coming into his knighthood, but he recalled the name.

"You still have received my land and my daughter."

"I did not ask for the land, as you know from the betrothal documents, but I did request permission from King Robert to marry Isa."

"Lady Isabella," Patrick corrected. Ric felt like snapping *my wife, my name,* but he knew that would only enrage the man further.

"Lady Isa," he could compromise, "is what is most important to me. The land could have been anywhere or not at all. I didn't marry her for the land."

"Perhaps not now. No, you married her for the heirs you would sire on her which would guarantee the land later." Patrick sipped from his mug. "I knew your father."

Ric was not prepared for the abrupt change in conversation and nearly choked on the sip he had just taken. "You did?"

"Yes. I fought alongside him more than once. A fine mon who chose a woman over his king. Sounds familiar."

"My parents were a love match. That is not a secret, and my father soon came around to the Scottish cause."

"And it got him and your mother killed. I would prefer that not happen to my daughter."

"Patrick," Agnes hissed.

"They aren't a love match." Patrick looked at Agnes but jerked his mug so hard in Ric's direction that some of the liquid sloshed onto his hand.

"Neither are we a political match. I care a great deal for your daughter, and her safety and happiness are more important to me than anything, or anyone, else." Ric's gaze hardened as he dared Isa's father to contradict him.

"The king sent you to spy for him." Ric did not respond, knowing it was a test to see which man he admitted to. Instead, he took a long draw on his mug and let the heat from the whisky burn a path to his belly. "You would do well to remember who granted a landless knight a prize far above his station."

"I am aware Isa is precious, and I've told you, she means more to me than aught else."

Patrick's laugh held no mirth. "I suppose we shall see." Patrick raised his mug to his son-by-marriage. "I shall pray you meet a better end than your father."

Ric brought the mug to his mouth to keep the curses from his lips.

"Sir Dedric," Agnes spoke up. "I remember your mother very well. We met on a number of occasions, and I actually met you when you were not more than two or three years auld."

Ric's eyes widened at this piece of information. He only knew his aunt and cousin, along with the MacLellans that he had met, who were familiar with his mother. "Ric, please, my lady."

"You are the image of your father, but there is a look aboot your eyes that is your mother. She was a woman of great determination and an iron will. She endured a great deal for the love of your father. He never once took it for granted." Ric nodded, aware that Agnes was making a point, though more subtly than her husband, but just as strong.

"We ride out tomorrow," Patrick announced.

"But we've only just arrived. I would like to see Isa for longer," Agnes countered, using her daughter's preferred name. She and Patrick stared at one another for a long moment before Patrick relented.

"The day after. Lord Dedric has patrols he needs to set. He is to depart immediately according to the king's wishes."

"I will leave once I am certain Isa is settled." Ric sat back and crossed his arms, daring Patrick to challenge him. Denying Ric would only make his father-by-marriage look worse.

———

After his exchange with Isa's parents, Ric felt like he needed a rest just as much as Isa. He made his way back to his chamber, but he found the room empty. He looked around, but the fresh kirtle Isa had laid out before he left to find her father was gone, and so were the slippers she intended to exchange for her riding boots. Ric walked to the landing and was prepared to take the stairs to the Great Hall, when he saw a flash of white-blonde hair and then heard Isa's laugh. He leaned to see who she talked to, and it stunned him to see her in the arms of another man. This man was of a similar build and size to Ric, but had sandy blond hair and a dimple Ric could see from across the room. His wife was still clinging to the man but animatedly chatting with him. It was the mystery man who Ric watched squeeze her waist and nod in Ric's direction. Isa spun around and beamed at Ric. There was no remorse or guilt for being found in another man's embrace. Ric was certain he would see stars, the blood pounded so hard in his temples. His vision tunneled as all he could take in was his wife with another man. He stalked forward but was unprepared for Isa to dash back to him and grab his hand to tow him behind her.

"Ric, I'm so glad you found me. I was just aboot to go look for you. It worried me that it might alarm you when you didn't find me in our chamber," Isa yammered as Ric's eyes narrowed as they approached the man who stood watching them. Ric could see he was a strikingly good-looking man, and his temper flared even more. "Ric, this is my cousin, Alasdair. I haven't seen him in years."

Isa's smiled slipped when neither man extended an arm in greeting. Instead they seemed to be sizing one another up, as though they were waiting for a chance to pounce.

"Alasdair, I'd like you to meet my husband, Sir Dedric Hartley." Isa unthinkingly wrapped her arm around Ric's and slid her hand into his, but when his fingers remained stiff instead of gripping her hand like he usually did, she looked up to see her husband was genuinely angry. She looked back at Alasdair and caught him smirking. "Ric, Alasdair and I grew up together. He's only a couple of months aulder than I am. We did everything together until he entered the lists and I was sent to court. It's been at least four years since we've seen each other. He was more like a brother than a cousin."

Isa looked between the men again. Ric's temper had not cooled, and Alasdair's arrogance had only increased. Isa was beginning to panic. She had hoped they would like one another upon meeting, and she would have family along with her husband at her new home.

"I'm your new captain of the guard," Alasdair finally spoke up.

"I already have one. The king's orders," Ric growled.

"That mon is to be captain when you ride out. My uncle has appointed me captain of the guard to defend the keep."

Isa looked up at Ric, and he finally looked down at her. He saw panic in her eyes as she shook her head. "I didn't know," she mouthed. "I'm sorry." Isa was not sure what she was apologizing for, but she suspected she had caused a rift between her and Ric and created a disaster of an introduction between Ric and Alasdair.

"Alasdair, I'm sure you'd like to get settled, and I planned to take Ric on a tour of the bailey and keep."

"I have little with me to settle. Perhaps you'd like a second tour guide since I've been here as often as you, if not more."

"No." Isa's tone made both men look down at her. "I haven't seen Ric for most of the afternoon as he was locked away with my parents, and I was resting. I'd like the time with my husband. I missed his company."

"While you rested?" Alasdair raised an eyebrow.

"Yes. Particularly while I rested." Isa raised an eyebrow in return.

"Bella," Alasdair hissed as his cheeks reddened.

"You need not pretend innocence for me. I'm married now. And it's Isa."

She looked up at Ric, pleading with her eyes that he agree to go with her and not reject her in front of her cousin. Ric nodded, and it was his turn to smirk at Alasdair as Isa led them toward the doors to the bailey. When they stepped outside, they both needed a moment for their eyes to adjust to the bright sunlight. Once they descended the steps, Isa practically dragged Ric to a storeroom across from the kitchens. She pushed the door open and pulled Ric inside. Once the door was closed, she fell against Ric and burst into tears. Ric had no idea what to make of Isa's sudden shift in mood. He slowly wrapped his arms around her, and when his hold tightened, she cried harder, trying to burrow into his chest.

"I'm sorry, Ric. I don't know what I've done, but I ruined your introduction to my cousin. I'd hoped you two would make friends. I'm sorry."

"Don't cry, my sweet." Ric tucked hair behind her ear and tried to lift her chin, but she shook her head and once more tried to burrow closer. Ric looked around and found a chair near a table covered in bags of what looked like flour. He led Isa to it and sat down before pulling her onto his lap. "Isa, don't cry. You're breaking my heart, and I don't know what to do to make you smile again." Ric kissed her forehead as she wiped her eyes.

"And I don't know why you're so angry at me. But I didn't mean it. Whatever it was. I didn't."

"I was jealous, Isa." Ric knew he had to confess, or his wife would not cease feeling guilty. "I saw you run past the stairs and then you were in another man's arms. I didn't know he was your family. I just saw my wife with another man."

Isa used her sleeve to wipe her eyes and dab her nose before placing both hands on Ric's jaw. "Don't you understand? I've never wanted anyone but you, my heart." Isa's hushed tones soothed Ric's nerves, and the term of affection was one he had not heard since the day they married. He craved hearing it more often.

"That's good to hear because I will never share you." Isa opened her mouth to ask if she could say the same but snapped it firmly shut. She knew she had no right to ask such a thing of her husband. "Isa, you can ask. You deserve to know, to be reminded, that I will not stray."

She nodded and raised her chin. "Kiss." The one word was all either of them needed. It was one of their tender exchanges of emotions neither was willing to speak aloud.

They sat together for a long time, enjoying the silence and one another's company. When they heard voices approaching the door, they knew they could not hide any longer. Isa took him on a tour that showed him the smithy, the stables, the areas where the laundresses hung the clean linens, the ovens used in summer to bake bread, and the chicken coop. She pointed out the postern gate and explained there was a paddock on the other side as well as a path to the loch. She offered to show him, but Ric pointed out that the servants would serve the evening meal soon. Isa promised to include it in the rest of the tour the next day.

The evening meal was more lighthearted than the last time Ric sat at the dais. He and Alasdair made proper introductions. When Isa turned away to speak to her mother, Alasdair leaned in to Ric.

"Good. It's good to see you're jealous, and not the type who looks at Isa as a possession. It means you care aboot my cousin. Fail her and she comes to any harm, I will kill you." Alasdair leaned away and was ready to step away, but Ric squeezed the forearm he still held from their warrior handshake.

"Fail to keep her safe while I am away, and I will disembowel you while you still breathe." The men nodded at one another before smiling. Isa turned back around in time to see a truce develop between the two men she cared for most.

By the time the meal ended, Ric had been most solicitous and ensured she had the best pieces of all the foods served. His arm rested against hers throughout the meal, and his hand lay on her thigh beneath the tablecloth. He had inched her skirts up, and when Isa realized what he was about, she helped gather the material. The feel of his bare hand against her bare thigh had them both shifting. They excused themselves and practically raced up the stairs.

The next day went quickly for both of them as Isa finished Ric's tour before meeting with her mother, the housekeeper, and the head cook. Ric went out to the lists with Alasdair and met the men King Robert had charged him to lead. He found the warriors were well trained and prepared for any attack that might be made against the castle. He inspected the walls and battlements before looking through all the weapons in the armory. Isa had briefly introduced him to the blacksmith, but he returned to speak with the man about his skills and experience. It impressed him to find the man made and repaired all the weapons and horseshoes as well as all the metal cookware for the kitchens with no apprentice or assistant. He decided he would send Robbie to help the man, since he had experience with maintaining both Ric's armor and weapons, as well as caring for their mounts.

Ric barely saw Isa until the evening meal, which went much like the night before. They ate with Ric's hand on her bare thigh, but Isa had covered his hand with hers and slid it much higher. She was nervous about being so forward, but the predatory look in Ric's eyes made her feel desirable and reassured her that Ric did not mind where she placed his hand. She placed her hand on his thigh but was about to snatch it away when Ric sucked in a whistling breath.

"Leave it," he muttered. Isa did as she was told until neither of them could sit without squirming. They left the dais before they served the final course, once again racing up the stairs.

The second morning dawned, and Isa stood with Ric on the steps to the bailey as they bid her parents goodbye. As her parents rode out through the gates, people from the village filtered in for market day. Isa squinted and tilted her head, sure she recognized one of the women as the beautiful English one who had appeared at Robert's court around the same time as Ric. She knew they had a past together, but she could not understand why she would be at Barsalloch, so she chalked it up to her imagination. Isa kissed Ric goodbye before he and Alasdair went to the lists. She spent the rest of the day working on the household accounts, which she and her mother discovered were in complete disarray.

· · ·

The third morning brought rain and Ric having to say goodbye to Isa. "I hope to be back within a week, my sweet. I need to survey the land which I now defend. I must see it from more than just the border."

"I know. I just ask that you be careful. Between the weather and the border reivers and the English, you have much to keep an eye open for."

"I will because I'm already impatient to return to you. Are you sure you will be well here?"

Isa nodded. She looked out at the people scurrying through the bailey and then back at Ric. "Alasdair will be here, and I have plenty to keep me occupied while you're away. There are several improvements within the Great Hall that I would like to make, and a number of storage rooms that have not been properly maintained. The time shall fly by."

Neither of them believed that, but Isa tried not to let her anxiousness show. Ric picked her up off her feet and kissed her much the way Magnus had kissed Deirdre, Edward had kissed Elizabeth, and exactly how Tavish had kissed Ceit. Alasdair cleared his throat several times, but neither of them was willing to be rushed.

Isa stood upon the steps alone as she watched Ric ride out of the gate. He turned back twice, and she waved each time. She pushed her wet hair away from her eyes, certain she saw the woman from the day before on one of the warriors' horses. She frowned but assumed the man knew her. Perhaps she was his wife, and he would return her to the village to avoid walking in the rain. When the line of twenty horsemen disappeared over the hill, Isa returned to the keep.

TWENTY

The week Ric anticipated being gone stretched first into a fortnight, then into nearly three weeks before the signal went up that the chieftain was returning. The sun had just set, and the sky was already dark. Isa called out for a bath to be prepared in her chamber before she took one of the torches from a wall sconce and rushed outside. She held the flame out high as she tried to make out the figures as they rode through the gate. Ric was seated on MacLellan and led the party into the bailey. Isa felt a bubble of excitement well within her chest, but she knew he would be cold and exhausted. She wanted to hurtle toward him and smother him in kisses, but she did not know what type of mood he would be in after sleeping outside for the better part of three weeks.

As the last of the men rode through the portcullis, Isa once again squinted at a figure on one of the horses. It was most certainly the woman from when Ric departed, and this time she rode her own horse. A knot formed in Isa's belly as she looked back at her husband who was already jumping down from his horse. He tossed his reins to Robbie and took the keep steps three at a time until he reached Isa. He swept her into his embrace and brought his mouth down to hers with need and hunger she gladly matched. Alasdair stepped forward and took the torch before Isa dropped it or lit them on fire. Once she had both hands free, she wrapped her arms around Ric's neck. He lifted her off her feet just as he had when he departed, and the kiss once more made people turn away.

"Need you," he mumbled against her neck. "Now."

"Yes," she moaned into his ear.

Ric looked at Alasdair long enough to bark, "Open the bloody door." He cradled Isa in his arms as he marched across the Great Hall. Neither of them noticed the clan members who stared at their chief and lady as he took the stairs three at a time just like outside. More than one person jumped at the sound of their chamber door slamming shut. Alasdair had followed them inside and just shrugged. While they were not seen until morning, they were easily heard.

———

Ric was only home for three days before he had to ride out again. During his time at the keep, he was virtually inseparable from Isa. He followed her around as she explained how she had kept busy. They were together in Ric's study where Isa resumed her research, her belongings having arrived from the royal castle while Ric was gone. While she poured over books and looked through vellums, Ric caught up on the clan matters that had accumulated in his absence. There was a list of complaints he would need to adjudicate when he returned the next time, and he needed to speak with the village farmers about the spring crops. There did not seem to be nearly enough time to spend on his duties or with Isa.

On the night before Ric was set to depart again, they lay tangled together among the bedsheets. Ric rubbed his thumb over the wedding band he had slipped onto Isa's finger more than a month earlier. He was surprised to realize so much time had elapsed, but then he remembered he had been away for most of it. He pledged to make it up to her when he returned from his next patrol. He did not want to tell Isa where he would be going, but he owed her the truth.

"Isa, I hate being away from you even for a morning let alone days and weeks. I wish this were a time when I could travel freely with you and not fear for you. I want you to know that I don't like leaving you."

"I never thought that you did, but this was the price we both had to pay."

"But I believe I got the better part of the deal." Ric kissed her knuckle just past the band with the deep emerald that matched her eyes.

"I have no complaints." Isa pressed Ric onto his back as she climbed onto him and guided his length into her.

Her moan signaled they were finished talking until the sun rose the next morning. Isa leaned forward, her hands resting on Ric's chest as her sheath slid up and down Ric's cock. She closed her eyes, enjoying each sensation as his rod filled her. She didn't want to think about him leaving the next morning, or all the days she would spend pining for him. She wanted to savor this time together. As Ric's fingers pressed against her backside, encouraging her to move faster and with more force, she pulled at one of his shoulders.

Ric gladly complied with Isa's silent request, sitting up and wrapping his arms around her. Their bodies pressed together, with Isa's thighs bracketing Ric's hips. The position offered a feeling of intimacy that few others did. Their gazes locked as Isa's fingernails grazed Ric's scalp. Her other hand lifted her breast to his mouth, and he latched on, suckling like a starving babe. They crested together before lying in one another's arms, their arms and legs still tangled as their skin cooled. They drifted off to sleep, content and refusing to think about the coming morning.

Isa's life began to take on a pattern. Ric's second patrol kept him away for over a month, while the third and fourth were considered short at a fortnight each. After that, she stopped keeping track. She oversaw the scrubbing of all the surfaces in the Great Hall that could be reached by a ladder or rod. She ordered the kitchen fires be extinguished, and the flues swept clean. She had the tapestries removed and beaten before airing them out. She looked through the attic and found furniture under sheets and more tapestries. She tugged down several and brought them to the chamber she and Ric moved into after her parents departed.

She gave up trying to take Bridei out for rides when Alasdair informed her that she could not go beyond the village without Ric beside her. Since he was never there, she never went anywhere. Alasdair and ten guards accompanied her whenever she left the castle wall to go to the village. She had looked for the mystery woman each time she went to the village but never saw her. She only appeared when Ric was leaving or returning. She tried not to think about why the woman traveled with her husband, but the sickening feeling ate at her. When Ric was home, he was devoted to her to the point where she sometimes had to ask for space. He did not act like a man who was disinterested in his wife, but then she reminded herself that he was away more than he was home. Perhaps he did not like to be lonely while traveling. That thought made her dash to a chamber pot more than once.

Ric's time at home was occupied with making love and their regular duties. There had been little time to talk about anything that was happening beyond the immediate, and they never spoke of their feelings, preferring to show them rather than articulate them. Isa knew she was in love with Ric, but she wondered how she could love a man who might prefer the company of his mistress to her own.

They had been married for nearly five months when Isa noticed an open missive on Ric's desk as she spread out the parchments she had been transcribing from Gaelic to French. Ric told her from the beginning that she was to use his desk or the table in his study any time she wanted. The handwriting on the missive was decidedly feminine, and it was addressed to "Ric" rather than Sir Dedric or even Sir Ric. Her stomach ached, and her hand shook as she picked it up. She had to read it twice to believe what she saw.

Dearest Ric,

The king grows anxious awaiting your latest report on the Maxwells' numbers. Graystone and Hargate await your word for the next attack. King Edward doubts your loyalty and insists you make your move on the Dunbars' main keep. You would do well to heed your king's desires and not continue to keep him waiting. I have seen for myself that the people within your castle believe your loyalty is to the usurper, so they will not expect your attack on their laird. You have the aid of Graystone and Hargate once they have trounced the Maxwells.

Do not keep me waiting any longer. I would see you soon for your latest news.

Ever yours,
Bella

Isa dropped the missive and ran to the nearest chamber she knew would have a chamber pot. She heaved into it, over and over, until there was nothing left within her. Her heart felt as empty as her stomach, and both ached with a pain that doubled her over. Her husband was a spy, not for King Robert but for Edward Longshanks. Everything about their marriage had been a lie. Everything since the very first time they met had been a lie. He had used her to gain land near the border and entry into another border clan from where he could run his nefarious operation.

She forced herself to trudge above stairs to their chamber to find a sprig of mint to freshen her mouth. She smoothed back her hair and forced herself to relax her face into the look of serenity she mastered while serving the queen.

She left their chamber and made her way to the stairs. She was halfway down when she noticed her husband standing close to the woman she had seen. It was clear they had a familiarity with one another that came only from intimacy. She watched as the woman put her hand on Ric's arm, and he did nothing to remove it. Ric shook his head several times before pushing her hand away and pointing to the door.

It was only then that Isa realized the woman could see her. The Englishwoman's look of smug satisfaction set Isa's teeth on edge. Isa was certain it was Bella. She had had her suspicions, but now that she saw the woman in her home with her husband, there was no doubt. Bella nodded to her, and Ric turned to see who Bella was looking at. The color drained from his face as he saw Isa watching them. He ran across the Great Hall to the stairs taking them faster than Isa thought any man could. Ric caught her arm as she made it to the landing.

"Let go," she hissed.

"Let me explain."

"Explain? You don't need to. I already know."

"It's not what you think."

"I don't need to think aught. I told you, I know." Ric had a sinking feeling as he looked into Isa's eyes, and the stare that looked back at him was filled with loathing. "What I don't know is which is worse. That you parade your mistress in front of me each time you leave and return and now she's in my home. Or that you're a spy. For King Edward."

"Isa, you don't know what you're talking about."

"Don't I? I see Bella with you each time you leave. At least you have her ride with one of your men, but she has her own horse when you return. She has been with you each and every day that you have been away. I think you never ended your affair with her. You duped me into believing you care so you could marry me all the while carrying on with the woman you really care aboot. I read her missive. I know."

Ric felt the blood run cold in his veins. He did not know where to begin to explain or what he could safely tell Isa. His mind screamed that he had to disabuse her of the idea that he was unfaithful. "I can't deny that the woman is Bella, but she is not my mistress."

"Then what do you call a woman who isn't your wife but who travels everywhere with you?"

"She doesn't travel with me. If you read the missive, then you know she is my go-between. She has stayed in the village at times. I know she's watched me ride out a few times and even caught up with the riding party when we return and pass the village. But she doesn't travel with me."

"You are a miserable liar, Dedric. I know she does. She is never, ever in the village when you are away."

"Then she is off finding her various messengers because she is not with me." Ric's voice was beginning to rise as his frustration increased. "I have always been faithful to you."

"You haven't a clue what that word means. You haven't been faithful to anyone but yourself. You weren't faithful to either of the kings you swore fealty to. You haven't been faithful to the pledge you made to my father since you intend to attack my clan. And you bluidy well haven't been faithful to me, whether it was swiving your mistress or lying to my face." Isa wrenched her arm free from Ric and turned toward their chamber, but Ric caught her again.

"You have no idea what you're talking about, Isa. Things are not as they appear."

Isa scoffed and crossed her arms as best she could with Ric still holding onto one. "You don't say. I believe I just learned that today. I hadn't even heard that you returned, and when I discover you have, I discover you brought Bella with you."

"Isabella—"

"Dedric," she sneered.

"You think you know everything, but you don't."

"Then tell me. Tell me the truth, and maybe I will believe you." Isa raised her eyebrows at him, and Ric could see that she was willing to listen, but he could not figure out what he could say that would not put her in danger. Ric knew he had taken too long when a wall shuttered in Isa's eyes, and her lips curled in disgust.

"You can bed me whenever you're home as is your right. I would be the liar if I said I could deny you. We both know at least my body can't. But don't speak to me. Don't touch me. Don't do aught near me beyond what you must."

"Isa, you're being irrational. I know you don't mean that."

"Don't I? Remain home long enough to find out."

Ric straightened to his full height and pushed his shoulders back. "I don't take orders from you, Isa. I'm your husband, and you should have a little more faith in me."

"Faith? I thought I'd already shown how faithless you are."

"There are matters of politics along the border that exceed your understanding, and they are not your concern."

Isa gasped before she closed her eyes for a long blink. "You pompous arse. I grew up along the border. I was the daughter of a border laird long before I made the mistake of becoming your wife. You do not have a monopoly on understanding what is at stake. How dare you speak to me as though I'm some insipid dimwit? You are not the mon I thought you were. You are so much less."

Ric reeled back as her words cut through him. He knew she was angry, and she had every right to be based on what she believed she knew. He just wished she would trust him more.

"You will regret what you're saying. That's not how you truly feel, Isa. We both know it."

"How I feel?" She shook her head. "Whatever feelings I might have had, you crushed. You keep dancing around the truth, telling me to trust you, but you won't give me any reason to. You have ruined everything. If only you could tell me that Robert put you up to this, or that you offered to spy for Robert instead. Something that could keep me from thinking the worst of you."

Ric panicked. She was too close to the truth, and he would protect her at any cost. If she knew too much, then she was in danger of saying the wrong thing to someone or be used against him. "Then you shall be disappointed. Perhaps it is best that your soft feelings end now before they go any further."

The color leached from Isa's face, and Ric feared she might faint. But it was her turn to stand to her full height with her shoulders back. "As I said before, you can claim your rights whenever you're not too busy swiving Bella. Other than that, stay away from me."

"You are developing a foul mouth, Isabella."

"You taught me the word and the deed. One of the only useful things you've done."

"What the hell does that mean?"

"Naught. As you pointed out, it all means naught." When she attempted to push past him, this time he let her. He knew they both needed time to cool off, and he needed to figure out how to resolve their argument while dealing with Bella's demands. He would kill the woman with his bare hands.

TWENTY-ONE

sa slipped into the kitchens near the larder and found a sack which she filled with three wheels of cheese and as many apples as she could find before she slipped into the main area. She spied loaves of bread cooling near the window. She inched closer, then knocked over a metal tray that clattered to the ground. As the women who had been busy working turned to see what caused the noise, Isa swiped three of them and pushed them into her sack, leaving the kitchen as inconspicuously as she entered. She kept the sack in front of her as she made her way through the bailey, taking an indirect route to the stables. She looked around to see if any of the stable boys were lurking in the stalls.

When she saw no one and heard nothing, she pulled an apple from the sack and stood before Bridei. She gave her steed the treat and quickly began to saddle him. She checked the saddlebags and breathed a sigh of relief that no one had found or removed the pair of leggings, tunic, and plain surcoat she kept in it for when she used to ride out from the royal court. She had convinced a few guards when she was still quite young to ride with her if she pretended to be a boy. She knew she could not leave unescorted, but if she looked like a lady-in-waiting, no one would let her leave, guards or not. She had taken to keeping them in her saddlebag, and now she was grateful.

She did not have time to change, nor would it matter since Bridei was so recognizable. She had to get through the gate before anyone could stop her. She knew Bridei could outrun any horses other than Ric's and Alasdair's. She had to get far enough away from the keep before either of them learned she was gone.

Once she finished saddling her mount, she led him from the stables and did not bother hiding her smile when she saw a hay wagon nearing the gate. She pulled Bridei around to the side farthest from the gatehouse and passed through with no questions. As soon as she was past the portcullis, she kept Bridei in the shade cast by the wall. She knew the guards would be looking out rather than down. She led her horse until there was no place to hide any longer. She mounted with ease and spurred him toward the east. Isa knew where she was going. She was glad that only one person might think of her destination, and she prayed it took Alasdair a while.

Robbie watched the chestnut horse leave the stables, but he could not see who led the horse. He frowned, knowing the horse was Lady Isa's and no one but she rode him. He followed the horse out of the bailey wall and nearly wet himself when he recognized Lady Isa mounting the horse then galloping away from the keep. He spun on his heel and ran back within the wall.

"Sir Alasdair!" Robbie ran toward the lady's cousin. "She's gone. She rode out alone."

"Isa?"

"Yes, Lady Isa rode out on Bridei without anyone to escort her. She was riding like the wind. I didn't even know her horse could run that fast."

"You have no idea. Where is your lord?"

"I don't know. I haven't seen him since we arrived in the bailey. He had a matter to attend to."

Alasdair narrowed his eyes. "What type of matter? If my cousin is riding away from him, then the matter was not their reunion."

Robbie looked away and shook his head. "I can't say. That is for Sir Ric to explain, but we must tell him about his lady wife sharpish."

Both men turned toward the keep as Ric burst through the doors. "Have you seen Isa? We had an argument, and I thought she would go to the study or the kitchens, but she's in neither, and no one has seen her."

"I have. Sir Ric, she just left." Robbie squeezed his eyes shut.

"Left? With whom? The guards know she isn't to leave without me, even if she has men with her."

"Ric, she left alone. Whatever you argued aboot must have been very bad. She's run away," Alasdair explained.

Ric blinked several times as he tried to understand what Alasdair and Robbie were telling him. "Was someone going to fetch me? Let me know that my wife is riding just miles away from enemy camps?"

"We were just going to look for you."

Ric pushed past them as he whistled loudly. He ran toward the stables. "Saddle and mount up. We ride again."

Alasdair followed him into the stables. "Let me come. I know the fastest way to Druchtag Motte."

"Is that where you think she went?"

"That's where I would check first."

"Splendid. Her father already hates me. Now I have to arrive looking for my wayward wife. I just pray she doesn't say the wrong thing."

Alasdair's eyes widened as understanding dawned. He was the only man with whom Ric had shared the truth. He had come to respect and like Isa's cousin, and with him in charge of her safety when he was gone, Ric felt the man had to know what to be prepared for. "Then you should definitely let me come."

"No, I can't. What if she returns while I'm gone? I need to know that she's safe if she is here without me."

Alasdair seemed to mull over Ric's words as the knight finished saddling his horse. "Very well. But if she isn't with our clan, then she could be anywhere. The weather could kill her if reivers or the English don't find her first."

"You don't need to tell me that," Ric snarled at Alasdair. Ric mounted and charged out of the bailey. He went in the direction that Robbie pointed. He could not understand why she would head east when her parents lived to the west. He wondered if she was trying to confuse him.

Isa gritted her teeth as the cold water splashed over her boots and along the hem of her gown. She had steered Bridei into the stream several miles back to hide her tracks. Her legs were freezing, and the water was soaking through the leather. She steered her horse up the bank and jumped down. She looked around and stood still as she listened for any sounds that did not come from forest animals. She pulled the dirk from where she kept it in her boot and reached behind her. She pulled the laces loose enough to not fear stabbing herself, and then cut through them just as Ric had the day they married. The memory made her pause as she swallowed her sob. She let the gown fall to the ground before unlacing her boots. She quickly pulled on the leggings, the tunic, and the surcoat. She was glad that she had already been wearing her plaid as it added an extra layer and would give her some protection when the temperatures dropped at night.

She relaced her boots and mounted Bridei. She looked at the gown and decided to leave it where it lay. It was a remnant and a reminder of a time she wished she could forget. She knew she never fully would, but it felt good to shed the past and leave it behind her. She spurred Bridei on as she continued to head east before turning north.

It took Isa four days of hard riding before she reached her destination. She had lived off the food she rationed and the animals she caught. She rode until it was too dangerous to continue in the dark. She had taught Bridei to lay on the ground when he was a colt. She and Alasdair often camped out with the other lads from their clan. Her uncle, Alasdair's father, once told her that if there was a danger of freezing to death at night, she should make her horse lay down so she could shelter against the animal. Bridei had grown used to it and now thought little of it when she gave the command. She dared a fire only long enough each morning to cook what she was able to snare the night before. She did not trust the smoke not to give her away at night.

She was sure Ric would chase her, but she did not want to alert anyone else to her presence. When she arrived at the Stewart keep, she was exhausted, hungry, and filthy. She wanted to fall into bed and sleep for a month of Sundays, and she knew this was the only place where she could do that.

Ric was at his wits' end. He had tracked Isa for the first few miles after leaving the keep, but her trail ended at the edge of the stream. He knew she must have entered it to keep him from tracking her, but knowing that led him to where her abandoned gown lay on the far bank. He thought his heart would give out when he recognized it and saw the laces had been severed rather than just untied. His mind flashed to how he had cut away Isa's gown the afternoon they married and why he had done so. He had been unable to wait another moment to see and feel Isa's body. He feared someone else had felt the same way. There were no signs of a struggle and no other hoofprints. They followed the ones that led away from the stream until they faded into mud from a recent storm. Neither he nor his most experienced scouts could pick up a trail after that.

Ric led the search party south, fearing he would find Isa being held hostage by reivers or English troops. Despite the number of men, they were able to go unnoticed as they traveled. Ric and a select few scouted ahead most days, and he had even sneaked to the edge of three English camps, but there was never any sign of Isa. They had a run-in with a pack of reivers who were more interested in their mounts than the men, but they would not get the mounts without killing Ric and his scouts. The outcome was not in the reivers' favor. Ric continued to ride east until he came to the border with the MacLellans. He met a patrol that recognized him, as he had come to his own clan's aid more than once since taking up residence at Barsalloch Pointe. The men said they had not seen anyone cross into MacLellan territory alone, and they had not spotted the remnants of anyone's camp.

Ric never questioned whether Isa would intentionally cross over into England, so he reasoned the only other choice was to turn north. They rode the boundary between Dunbar and MacLellan territories for three days, asking any of the patrols they spotted if they had seen anything that made them suspicious, or a lone rider moving across their land. No one had any information to share.

The men had been searching for nearly three weeks when they made their way onto Stewart land. One of his men suggested that they at least inquire in case she was trying to make her way back to Stirling and was disoriented. Ric agreed, but held little hope of gaining any further news about Isa. He feared she was dead, and he would never find her body.

He trudged up the steps to the main doors of the Stewart keep and was led into the Great Hall. He was unprepared to see his wife sitting next to a man on the dais, leaning into him as they conversed.

"Isa?" Ric whispered then bellowed. Isa and the man sitting next to her turned to the commotion at the door as a man drew his sword and guards leaped forward to restrain him. "What the devil are you doing sitting with my wife?"

"She is a guest in my home." The handsome dark-haired man stood. Ric quickly noticed that he was taller and heavier than the man, but he would not underestimate any laird who survived in Scotland. Between the war with England and the clashes between the clans, surviving as a laird required cunning and fighting skills.

"My wife is returning to her own home. Now." Ric broke loose and charged toward the dais.

"I don't believe she wishes to go anywhere with you. I believe that's why she is here to begin with."

Ric halted as he looked at the man and then at Isa who seemed to sit in suspended animation. She looked ready to rise from her seat, but she also had a staying hand reaching for the man's arm. Ric looked at Isa and could not put his finger on what bothered him most. Perhaps it was the way she sat so cozily, or maybe the fact that she had traveled directly there apparently unharmed when he had spent three weeks failing to track her. Ric was fairly certain it was the fact that she looked relaxed and happy, or at least had before she saw him. She was in a gown that fit her perfectly and her hair was styled as it had been at court.

"Where is the lady of the keep?" Ric looked around but saw no other lady who fit the rank of a laird's wife.

"She is right here," the impertinent man looked over at Isa.

"Where the hell did you get the clothes, Isa, if he has no wife to share them with you?"

"They're mine."

Ric was certain he saw red. He surged forward ready to impale the man who was not only harboring his runaway wife, but was clothing her, too. Isa leaned back in her chair, growing nervous as she saw rage fill Ric in a way that even his first encounter with Alasdair had not done.

"You're frightening my sister. She ran from you, and now you're scaring her. Get out." Andrew Stewart stepped toward the edge of the dais, and Isa pushed back her chair so hard that it clattered to the ground. She skirted around the table and tried to get between the two men.

"Lady Isabella doesn't have any brothers. Sisters yes, but brothers no."

"Actually Ric, I do. Put your sword away before one of Andrew's guards runs you through for threatening the laird in his own keep." Isa remained between her husband who had his hand on his sword hilt and her brother who carried more knives than even most Highlanders. Both Ric's physical appearance and his arrival in her brother's keep discomfited her. She waited until he let go of the hilt of his sword. "Andrew is my half-brother. Before my mother married my father, she was married to Andrew's father, Laird Stewart. After his death, the king allowed my mother to remain here until Andrew was auld enough to foster, then he ordered my mother to return to her clan, which she did. My mother was a Comyn, and her father arranged the marriage to my father as a way to form an alliance."

Isa did not need to add that the alliance was to fight against King Robert and to aid the English.

"You never told me you had a brother."

Isa's gaze hardened as she glared at Ric. "There is a lot we didn't tell each other."

Ric seemed to go hollow before her eyes as he nodded. "That is true. Are you happy here, Isa?"

Isa looked at Ric and wanted to tell him that she had been miserable, but she also wanted to protect herself. "Happy enough."

The moment the words left her mouth, she knew she had made the wrong decision. Ric looked at Andrew before looking at her. "If you're happy here, Isa, I won't force you to leave. I don't wish to leave you here, but I don't want to make you miserable either. If my men and I might benefit from a night's rest in the barracks, we'll ride out at dawn."

"You can't sleep in the barracks." Ric would have laughed at Isa's appalled expression if he had not felt like he had just come out the losing side of the worst battle of his life. "Ric, you should have a chamber within the keep."

Ric shook his head, but Isa stepped down from the dais. "Ric, you don't look well. Please stay in a chamber," she whispered.

"Why does what I look like matter to you?"

Isa jerked back as though he had slapped her. She shook her head as she backed away, and Ric wanted to reach out to her, bring her back to where he could embrace her like he had so many times before. "Do as you like. You always do."

Neither Isa nor Ric had noticed Andrew speaking to the housekeeper until Isa turned back to the dais.

"Sir Dedric, Mary will show you to a chamber. You are welcome to spend the night and be on your way in the morning." Ric looked between Isa and Andrew before nodding. He trudged up the stairs behind the older woman, and Isa once again worried about how defeated he looked. "So how much longer are you going to punish the poor sod?"

"Andrew, this was never aboot punishing him. I simply cannot live with him any longer."

"When are you going to tell me what happened? You arrived here in the middle of the night looking like a drowned rat, then slept for nearly two days and have barely eaten in a fortnight. Today was the first time you've laughed, and it ended when he arrived. What the devil did he do? You assured me he never raised a hand to you. Was that not true?"

"He's never struck me, and I'm sure he would kill any mon who tried to."

"Was he unfaithful to you? Isa, you can't expect that."

"That was part of it, but not the entire reason. Andrew, I can't tell you."

Andrew pulled Isa in for a brotherly embrace, and she welcomed the comfort that he had always offered as a sibling ten years her senior. "Well, I think you will have little choice but to resolve this one way or another."

"It is resolved. He leaves in the morning."

"That's not what I meant. Mary showed him to your chamber."

"Andrew, no! Dear God, what have you done?" Isa pushed past Andrew and bolted for the stairs. She ascended as quickly as she could and raced down the passageway before bursting through the last door along the corridor. She found Ric looking into one of her chests as he fingered the sleeve of a gown hanging on a peg.

"You already have a life started here. How could you have had so many clothes made so quickly? Did you plan to come here even before we argued?"

"No. I didn't know this was where I would go until I'd led Bridei out of the keep. I–I thought you might get here sooner. Is Alasdair not with you?"

"No. I made him stay behind in case you returned. I didn't want you in the keep alone."

"Alone? With more than a hundred people coming and going each day, with an entire barracks full of warriors. I was never alone."

"You were if I wasn't there to protect you, and the only other man I trust was gone too."

"Ric, you see danger where none exists. You seem to so easily forget that I grew up on that land. I know what life is like there just as well as you do. I may not have fought any battles, but I remember the raids when I was a child. I remember my father riding out and none of us knowing if he would return. I know the risks, but not every corner has someone waiting to jump out and slit my throat."

"You don't know that," Ric whispered.

"Then maybe you should have told me the truth. Maybe then I would have been appropriately cautious, but I never suspected I might be the target of both English and Scottish fighters."

"And making you a target is why I didn't tell you aught that might be used against you or me. If one of Edward's men thought he could gain information from you or kidnap you to coerce me, I might truly lose you. The less you know, the less anyone can force out of you."

"And if there's a raid while you are gone? How do I know who to trust? How do I know if the warriors who arrive are friend or foe, there to kill me or there to save me?"

"That's why Alasdair remained at the keep whenever I rode out."

Isa threw her hands up in the air with an aggravated growl. "And this is why I left. You expect me to trust you, a spy, implicitly, when you don't trust me at all."

Ric moved to reach out for her but dropped his hand when he was not sure how she would respond. She took a step closer but then caught herself. "You never did say how you came to have so many clothes here. How could you if you didn't plan to be here?"

"Because I often came here while I was at court. The king visited many times. Andrew's father swore fealty to Edward, but much like my father, reversed his position. Unlike my father, Andrew's father picked up the banner for Scottish independence, fighting alongside King Robert beyond just the days he owed as his fealty. Andrew has always been loyal to Robert. I came here for many holidays too, since my clan is not always in favor. It eventually became easier to leave clothing here than have chests hauled back and forth. This keep feels almost as much like home as Druchtag Motte and far more like home than court ever did."

"And you will serve as your brother's chatelaine?"

"If he asks me to, and I choose to remain here."

"You still haven't decided?"

"It will likely not be my choice to make in the long run."

Ric did step toward Isa until they came toe to toe, but he still did not reach for her. "I won't force you to come back with me, Isa. I won't hold you captive in the name of being married. But you are still my wife, so I won't allow anyone to dictate where you live. It is your choice."

"Then why are you making it so impossible?" Isa's eyes filled with tears. "I believed you all those times you said you would be faithful. Then the moment we arrive at what is supposed to be our home, you bring your mistress to it. You've hidden a horrible truth from me that could just as easily get me killed for treason as it could you. You've lied over and over. Everything has been a lie. The mon I fell in—"

Isa slammed her mouth shut and tried to turn away, but Ric's hand lightly gripped her waist. It was the first time he had touched her since he arrived. Electricity sparked between them as Ric pulled her against him, and she did not resist.

"I love you, Isabella."

Tears streamed down Isa's cheeks as she shook her head. "Don't say that," she croaked. "No more lies. Please, not that one."

"I have never meant aught more than I mean those." Ric took her hand and led them to the edge of the bed. "Sit with me, please, and I'll explain everything."

Isa suddenly felt too tired to fight Ric, so she sat beside him. She wanted to lean against him but fought the pull until he wrapped his arm around her. She rested her head against his shoulder as the tears continued to fall.

"Isa, I barely remember my father. He's more like a mythical figure than a real man in my mind, but I do remember my mother. Clearly. I remember how she smelled, the sound of her laugh, the way she would offer me the first bite of the fresh loaves she baked. I remember the chamber I shared with them, and then only my mother after my father was killed. It's where I watched the English assault, then murder her." Ric's arm reflexively tightened around Isa. "I'm terrified the same will happen to you. I was too selfish to leave you at court. I couldn't overcome my need to be near you, but now I can't stomach the idea of you dying the way my mother did. And for the same reasons. Isa, my father loved my mother, but he failed to protect her. He didn't ensure she would have the protection she needed if he was gone. He shared things with her that the English tried to force from her. I won't make the same mistake as he did. I do love you, Isa. More than my own life. I've told you from the beginning that there is naught I won't do to protect you, and I thought that meant keeping the truth from you."

Isa snaked her arms around Ric's waist as she sobbed. He waited until her tears slowed, and she sat up. "But that isn't love, Ric. Not completely. Maybe if I was your child, but I'm your wife. I'm the lady of the keep and responsible for the lives of our clan when you are gone. Besides myself, how can I keep our people safe when I don't whether I can trust you or anyone else? Whose side are you on?"

Ric looked into Isa's watery green eyes and knew there was no avoiding explaining everything from the very beginning. He wiped the tears from her face before lifting her onto his lap. When she did not resist, he positioned them so they leaned against the headboard and stretched out their legs.

"You know my past as far as being forced into service for Edward. When my tenure drew near to the end, I began to think about what I would do next. I considered moving to France, but there was no one there who I wished to serve, and there was no home for me either. I did not want to wander from village to village hiring myself out as a mercenary. I wanted to come home. I wanted to come back to Scotland and not to fight against my own people."

"I'm glad you chose to come here rather than France," Isa whispered as a shiver ran through her at the thought of never meeting Ric.

"When I fought for Edward, I fought more to stay alive than to defend his cause. I never believed he had a righteous calling to be the Hammer of the Scots. Lord Geoffrey Wingate was who I fought for when I first became a knight, and I did mean my allegiance to him. He was the closest substitute for a father that I had. I was his squire, and he taught me how to control my anger and grief and make those my weapon rather than what consumed me."

"I suppose one should count even small blessings. At least you had someone you could trust and respect."

Ric shrugged as he remembered how tenuous his relationship with Geoffrey had been in his early days as a squire. He had to admit that he missed the man who was a surrogate father. "Shortly after I received my spurs, the king summoned me to his direct service. I had little choice but to go, as I'd been forced down the path of knighthood before I understood what that commitment would mean. I felt I owed Geoffrey for the time he spent raising me and training me. Then I was bound to Edward. Within weeks of being at court, I met Bella."

Isa made a sound of disgust but nodded her head when Ric's eyebrows shot up.

"She flirted and fawned over me, and I thought I was in love with her. We began an affair I believed was leading to marriage. A month later, I learned that not only was she engaged in affairs with several courtiers, she had been tasked with seducing me, so Edward could measure my commitment to him. Obviously, the connection I believed I had with Bella was one-sided."

Isa remained tense as her dislike of Bella grew with Ric's retelling of his past.

"That was eight years ago, and I haven't touched her since. After that, I wished to be away from court and Edward as often as I could. Time away quickly made me realize two things. First, I never loved Bella, but I was infatuated with her and the attention she paid me as a young, landless knight. Second, it confirmed that Edward is a man to never trust, not even the slightest."

"I count myself lucky then that the luster wore off all those years ago, or I would not be here with you," Isa mused. "Sorry. Please, go on."

"I would see Bella when I returned to court, but I kept my distance, and she had moved on to more important and influential men. She flirted once in a while, but she had about as much intention of bedding me again as I did her, which was none."

"Good," Isa muttered under her breath before flashing a guilty smile.

"I thought I was about to gain my freedom, but Edward sent me on one final mission. I was to spy for him among my clan. I was to become a MacLellan in truth, or the truth I presented, and then report to Bella what I learned. She has a relay of messengers and go-betweens that I'm sure exceeds aught the king has contrived on his own. Once I met the Mac-Lellans, however, I couldn't do it. My cousin is the exact image of my mother. It was like seeing a ghost."

"I can't imagine how that must have felt after all these years." A tremor passed through Ric, and she ran her hand soothingly over his broad chest as she waited for him to continue.

"It would have been like I was the one to kill my

own mother if I shared aught that endangered them. And once they got past my accent, I was welcomed as a member of the clan. It was there and then that I decided I couldn't go through with Edward's orders. Bella kept appearing at the most inopportune times, but it was intentional, so as fair turnaround, I intentionally fed her misinformation. I went to Robert's court because I did want to make my home here, and I wanted to be done with England. If I had to fight for Robert in order to earn a plot of land, then so be it. I never imagined I would meet a woman that I fell in love with within moments of meeting her."

"I never believed it was possible to fall in love with someone so quickly, but I've hated every second of imagining my life without you. It's an agony unlike aught I've ever endured." Isa placed a kiss over Ric's heart as their arms wrapped tighter around each other before Ric continued.

"When I met with the king to arrange our betrothal, he named me a spy for Edward, but did not harbor any animosity to me. I'd proven myself before his brother and the Sinclairs. He did hold your hand in marriage hostage."

"What?" Isa broke in. Her stunned expression turned dark as Ric watched her anger begin to build. He rubbed her back until he felt some of the tension dissolve, and he was confident he could resume his story.

"He decreed that I could only marry you if I were to agree to live near the border and spy for him. I agreed without hesitation but insisted that you were to accompany me. I couldn't imagine leaving you behind, but the moment we rode out of Stirling, even before, I became terrified that you would die like my mother did. And I believed you would never love me if you knew I was supposed to spy for both sides."

Isa covered Ric's lips with her finger. "Do you

know why I love you? I love you for your kindness to me, and how you take my interests seriously. You've spent hours listening to me discuss things that probably are trivial to you, but you know they aren't to me. I love you for putting me ahead of yourself. I knew you rode patrol for Robert and that was part of the betrothal agreement, but I had no idea that he expected you to spy for him. I love you for your bravery and strength. I love you for trying to do what's right despite the obstacles. I love you for recognizing a wrong and trying to right it. I understand your need to keep me safe. How do you think I feel every time you leave? I just wish you trusted me enough share your burdens. If we were distant and married by arrangement, if you believed I was incapable of handling the truth, then I could understand why you wouldn't share this with me. But you believed that my fate rests solely in your hands. You aren't God. You can't control everything. I can't live like a prisoner in my home because you're always gone, and I'm not even allowed to venture to our own village. I can't live in ignorance when it is my life at risk. I deserve to know. And I want to be by your side, not always left behind."

Isa tugged on Ric's surcoat until he leaned forward enough for her to kiss him. She hoped he understood all the unspoken emotions she felt. Ric swept his tongue against the seam of her mouth, and she opened for him immediately. Their need to reconcile created an urgency between them that turned into a blaze as their hands roamed over each other. But before Ric could let it go further, he had to finish his apology.

"Isabella, I love you, and I thought I was doing what was best. I'm sorry for the pain I caused you. I'm sorry for shutting you out. I'm sorry for being so controlling, and I know I was unreasonable, but I couldn't shake my fear. I'm sorry for not being the husband you deserve."

Isa sat up and pulled her skirts to her waist before straddling his lap. She wanted to look into his eyes as they hopefully put the difficulties in their marriage behind them. "You are the husband I deserve and the only one I want. I want to come home with you. I understand now the position you were placed in and what you did to try to make the best of it. Do you promise to include me when you have a decision to make that affects both of us, affects our people?"

"Yes. You have no idea how many times I wished I could come to you for your opinion."

Isa nodded as she rested her hands over Ric's heart. "What are you going to do aboot the kings?"

Ric took a deep breath before blowing it out slowly and scrubbing his hand over his face. "If I truly had my choice, I would take you to live on Sinclair land. I would get us as far away from the border as I possibly could. You would be near your friends, and I could offer my services to their laird. I would leave this Godforsaken strip of land and never look back."

"How long did Robert say you have to serve?"

"Indefinitely. He gave me Barsalloch Point to govern and protect as part of our marriage. I assume that means I am to be there until I am no longer able to fight. Then it would revert back to your father or perhaps be inherited by any sons we might have. I would hope it would remain your dower lands, so you have somewhere to live with any daughters we might have until the king arranges a new marriage."

Isa shook her head so hard wisps of hair flew about her ears. "I will not marry anyone else. You are the only husband I will ever have. And don't speak as though you will leave me a widow. I don't like it."

She knew she sounded petulant, but she was still angry and frustrated. Her feelings were directed at the two kings who manipulated her husband, but there were certain things that held her resolve.

"Isa, you know that won't be your choice."

Isa's jaw set, and her emerald eyes hardened. "I no longer care what Robert thinks. He sentenced us both to an indefinite servitude with death as a daily possibility. You came to Scotland to escape the fighting, and he sent you back. If I lose you, I consider my life of service to the crown to be done. I will have given more than enough. I will retire in solitude if I must, but I will not remarry."

"A life of solitude is what I wanted in the beginning. Then I met you, and all I want now is to build a family and grow old with you. If I lose you, then there will be naught but solitude. I never wanted to marry until I realized I couldn't live without marrying you. There will never be another, Isa."

Isa lifted the hem of Ric's surcoat and tugged until he leaned forward enough for her to lift it over his head. She sat back as she frowned at the hauberk.

"I haven't a clue what to do with that." Isa's puzzled expression made Ric laugh. He set her beside him on the bed before standing. He pointed out how he could tighten it at the sides but preferred to wear it loose so his arms could move more freely. He showed her where to grasp, so it could be lifted over his head without tearing into fingers.

When he was free of the chain mail, Isa kneeled on the edge of the bed and lifted his tunic as he bent to let her pull it off. He lifted her chin for another searing kiss as he drew his dirk through the laces of her gown. Isa felt the tug then the material slipping off her shoulder.

"You didn't ask if I like this gown."

"I'll buy you another set of laces." Ric resumed

their kiss as he pushed the gown down her arms, then tugged at the ribbons on her shoulders that held her chemise in place. His hand kneaded her breast as his mouth descended to the other. She grasped his shoulder and ran her hand through his hair as she leaned back. Ric looked up and watched Isa with her head thrown back in pleasure.

When his ministrations paused, Isa looked down at him. Ric felt his cock throb at the arousal he saw in Isa's gaze. He lifted her from the bed, pushing the gown from her hips. She kicked off her slippers as she yanked at the laces of his leggings. He pulled his boots off before stripping off his leggings. Isa rolled down her stockings, and they stood gazing at one another's naked form, appreciating the beauty before them. Ric lifted Isa so her legs could wrap around his waist as he slid into her. The same fire that had always roared to life when they came together surged between them once more. Isa clung to Ric as they tumbled to the bed. Nothing either of them did was enough to satisfy their mutual need as they clawed at one another, starving for the connection they always found together.

"I love you, Isa. I want to prove that to you every day for the rest of my life. I want everything with you. A life with a family and a happy home. I want to give you that as much I want it for myself."

"We will, Ric. We were halfway there. If we can move beyond this, then we'll have that."

"I'll do aught that you ask, tell you aught that you wish or feel you need to know. There will be no more secrets, lies, or half-truths from me. None of it is worth it if it'll put a divide between us."

"Make love to me. That's all I need or want right now. Just hold me."

Ric buried his nose along Isa's shoulders as she wrapped her arms and legs around him. Their movements were frantic as their bodies crashed against one another, starving to be closer. Isa begged for more, and Ric gladly gave her everything he could. He feared he was too rough, but each time he tried to gentle his motions, Isa urged him on.

"I need to know you want me as much as I want you. I feel out of control, Ric. That naught is enough to show how much I want you."

"You want to know how desperate I am to be inside you, to spill my seed and prove you're mine."

"I do," Isa cried out. "I want to claim you as only mine, the only woman you're with. Do you feel as out of control as I do?"

"Isa, how can you not know?" Ric surged into her over and over, letting go of any restraint he might have had, if he'd wanted any. Isa's pants and moans made his cock throb inside her, and when her sheath clenched around him, and her body went taut, he was certain he was close to passing out.

"Ric!"

"Isa!"

Ric followed her over the cliff as his release sprung from him. He rolled to his side, bringing Isa with him as their bodies remained fused together. Their kisses were soft as they basked in the afterglow of their frenetic coupling.

"Making love to you is unlike aught else I've ever done. I never made love before being with you." Ric knew he risked a dicey topic after what they had just shared. "I want you to know I don't use that term loosely."

"I admit I've wondered more than once."

Ric kissed her forehead, and they lay embracing in silence until their clammy skin chilled. Ric pulled the covers over them as they nestled together.

"I haven't slept well since I left. I never sleep well

when you're gone. It's never as comfortable," Isa yawned. "Do you mind if I nap?"

"I've barely closed my eyes since I thought I lost you. I'm rather tired, too."

Isa stroked his chest as Ric rolled onto his back, and Isa settled her head on his shoulder. "I'm sorry I ran away. I was scared and angry. I've pulled you away from where you should have been patrolling, and I know I made you worry." Isa sat up on her elbow. "I know we will argue in the future. I don't want you to fear that this is how I will react every time we disagree."

Ric pressed her back against him as he worked his finger through her braid then stroked her hair. "I didn't think you would. I understand why it drove you away, Isa. It was reasonable to want to escape when you believe you're married to a traitor. I can't deny that I am a traitor."

Isa's hand paused. Suddenly not as sleepy as she had been a moment ago, Isa sat up once more and looked at Ric. "You are not. You served your time for Edward after being conscripted. He may have sent you to spy, but you are not English. Your father chose a Scottish wife and made a home in Scotland. He made that choice for you. You told me that you gave Bella information that wasn't true. Your loyalty to Robert came by choice, not by force. You have served Robert loyally, for there has been no news of attacks along the western border. Even if you hadn't told me, I would have heard from the servants or on market day. You are not a traitor. Don't say that."

Isa laid down again once more and resumed her lazy circles over Ric's chest as he stroked her hair. "I'd like to move north to the Sinclairs as soon as we can leave."

"I thought you were excited to live among your clan again."

"I was," Isa yawned. "But I'm more excited aboot you living."

"I will grant your wish, if I can."

The couple fell asleep and remained that way well into the evening. Andrew sent up a tray with enough for at least three meals, and they took advantage of it, remaining sequestered away the entire next day and night.

TWENTY-TWO

I sa and Ric set off for Barsalloch Point the third morning after Ric's arrival, having spent a day alone and a day with Andrew. Isa and Ric felt reconciled and stronger than they ever had. The journey back to their home was uneventful, for which they both breathed a sigh of relief. Robbie and Alasdair were in the bailey as they rode under the portcullis. Their faces were grim even when they saw Ric lift Isa from the saddle and kiss her before placing her feet on the ground. They walked hand in hand to Alasdair after Robbie took the reins and shot Ric a glance that had the hair standing up on Ric's neck.

"What's happened?" He asked Alasdair before anyone could greet one another.

"There was an attack along the border between us and the MacLellans. Apparently, the English tracked a group of scouts that had gotten too close to their camps. They attacked the MacLellan patrols and burned our crofters' homes and fields."

Isa turned wide eyes toward Ric and backed away as she shook her head. She covered her mouth with her hands as she looked between the two men.

"This was my fault," she whispered. "You tracked me east. You must have feared I'd been taken and scouted the English camps to check. They wouldn't have been after you, and they wouldn't have killed those people if you hadn't been searching for me."

Ric pulled her into his arms and glared at Alasdair over her head.

"Don't blame him," Isa mumbled against Ric's chest. "You would have told me now anyway."

Ric did not know how she could tell he was glaring at her cousin, but she could read him better than he could read himself some days. "It's not your fault, Isa. I was able to get that close to their camp because they've been planning that attack for weeks. It was bound to happen sooner rather than later."

"And you could have been there to stop it, but instead, you were chasing me."

"I am not the only border lord King Robert has. He could have sent more forces there to fight, but he didn't."

"You have to go! They need you there."

"But I don't want to leave you behind."

"I'll have Alasdair here with me. You have to go."

Ric scrubbed his hands over his face before running them through his hair. He looked back at the stables and the men who had just arrived with him. He looked forward and found Alasdair standing there waiting for his directions.

"Round up the other men. We'll ride out within the hour." Ric took Isa by the hand and led her into the Great Hall and into the solar they shared. "I don't want to leave you now that you're home, but I know that you are right, and I have little choice. I will return to you as soon as I can, Isa. I love you."

"I love you, Ric."

Isa and Ric left the solar and returned to the bailey where Isa watched Ric mount his horse and the men followed him through the gate. He turned back twice just as he always did, and Isa waved.

Ric rode hard for three days as he and his men raced to the border with the MacLellans. As they came within miles of where the skirmish was supposed to have happened, Ric looked around. He saw no evidence of a recent battle and began to grow suspicious. They passed through villages where people said that they had not seen any sight of the English in months. When they arrived at the border with the MacLellans, he recognized some of the men who were on patrol as ones he met while staying with his cousin.

"We were told that there was a battle here. We were told that some of your patrols died and that the English burned out many of my people's fields and crofts, but we haven't seen any evidence of that."

The MacLellan patrol looked amongst themselves and shook their heads. The leader spoke up as he looked to the south. "We know the English are just beyond the line and not far from here, but they haven't crossed the border recently. We've been expecting an attack, but naught has come."

Ric looked around and tried to deduce why they were given inaccurate information. He felt like he was on the receiving end of one of his own distractions, but Robbie had confirmed that they were told about the attacks from people who arrived on market day. Ric had wondered momentarily if Alasdair had set him up as a way to get back at him for Isa running away, but he knew that Isa's cousin would never hurt her by risking Ric's life, so he knew that Alasdair had spoken what he believed was the truth.

Ric chose to scout along the border with England for another day then turned back toward his home. As they rode back on the second day, Ric found his senses warned him of an impending ambush. He kept his head on a swivel, scanning his surroundings, but there was no sign of anyone lying in wait for them. But he could not ease the intuition that screamed that he must remain vigilant. As dusk arrived on that second day of their return home, Ric's suspicions were proven true. They had just made camp when they heard a rustling in the bushes. He had already warned his men that he suspected an imminent attack just before they stopped for the evening. Ric expected Hargate's or Graystone's knights and soldiers, but he did not expect Bella to appear along with Lord Hargate himself, followed by twenty of his warriors and knights.

The battle was short, with the Scots coming out the clear victors. Only a few of Ric's men bore injuries, while most of the English were dead or mortally wounded. Hargate targeted Ric, but the latter was used to Hargate's maneuvers as they were the choreographed moves every knight learned. Ric had the smug satisfaction of being able to run Hargate through himself. The man's arrogance led him not to wear armor for the ambush.

After Ric wiped his sword clean on Hargate's surcoat, he turned to look for the woman he was certain was at the heart of the attack. Bella was held captive by two of his men until Ric was available to question her.

"You are easily duped," Bella said before Ric had an opportunity to begin his questioning. "There was never any reason for you to leave your pretty little bride behind except for the fact that you are at the usurper's beck and call. Perhaps you should have stayed home and kept an eye on your wife rather than running to aid your new king. Perhaps then she would have lived."

Ric listened to everything Bella spewed, but it was her last words that registered with him. He reached out and wrapped his hand around her throat and lifted her off the ground before shaking her. "What the hell did you just say?"

When Ric dropped her back to the ground, Bella rubbed her throat where Ric could see angry red marks from where his fingers had pressed against her. "I said your wife is dead by now. Your game of distraction and diversion has been turned on you. Did you really believe I hadn't figured out you turned? I've known for ages, but it didn't suit Edward's cause until now. You should have paid more attention to your own fears. She might have lived."

Ric saw stars as the world felt as though it was closing in to a few pinpricks of light before his eyes. There was a ringing in his ears as he tried to clear the fog from his mind and understand everything Bella told him. His blade was against her throat before he realized what he was doing. "It was one thing when I was the only one you targeted, but you've made a grave error if you think I will let you live when my wife doesn't. You have played me for a fool twice now, but you never will again."

Bella's eyes widened as she realized Ric intended to end her life. She tried to twist away, but his hand clamped around her upper arm in a vise so tight it hurt to move. Then she attempted to talk her way out. "Edward will not forgive you if you kill me. He already planned to wipe out your clan and your dimwitted little bride's. Now he will pursue you to the ends of the earth before he lets you live in peace."

"That may be so, but that doesn't change the fact that your life is forfeit."

Before Bella could try anything else, Ric thrust the blade into her belly and twisted. He watched the shock sweep over Bella's face with grim satisfaction. Watching Bella know the life was seeping from her was why he had not slit her throat. He would not give her an easy death when she would be the reason he would return to Barsalloch Point without his wife waiting for him.

<hr>

Isa awoke to the sound of the warning bells sounding the alarm. She jumped from bed and ran to the window, where she could see smoke rising in the distance and horses racing toward the keep. She grabbed her robe and pulled it over the thick chemise she wore to sleep in when Ric was away. She knew there was no time to dress before she ran down to the Great Hall in her bare feet. Isa looked around as villagers poured in, running for the safety of the keep when they heard an attack was under way. She guided the women and children to storerooms that had false floors and to the cellars below the kitchens where they kept root vegetables throughout the winter. As she ran to the bailey for her third time, looking for anyone who needed a refuge, she watched the gates vibrate from the attackers attempting to break through.

"Isa! Isa! Go inside!" Alasdair ran toward her as she pointed a woman in the direction of the kitchens.

"I can't. I have to make sure the women and children are hidden. Then I will."

"No. Ric told me you are to be hidden the moment we know of an attack. You have to go inside."

Isa pushed Alasdair away. "No. Whether Ric likes it or not, I'm the lady of the keep, and it's my duty to protect our people just as much as it is his. I will deal with him when he returns. Now move, Alasdair."

Alasdair lifted Isa around the waist and began moving toward the keep's steps. He had just taken the first two steps when he lurched forward, pinning

Isa beneath him. He rolled to the side, groaning, and Isa looked over his shoulder. An arrow was protruding from his shoulder blade.

"Bluidy hell that smarts. The bone stopped it, but it hurts. Isa, break off the arrow." Isa rolled Alasdair back onto his belly as she placed one hand on his back and the other around the arrow. She snapped off as much of the shaft as she could before helping him to sit up. "Isa, you must go inside. They're going to breach the gate, and the arrows are already landing."

"Who are they?"

"I don't know, other than they're English."

"They must know Ric is away."

"I believe you're right. Isa, lock yourself in your chamber. I have to go. Lock and bar the door. Don't open it for anyone but me."

Isa nodded and watched as Alasdair ran toward the battlements. Isa looked to the wall walk, where she could see men shooting their own arrows into the hoard of attackers. She watched two men push a ladder away from the wall and heard the screams of the men who fell. Isa's eyes swept the bailey once more, and she did not see any more women or children who needed sheltering. She saw villagers equipped with trowels, spades, and pitchforks ready to defend the keep when the walls and gate were breached. Confident that there was no one left to hide, she ran toward a storeroom where she had hidden several children.

Just as she reached the door, a tremendous creak then the sound of splintering wood filled the air. She looked back in time to see the gate burst open. She looked toward the storeroom but knew she could not make it before the enemy saw her. She would not lead warriors directly to unarmed children. She changed directions and attempted to make her way to the kitchens. If she could get inside the keep, she could get to her chamber. The smell of burning thatch caught her attention, and she spotted flames rising from the stables. Stable hands were leading the spooked horses out of the stalls as fast as they could.

It was complete bedlam as the first wave of enemy warriors surged forward and met resistance from the men who remained to defend their homes. She watched Alasdair leap down the final three steps from the battlements and swing his sword as a man charged toward him. Alasdair sliced through the man's ribs, and Isa felt nauseous as blood squirted from the wound. The man had been a foot soldier and did not have the armor of a knight. Isa turned back to the kitchens and began to run, her robe and chemise lifted above her feet to keep from tripping. She reached for the door, but a weight pulled her back. She spun around, swinging her fist and landing it on her attacker's throat. She lashed out again, this time with her knee aiming for the man's bollocks.

"A wee wildcat we have here." The man crowed in his English accent. "And a beauty at that. Graystone shall be happy to have you. Once I'm done."

The man's other hand reached for her breast, but Isa wrenched his pinky backward then down, forcing his arm away. Rather than aim for her breast again, his gloved hand landed across her cheek. Isa continued to struggle until she noticed the handle of a knife at the man's waist. She twisted one way then another, distracting him, until she was able to pull it free of its sheath. The next time the man raised his arm, she stabbed into his armpit where she remembered Ric's mail did not protect him. Then she stabbed at the gap between his neck armor and collar of his hauberk.

"You bitch. You will pay for that."

Isa saved her breath for her fight. She continued

to lash out until the man raised his visor and gave her opening. She changed her grip easily and thrust the end of the blade into his eye. He staggered back, roaring in pain. Isa did not wait to see what happened to the man; she attempted to get to the kitchens. But a searing pain burst between her shoulder blades, then another beneath her ribs. She knew what had happened. She knew someone had recognized her in her finer fabric, perhaps even her face, and knew she was the lady of the keep. She had been struck by two arrows. She staggered several more steps before she fell against the door to the kitchens. She tried to summon the strength to pull it open, but she sunk to her knees. She heard English voices running toward her, so she allowed herself to fall forward like a dead weight. She stifled the groan and lay there without moving. As they came close enough for her to smell their body odor, she drew in a deep breath then waited.

"She fought like a trapped she-wolf. A shame that she's dead. I would have quite enjoyed her. I might have even waited for Hartley's return before I had my way." There was a pause before the man carried on. "Or probably not. I doubt I would have wanted to go without a woman for that much longer."

"My cods ached just watching her run. Hartley is a lucky man to have her in his bed. I heard they are like rabbits. She's better than a tavern whore." A new voice spoke, and Isa struggled to remain still as her temper rose.

"Was. Hartley was a lucky man." A third voice came from the other side of her.

Isa had purposely landed so her face was mostly covered that way they would not see her eyes twitch or move if she could not help it. Her lungs burned with a need for another breath, but she dared not let her back or chest move with the arrows sticking out.

If they wobbled or vibrated, the men would know she lived.

"What do we do with her, Lord Graystone?"

"Leave her," came the voice she had heard addressed as Graystone. She recognized the name. "Let Hartley find her just as he did his mother when I was done with her."

Isa wanted to be sick. She felt the bile in the back of her throat as she heard the man who murdered Ric's mother admit to the crime as though he spoke of what he ate the night before. The voices moved away from her but she still remained still. She could hear metal still clanging and the screams of the injured, so she knew the battle had not ended. The men had recognized her and come to investigate, but the fight was not lost yet.

The battle raged on, with the Dunbars pushing the English out of the bailey and back toward the open land that surrounded the keep. With more space to move, the fighting drew out. A second wave of English fighters poured over the rise, but reinforcements came from Isa's parents. Laird Dunbar led the charge after a messenger arrived with news of the attack. The two keeps were far enough apart for daily visits to be unreasonable, but not so far that Isa's father could not come to her aid. It was only moments later that Ric and his men followed the English over the rise. The Dunbars defended themselves from every side.

TWENTY-THREE

Isa moaned in pain as gentle hands lifted her body and legs from the ground.

"We need to get the lass to her chamber before she bleeds to death." Isa recognized the voice of her head cook. "She's a slight thing but sturdy. She has a good constitution. If this fever doesn't take her, then we should be able to get her stitched up good as new."

"I doubt the chief is going to see it that way. They're saying the mon come racing over that hill, sword raised over head like the devil himself. I'm sure I heard his war cry," her housekeeper warned.

"Ric," Isa moaned.

"Aye, lass. Your mon is on his way. We will just make you a bit more presentable before he finishes this nasty business outside," the cook said.

"Hurts."

"I know, lass. We have Hagatha coming to tend you. She went for her medicinals and will be back in two shakes of a lamb's tail." This voice came from her housekeeper.

"I love him. Tell him." Isa forced out. "I love him."

Everything faded to black, and Isa went limp.

The women rushed her inside where other warriors were beginning to trickle in or be carried in. They decided the laird's chamber was too far to carry Isa, so they found a table and ordered screens be brought down from the upper chambers. The women cordoned off an area where Hagatha could work on Isa without anyone seeing the lady of the keep being stripped to the waist. Isa remained unconscious for the entirety of the time it took the healer to tend her wounds. A hint of fever concerned the older woman more than the actual wounds, which she packed with yarrow roots before stitching them as best she could. She spooned a tincture of willow bark tea into Isa. She had only finished moments earlier when a new form of hell broke loose in the Great Hall. The chief was home and looking for his wife.

Ric raced over the hill as the smell of smoke and the plume reached him and his men. He cursed himself for not riding through the night again. After the incident with Hargate and Bella, Ric ordered his men to break camp and then rode throughout the night. He was not able to do the same the next night as the terrain was rougher, and he knew both man and beast were exhausted. But as he raced toward his home and Isa, he could not remember his rationale for slowing. With his sword swinging both left and right, he cut through the warriors who were on foot, aiming for any man with chain mail or no plaid. He unhorsed three knights as he charged toward the portcullis. His stomach dropped to his stirrups when he saw the battered gate and the bodies strewn about the bailey. Ric spotted Alasdair and kneed MacLellan toward his captain of the home guard.

"Isa?"

"Inside." Alasdair had not seen her since he sent

her to the keep. Since he had not seen her in the bailey after the gates were breached, he assumed the only place she could be was safely locked away.

Ric nodded and spun MacLellan around and charged back out the gate. He saw the arrival of more Dunbar warriors and was not sure if he should cheer or shudder that his father-by-marriage led the party. He targeted as many of the mounted knights as he could. When there did not seem to be any left to fight, he slid to the ground and slapped MacLellan on the rump, sending the horse back to the keep. Alasdair made his way to Ric's back, and they fought together as the numbers began to dwindle.

A flash of white emblazoned with red shot through with gold caught his eye. He knew immediately that he had found the man who was the cause of the destruction and death that filled his home. He charged toward Graystone as the man sneered at him.

"I saw you ride into the bailey. Did you see your dead wife? She looked so much like your mother did when she died." Graystone taunted Ric. "The only difference is I gave your mother a good rogering before I killed her. I didn't get the chance to do the same with your wife. A pity really because I heard she was even lustier than your whoring mother."

Ric picked up his pace but dropped his sword in favor of leaping at Graystone. The older man tumbled backwards as Ric's weight landed on him. Unprepared for this type of attack, Graystone could not swing his sword nor reach for a knife. Ric pinned him to the ground then lifted his head before banging it into the ground. The metal helm rang as Graystone's skull rattled about. Ric knew it would be worse than standing within a church bell. He ripped the helm from the man's head and flung it away from them both. Ric lifted his opponent's head and slammed it into the ground three more times before wrapping his hands around the older man's throat. While Graystone was an experienced knight and still in excellent condition, he was no physical match for Ric's larger body and superior strength. He tried to flip Ric off of him, but it only gave Ric more leverage to press his neck to the ground. Ric's eyes caught sight of a large rock that was within reach. He brought it down over and over until Graystone's face was no longer recognizable.

"You thought about touching my wife. You defiled my mother. You will die, Graystone, but it won't be here, and it won't be now. I shall make you suffer for what you've done to my family. I will make sausage with your entrails and feed it to the wolves. You will know what it is to be drawn and quartered. Each part of you sent to a different corner of Edward's realm. But before I do that, you shall dangle from the top of my pillory pole for a few days. Once the magpies have plucked out your eyes, I will bring you down. Without your sight, you won't know what part I will hack off next."

Ric stood and spat on the man who he had long suspected orchestrated the raid that killed his mother. But he had never known Graystone to be his mother's rapist and murderer. He bellowed orders to Alasdair as he pushed his legs to carry him as fast as they could back to the keep. He would find his wife's body, and God protect anyone who attempted to keep him from her.

Ric stormed through the doors of the Great Hall. He flung them open so hard that they slammed against the wall, making a sound that echoed even in the crowded space. He looked around but could not see anyone with the pale blonde hair that belonged to his wife.

"Where is she?" He roared. "Where the devil is my wife?"

He pushed past people who did not move out of his way quickly enough. He scanned the tables covered with wounded and looked at the dead bodies on the floor. When he could not find her, he headed toward the stairs.

"Chief, she's here!" Hagatha, the clan's healer, called out. "She's poorly, but she's breathing easier."

Ric's world tilted and then spun as he repeated the word "breathing" over and over.

"She's dead. How can she be breathing?" He muttered as he staggered toward Hagatha and two other women he recognized but whose names he could not recall.

"Lady Isa was injured and has a fever, but she never died." Hagatha stepped aside, so Ric could move between the screens. Ric looked at his wife who appeared so tiny laying on her stomach with bandages wrapped around her entire midsection. He could see her back moved with each shallow breath, but she did not move. He dropped to his knees beside her and took her hand.

"Isa? Can you hear me? I'm home. I've come to take care of you, but you must promise to get better." Ric's voice cracked as he whispered to his wife. He looked up at the women who had clearly tended to their lady. He could not bring himself to ask what happened.

"She was still in the bailey when the gates gave way. She'd made sure all the women and children were hidden. When Alasdair tried to bring her inside, he took an arrow in the shoulder. One of the men said they saw her break the shaft off before turning toward a storeroom. When the English stormed in, she chose to run toward the kitchens. Turns out the storeroom hid children. She refused to risk leading the English to them. She was reaching for the kitchen door when two arrows went into her back. I don't know if they were ones shot over the wall or from a man inside, but they struck bone and muscle, not aught vital within. She has a fever already, but she's a strong lass." Hagatha stepped forward and rested a gnarled hand on his shoulder. "Stay with her, Chief. Talk to her like you were. Give her something to fight for, something to return to."

Ric nodded as he looked down at Isa's unconscious form. She looked as peaceful as she did when she slept next to him in their bed. He brushed hair from her face and kissed her cheek. "Can she be moved? Can I take her to our chamber?"

Hagatha nodded. "Just be slow and gentle."

Ric slipped his arms beneath Isa and eased her off the table. She moaned in pain, and Ric wanted to weep. He was not sure if the tears would be from guilt that he left her unprotected or joy that she was alive. He walked slowly up the stairs and stood aside as Hagatha opened the door to his chamber and then pulled down the covers. He had just laid Isa onto the mattress and covered her when her father barged in.

"What the bluidy hell happened to my daughter? What were you thinking leaving her alone?"

Ric straightened from leaning over the bed, and the older man took a step back. "Your daughter was doing her best to protect our people, yours and mine. She put herself at risk to ensure the women and children of this keep and village were safe. I was away fulfilling my duties to you. I was away investigating claims that crofts had been attacked near the border with the MacLellans. I had no way of knowing it was a ruse to leave Barsalloch open for attack. Men of this clan fought valiantly and were successfully pushing the English back. Isa got caught in a line of arrows." Ric lowered his voice as he looked once more at Isa and thought she looked more like she was napping than fighting for her life. "My worst nightmare has come true. She may die just as my mother did."

Patrick Dunbar's eyebrows went up at the reminder of how his son-by-marriage's mother was killed. He had to admit to himself that he had not made the connection between Isa and Ric's mother. Dunbar walked forward to stand beside Ric as the younger man steeled himself for the next onslaught of demands or allegations.

"I saw and heard you and Graystone. I knew he was the reason for your mother's death, and I assumed you knew, too. I'm relieved to know the bluidy bastard shall suffer until the very end. Ric, Isa is not your mother. She will pull through if for no other reason than because she loves you. That was obvious the moment I saw you arrive with her."

Ric looked at the older man in surprise.

"Well, she said she prefers Isa now, and you are part of the clan." A smile tugged at the corner of his lips. "Part of the family. I have failed my daughter on several accounts, but I believe I made up for some of it when I agreed to your marriage. The king told me it was a love match, but he also reassured me that it was a strong political match. As long as you continue to care for my daughter, then I release you from my service. I don't want her near the border any longer. She was sent to court not only as part of my truce with the king, but to keep her from the instability here. Her sisters are auld enough to follow suit and will be joining the queen's ladies in the spring. I want all of my lasses away from this damnable war."

Laird Dunbar stepped closer to the bed and

looked down at Isa, and a true smile broke through even for a moment. "She looks like her mother, and she has the woman's spirit. Agnes defended our castle once, and it was the story of legends. She had stones thrown down upon the men who attempted to break through the gate. The standoff lasted for weeks while I was on campaign for Robert. We'd only put aside our animosity months earlier, and I owed him my time and my fealty. The English eventually retreated when they began to starve. They thought they could lay siege and force my people out, but Agnes ensured I had a home to come back to that was still solidly within Scotland. Isa is much like her mother. She can withstand life on the border, but I don't want her to have to." Dunbar laid his hand on Ric's shoulder and squeezed. "Take her back to court or offer your sword arm to another clan, but don't stay here."

Ric nodded, unsure of what to say. He wanted to accept Dunbar's word, but he could not be sure that it was not spoken out of fear and worry that would later dissolve, leaving him still bound to the clan, nor could he be sure that King Robert would allow him to walk away. The men nodded to one another, and Laird Dunbar slipped from the chamber.

TWENTY-FOUR

The next fortnight dragged on as though Ric had been caught in a bog. He did not leave his chamber once. Food was brought to him that he barely touched. He bathed with an eye on Isa at all times. He slept in a chair beside the bed, his hand resting on her arm, until Hagatha declared it was safe for him to sleep beside Isa without worrying about jostling her. He did everything to care for her, feeding and bathing her as well as talking to her throughout the day. He ordered Isa's books be brought up, and Ric read to her for hours.

Alasdair had been ill from his injury but recovered sooner than Isa. Ric tried to convince himself it was because Alasdair was stronger, but he struggled not to hold the man's speedy recovery against him when Isa barely made any sign that she was alive besides her shallow breathing. Alasdair sat with Ric every day, often taking turns reading, so Ric's voice could rest. He kept Ric informed of clan matters and brought documents for him to sign and passed along Ric's adjudications on disputes that Alasdair relayed to him. Ric appreciated the man he once wanted to throttle. He knew he would make the recommendation that Alasdair assume the role of chieftain at Barsalloch Point until he inherited the lairdship from his uncle.

It was on the seventeenth day after Isa's injury that Ric finally knew they were making progress. The worst of Isa's fever had broken after the first week, but it would come back at night. She remained listless even after the fever ceased plaguing her. Ric knew from his own experience that her body was still recovering from the wound, and the infection and fever, but he was on the verge of panic when Isa did not appear to be making any progress. Hagatha had been to see Isa twice a day since the fever broke, but she had no answer as to why Isa did not seem to be improving. She could only reassure Ric that Isa was not worsening.

Ric dozed beside Isa, his hand on her arm, when he awoke to her trying to shake it off. Her arms twitched then twisted before he could tell she was attempting to lift it.

"Isa? Isa, are you awake?" No response came to his questions, but he noticed a healthier color was replacing the pallid tone her sunken cheeks had taken on.

The next day, Ric noticed that Isa moved her legs as if to kick off the covers. He asked if she was too hot, and when he removed the heavy blankets, she settled again. For the next three days, Ric witnessed small things that finally assured him that Isa would recover.

"Ric?" Isa's throat felt raw and swollen, but she forced herself to say her husband's name. She was too thirsty to ignore. "Ric?" She knew she was barely whispering as she could barely hear herself, but Ric was at her side immediately.

"Isa? You're awake?"

"Mmm," was the best that Isa could respond. Ric looked down to see Isa's emerald gaze was clear and bright. "Wa–" Isa grimaced as pain tightened her airway.

"Water? I have some here for you." Ric eased her into a sitting position and put the mug to her lips. He only allowed a dribble at a time, knowing that too much too soon would make her ill, and he could remember how badly his throat had hurt the various times he recovered from an injury. Isa sipped the cool liquid and it amazed her how much better she felt within moments of drinking the water. She reached for Ric's hand when he put the cup back on the bedside table.

"You. Here. Always." She could not form a complete sentence, but she forced the words out wanting Ric to know she was aware he had taken care of her.

"Yes. Of course. There was nowhere else I was going to be but beside you."

"Crofts?" She tried to clear her throat but winced.

"Shhh. I will tell you everything, but you must continue to rest." When Isa scowled, Ric chuckled. "I know you feel like you've been resting for ages, but you can't expect to jump out of bed after three weeks of being unconscious."

Isa gasped and shook her head. "Not that long," she mouthed.

"Today marks day twenty-one." Isa was not sure how to react to the news that she had been unconscious for so long and that her husband had remained by her side for the entirety of her recovery. She had often heard him reading to her or talking to her, and she even remembered Alasdair being there." Do you remember being injured?"

Isa nodded but then frowned as a memory niggled at the back of her mind. Suddenly, the conversation that had taken place over her as she pretended to be dead came rushing back.

"Graystone," she croaked.

"I know he orchestrated the attack here and the one that killed my mother all those years ago. He, Hargate, and Bella concocted rumors to lure me away. Hargate attempted to ambush me on my way from discovering that there had never been an attack on our crofters or the MacLellans. Bella led me to believe you were already dead, and for that, among her other sins, she lost her life. I was horrified to see the castle under siege. I'd already believed that the keep had fallen and that Graystone would be in control. It came as a shock to me and to the men when the battle was in full force as we approached. I fought my way into the bailey, and Alasdair told me you were inside. He thought you were safely hidden, not being sewn back together. I rode back out and eventually found Graystone. He confessed to what he did to my mother and suggested that he wished he'd had the opportunity to do the same to you. He died two days ago."

Isa furrowed her brow and shrugged her confusion as she shook her head. She thought the man would have been dead before the battle ended.

"He paid recompense for what he's done to my family." Ric would not tell Isa details then, but he knew she would find out inevitably sooner more likely than later. She nodded and accepted his explanation.

"I love you, my heart," she rasped. "So frightened you wouldn't return in time." She grimaced from trying to say too much.

"I love you, too, my sweet. I knew I did before this, but I didn't understand its depth until I nearly lost you. Your father was here." Isa jerked, unprepared for the shift in conversation. "He has released me from his service. He is sending your sisters to serve the queen, and he'd like us to escort them there. He doesn't want you to live here anymore. He suggested that we either remain at court, or I find a clan to hire my sword arm out to."

Isa's mouth made a perfect circle in surprise. "Don't do that. You know what it makes me think of," Ric teased.

"Maybe tomorrow. When I can swallow," Isa mouthed, and Ric coughed.

"You're horrible," he declared, but Isa shook her head.

"No. Very good. You've said so." Isa grinned as Ric coughed again.

"Did you not hear the part about me finding a new clan for us?"

Isa nodded. "Sinclairs?"

"Yes. That's where I hope we can go. I don't know if Magnus and Tavish have left yet. I suspect they will have after all this time, but I will send a message to their father if the king agrees."

Ric's breath caught as the full radiance of Isa's smile was turned toward him. He wrapped his arms around his wife, and she nestled against him as she had so many nights before, and it was only moments later that they were both asleep.

It was another fortnight before Ric was convinced Isa was well enough to travel. She had made rapid improvements from the day she awoke. Ric sent a missive to her parents as well as the king. He informed the Dunbars that he would be taking Isa back to court and was prepared to escort their other daughters. He requested an audience with the king to discuss his release from owing Laird Dunbar his fealty.

Isa was excited to see her younger sisters for the first time in nearly three years. They were young women and ready for their duties at court. Lady Agnes oversaw the packing and preparations while Isa continued to recuperate. Isa spent as much time with her mother and sisters as she was able to manage, but she was always happiest when Ric carried her to their chamber each night. They slowly resumed their intimacy, able to do more each night. They found they enjoyed the exploration of different ways to share their need and demonstrate their love. With limitations still keeping them from the vigor they had always experienced before Isa's injuries, a deeper bond formed between them as they took their time.

When Ric finally agreed that Isa was ready for the long journey and Lady Agnes was convinced they were well prepared, Ric wrapped Isa in a plaid and passed her to Alasdair before he mounted MacLellan. Alasdair handed Isa up to Ric, where her husband wrapped a second plaid around them plus his cloak.

"I shall suffocate! You're like a raging fire to begin with. I shall swelter under all these layers," Isa argued.

"We shall see." Ric nudged MacLellan forward and led their party out of Barsalloch Point gates. Neither Ric nor Isa looked back. "Let me enjoy holding you. I don't get to do that nearly often enough."

"Only every morning, noon, and night," Isa scoffed.

"Precisely. Not nearly enough. There is too much time in between."

Isa gave up and burrowed into the warmth of

Ric's body and the many layers. She slept most of the journey, but she could tell she was getting stronger. By the time they reached Stirling, she felt almost like her old self, but even with her returned energy, she was not looking forward to seeing the king.

TWENTY-FIVE

Isa slipped away from her chamber while Ric thought she was napping. She wound her way through the passageways until she arrived at the door to the scriptorium. She pushed the door open and looked around, pleased to see the monks had already left for afternoon prayer. Isa slipped inside and made her way to the bookshelf where her favorite book of history on the Romans in Britannia sat. She struggled to reach the tome, so she pulled a chair over to the bookshelf.

She had just wrapped her fingers around the spine of the books when two strong hands plucked her from the chair. She squealed and pretended to pull away, but she suddenly came face-to-face with her husband's menacing glare. She wrapped her arms around his neck and pressed her lips to his. Their kiss grew immediately into the uncontrollable passion that had always existed between them.

"I think I shall finally have my greatest fantasy come true." Ric stepped away from the chair and swept his arm across the table before seating Isa on the edge. "I've wanted to make love to you on this table since I first discovered you in here."

"And if someone walks in?"

Ric held up the key to the only door to the chamber. Isa grinned as she reached for the laces to his leggings. Isa's head fell back as she moaned, but she needed to see Ric, needed to watch him. Ric grinned at her and shook his head before continuing to work Isa into a frenzy with his tongue and fingers. When her breath shuddered, Ric knew she was ready for him. He slipped into her sheath as her muscles spasmed around him. He circled his hips each time she lifted her hips to meet his thrusts. Their breathing was labored as they both sunk into the pleasure of making love. They tumbled over the edge into their release together, and afterwards, Ric leaned over Isa as she reclined on the table. She stroked his hair as he kissed the exposed skin of her chest.

"At least we didn't get caught this time," Isa laughed.

"I remembered to lock the door this time."

"That doesn't do us any good when we're in the alcoves."

"You shouldn't have wriggled so much, then the tapestry wouldn't have moved."

"That wasn't me!" Isa swatted at him indignantly. "That was entirely your fault then, too."

"And the gardens?" Ric gave her a stern look but could not keep a straight face.

"Well, that time might have been my fault. But it was only Lady MacAdams and Lady Gordan who found us. They're both looser than an auld mon's gums."

"With their favors and their gossip," Ric admonished, but once more, he could not keep from smiling.

Neither of them had felt any guilt over the times they had been discovered, or nearly discovered, trysting since they arrived at court. It cast no doubts in anyone's mind that they were a happily married love match. Women gave up trying to catch Ric's eye as it never strayed from Isa, and the men quickly learned that their life was more valuable than flirting with Ric's wife. Isa was far less tactful in letting the men know that she was not interested than Ric was with the women. She had nearly gelded more than one man within their first week back at court.

"I came to tell you that the king has called us for an audience," Ric stood up and refastened the ties at his waist.

"And we've kept him waiting while we—" Isa gestured between them and then at the table.

"I told him it might take me awhile. I believe the king understood my meaning."

"Ric!" Isa spluttered in exasperation as she hurried to right her skirts and smooth back her hair. They gathered up the parchments and books that were strewn on the floor near the table then left the scriptorium hand in hand. They made their way to the Privy Council chamber where they were admitted immediately.

"Good of you to join us, Lady Isabella." The Bruce looked up from where he poured over missives. "I was beginning to wonder if you'd gotten lost." Isa dipped into a curtsy but refrained from speaking. "Sir Dedric, it is my understanding that you wish to live somewhere other than at Barsalloch Point. Lady Isabella, are you in agreement with this?"

Isa wanted to look at Ric before she spoke, but she would not let the king think there was any doubt in either of their minds. "I believe the Highlands are beautiful in spring. In fact, I've heard they're quite lovely during all the seasons."

Robert guffawed as he looked at the woman who had arrived at his court as barely more than a girl. She stood before him, an experienced courtier, but what struck him most was how happy the couple was together. He thought back to his own wife, Isabella, who died too soon after they were wed. She had been a Highland lass through and through, having married Robert well before he made his fight for the throne. Now his only reminder of her was their daughter Marjorie. Robert cleared his mind of his rambling thoughts and looked once more at Isa.

"And did you have a particular place in mind?"

"Why, the wildest part of the Highlands must be the most beautiful. I believe Dunbeath would be a rather nice place to settle."

"You'd like to go as far north as one can before falling into the sea," the king mused.

"I would hope the Sinclairs would let us through their gates before that happened," Isa played along with Robert's teasing.

"Sir Dedric, is this where you had in mind?"

"It is, Your Majesty. I found I got along rather well with the Sinclair brothers, and I would be honored to serve Laird Sinclair."

"And what of your other commitments?" Robert's comment was vague, but no one in the chamber misunderstood.

"You may have noticed that I walk much more quietly these days. My spurs were returned, entrusted with Lord Graystone's head for safekeeping until both reached King Edward."

"And where did the other parts of Graystone wind up?"

"The four corners of England, just as I promised him."

"And Dunbar?"

"My father-by-marriage released me from my obligations several weeks ago with his express wishes that I take his daughter far from life on the border. Lord Alasdair has taken over as chief at Barsalloch until such time as he becomes laird."

"As the husband of the laird's eldest daughter, you could have made the argument to become laird upon the Dunbar's passing."

"Perhaps, but my wife is more important, along with our family." Ric cocked an eyebrow and waited for the king to follow his hint.

"Are felicitations in order, Lady Isabella?"

"They are, Your Majesty. We learned of it yesterday."

The king pursed his lips and glared at Ric. "I would venture to say this situation was not such before Lady Isabella's injuries, and I believe it has only been two months since she became alert again."

"Nearly three months, Your Majesty?" Isa inserted. "We've been here for nearly a month of that time."

Isa ducked her head, embarrassed that she had spoken of something so private before the king. She wished she had let Ric carry on this part of the conversation, but she did not care to hear anyone accuse him, whether out loud or insinuated.

"Is your wife always so protective of you, Sir Dedric?"

"Yes," Isa and Ric responded as one. Isa snapped her mouth shut and looked down again, shutting her eyes as she bit her tongue.

"The final thaw in the Highlands should be through. I would say you shall have your wish to see spring in the heart and soul of Scotland." Robert nodded and then gestured for a scribe to step forward. Robert took a piece of vellum from the young man and held it up. "This needs only my signature and my ring."

Isa and Ric watched the king sign the missive and then press his signet ring into the warm wax that sealed it.

"We shall have our answer from the Sinclairs

within a month. In the meantime, perhaps you would keep in mind the impressionable ladies within my wife's court. Some seem to be receiving lessons meant to be saved for their wedding night."

Isa felt her face catch fire as she looked at the king, then Ric, then the king again. She dipped into a curtsy and prayed they would be dismissed soon.

"You may go, but let it be to the privacy of your chamber. The monks will not appreciate having to tidy up." This time even Ric blushed at the king's rebuke. Neither of them knew how the king had already learned of their tryst in the scriptorium, but they were glad to escape the Privy Chamber and make their way to their own. Once inside, Ric wrapped his arms around Isa's waist, resting his hands on her belly as her back pressed against his chest, and they looked at themselves in the mirror.

"I never imagined that arriving at Robert's court would so drastically change the course of my life. I thought I might fight for him a few times and then retire to the country. Little did I know that agreeing to be a spy at his Highland court would grant me the opportunity to meet the only woman I have ever loved."

Isa covered Ric's hands with hers and twisted to kiss his cheek. "The only thing you need to continue spying on is me in my bath." Isa turned in Ric's arms and the couple kissed, just as they had the night they met and many times since.

"Do you think Laird Sinclair will like us?" Isa asked as she and Bridei trotted alongside Ric and MacLellan.

"I'm not worried about whether he will like you. Everyone likes you. I'm more concerned about him welcoming me into his guard. I read his response to the king. At best, it was tepid."

"I suppose we shall see soon enough." Isa pointed to movement in the distance. "We're aboot to be welcomed one way or another."

Ric and Isa continued to make their way toward the Sinclair keep as a welcoming party rode toward them. It was not long before they recognized Magnus and Tavish, who were accompanied by two other men who were so similar that they looked like the same face four times.

"It's aboot time ye arrived," Tavish snapped. "Ceit has been chewing ma ear for days."

"Hello, Tavish." Ric chuckled, but his friend scowled.

"Deirdre hasnae been much more patient either." Magnus elbowed his older brother. "But she still likes me, so I canna complain."

"Since neither of ma younger brothers have any

manners, I'll make the introductions." It was clear that the man speaking was the oldest by the air of authority he carried, but it was the man between him and Magnus who seemed to be the most astute as he watched Isa and Ric. "I am Callum Sinclair, heir and tánaiste. This is ma brother, Alex, who is ma second. Ye ken the other two, unfortunately. Dinna judge us by our worst examples." The man who introduced himself as Callum rocked forward in his saddle to look past Alex and smirk.

"Och aye, well from what I hear, ye and Ric have something in common. Dinna lose track of yer wives," Magnus winked.

At Isa's confusion, Alex finally spoke up. "Both ma wife and Callum's took turns running away," Alex grimaced.

"But they returned?" Isa asked softly.

"Aye," Callum and Alex answered together, wide grins hinting at happy marriages.

"If you don't mind, I'd like to get Isa inside. It's been a long journey."

"Where's that squire of —" Tavish trailed off as she saw Isa's eyes widen, and she shook her head beneath her hood. Ric placed his hand over Isa's and squeezed.

"It's all right, my sweet." Ric turned to look at his friends and their brothers. "Since I am most certainly not in King Edward's employ and have decided to move to the far north, Robbie had no choice but to return home. I managed to arrange for him to squire for the man who trained me. He is in good hands."

It had been a risky journey smuggling Robbie back across the border and to Geoffrey Wingate, but it pleased Ric to know Robbie was safe and in good care. The six riders cantered to the gate of a castle that perched on a cliff overlooking the North Sea. Isa smiled as she heard the waves crash against the rocks, and she was sure she heard a seal barking. When they came to a stop in the bailey, Isa and Ric saw four women and an older man waiting on the steps. It took no effort to see where the Sinclair brothers got their good looks. Laird Sinclair looked more like a much older brother to the men than their father. He was still fit, and it was clear he joined his sons in the lists regularly. Isa recognized Deirdre and Ceit, but she did not know the other two women.

When Ric lifted her from her saddle and placed her feet on the ground, her cloak gaped, and four happy gasps came from the steps. Deirdre and Ceit ran to meet her while the other two women picked their way more carefully down the steps, both clearly pregnant.

"Ye're having a bairn, too?" A woman with fiery hair asked quietly. She glanced at Deirdre then Ceit and nodded.

"I am," Isa blushed.

"These are our sisters by marriage. This is Siùsan," Ceit gestured to the woman who just spoke. "And this is Brighde. Siùsan married Callum, and Brighde married Alex."

"Welcome to our home," Brighde smiled warmly.

"It's still rather brisk out here. I dinna want to have to worry aboot ma sons' poor constitutions," Laird Liam Sinclair boomed. "It was most inconvenient when all four suddenly fell ill and were in need of their wives' constant nursing."

The four brothers grinned as each greeted their wife as though they had been gone fifteen years rather than fifteen minutes.

"I think we shall fit in well here," Isa whispered as Ric wrapped his arm around her waist.

"I couldnae agree more, lassie." Ric offered her a crooked grin as he practiced his Highland brogue. "I ken we've found our home."

Celeste Barclay, a nom de plume, lives near the Southern California coast with her husband and sons. Growing up in the Midwest, Celeste enjoyed spending as much time in and on the water as she could. Now she lives near the beach. She's an avid swimmer, a hopeful future surfer, and a former rower. When she's not writing, she's working or being a mom.

Subscribe to Celeste's bimonthly newsletter to receive exclusive insider perks.
Subscribe Now

Have you chatted with Celeste's hunky heroes? Are you new to Celeste's books or want insider exclusives before anyone else? Subscribe for free to chat with the men of Celeste's *The Highland Ladies* series.
Chat Now

A Spinster at the Highland Court
BOOK 1 SNEAK PEEK

Elizabeth Fraser looked around the royal chapel within Stirling Castle. The ornate candlestick holders on the altar glistened and reflected the light from the ones in the wall sconces as the priest intoned the holy prayers of the Advent season. Elizabeth kept her head bowed as though in prayer, but her green eyes swept the congregation. She watched the other ladies-in-waiting, many of whom were doing the same thing. She caught the eye of Allyson Elliott. Elizabeth raised one eyebrow as Allyson's lips twitched. Both women had been there enough times to accept they'd be kneeling for at least the next hour as the Latin service carried on. Elizabeth understood the Mass thanks to her cousin Deirdre Fraser, or rather now Deirdre Sinclair. Elizabeth's mind flashed to the recent struggle her cousin faced as she reunited with her husband Magnus after a seven-year separation. Her aunt and uncle's choice to keep Deirdre hidden from her husband simply because they didn't think the Sinclairs were an advantageous enough match, and the resulting scandal, still humiliated the other Fraser clan members at court. She admired Deirdre's husband Magnus's pledge to remain faithful despite not knowing if he'd ever see Deirdre again.

Elizabeth suddenly snapped her attention; while everyone else intoned the twelfth—or was it thirteenth—amen of the Mass, the hairs on the back of her neck stood up. She had the strongest feeling that someone was watching her. Her eyes scanned to her right, where her parents sat further down the pew. Her mother and father had their heads bowed and eyes closed. While she was convinced her mother was in devout prayer, she wondered if her father had fallen asleep during the Mass. Again. With nothing seeming out of the ordinary and no one visibly paying attention to her, her eyes swung to the left. She took in the king and queen as they kneeled together at their prie-dieu. The queen's lips moved as she recited the liturgy in silence. The king was as still as a statue. Years of leading warriors showed, both in his stature and his ability to control his body into absolute stillness. Elizabeth peered past the royal couple and found herself looking into the astute hazel eyes of Edward Bruce, Lord of Badenoch and Lochaber. His gaze gave her the sense that he peered into her thoughts, as though he were assessing her. She tried to keep her face neutral as heat surged up her neck. She prayed her face didn't redden as much as her neck must have, but at a twenty-one, she still hadn't mastered how to control her blushing. Her nape burned like it was on fire. She canted her head slightly before looking up at the crucifix hanging over the altar. She closed her eyes and tried to invoke the image of the Lord that usually centered her when her mind wandered during Mass.

Elizabeth sensed Edward's gaze remained on her. She didn't understand how she was so sure that he was looking at her. She didn't have any special gifts of perception or sight, but her intuition screamed that he was still looking.

A Spy at the Highland Court **BOOK 2**

A Wallflower at the Highland Court **BOOK 3**

A Rogue at the Highland Court **BOOK 4**

A Rake at the Highland Court **BOOK 5**

An Enemy at the Highland Court **BOOK 6**

A Saint at the Highland Court **BOOK 7**

A Beauty at the Highland Court **BOOK 8**

A Sinner at the Highland Court **BOOK 9**

A Hellion at the Highland Court **BOOK 10**

An Angel at the Highland Court **BOOK 11**

A Harlot at the Highland Court **BOOK 12**

THE CLAN SINCLAIR

His Highland Lass **BOOK 1 SNEAK PEEK**

She entered the great hall like a strong spring storm in the northern most Highlands. Tristan Mackay felt like he had been blown hither and yon. As the storm settled, she left him with the sweet scents of heather and lavender wafting towards him as she approached. She was not a classic beauty, tall and willowy like the women at court. Her face and form were not what legends were made of. But she held a unique appeal unlike any he had seen before. He could not take his eyes off of her long chestnut hair that had strands of fire and burnt copper running through them. Unlike the waves or curls he was used to, her hair was unusually straight and fine. It looked like a waterfall cascading down her back. While she was not tall, neither was she short. She had a figure that was meant for a man to grasp and hold onto, whether from the front or from behind. She had an aura of confidence and charm, but not arrogance or conceit like many good looking women he had met. She did not seem to know her own appeal. He could tell that she was many things, but one thing she was not was his.

His Bonnie Highland Temptation **BOOK 2**

His Highland Prize **BOOK 3**

His Highland Pledge **BOOK 4**

His Highland Surprise **BOOK 5**

Their Highland Beginning **BOOK 6**

The Blond Devil of the Sea **BOOK 1 SNEAK PEEK**

Caragh lifted her torch into the air as she made her way down the precarious Cornish cliffside. She made out the hulking shape of a ship, but the dead of night made it impossible to see who was there. She and the fishermen of Bedruthan Steps weren't expecting any shipments that night. But her younger brother Eddie, who stood watch at the entrance to their hiding place, had spotted the ship and signaled up to the village watchman, who alerted Caragh.

As her boot slid along the dirt and sand, she cursed having to carry the torch and wished she could have sunlight to guide her. She knew these cliffs well, and it was for that reason it was better that she moved slowly than stop moving once and for all. Caragh feared the light from her torch would carry out to the boat. Despite her efforts to keep the flame small, the solitary light would be a beacon.

When Caragh came to the final twist in the path before the sand, she snuffed out her torch and started to run to the cave where the main source of the village's income lay in hiding. She heard movement along the trail above her head and knew the local fishermen would soon join her on the beach. These men, both young and old, were strong from days spent pulling in the full trawling nets and hoisting the larger catches onto their boats. However, these men weren't well-trained swordsmen, and the fear of pirate raids was ever-present. Caragh feared that was who the villagers would face that night.

The Dark Heart of the Sea **BOOK 2**

The Red Drifter of the Sea **BOOK3**

The Scarlet Blade of the Sea **BOOK 4**

Leif **BOOK 1 SNEAK PEEK**

Leif looked around his chambers within his father's longhouse and breathed a sigh of relief. He noticed the large fur rugs spread throughout the chamber. His two favorites placed strategically before the fire and the bedside he preferred. He looked at his shield that hung on the wall near the door in a symbolic position but waiting at the ready. The chests that held his clothes and some of his finer acquisitions from voyages near and far sat beside his bed and along the far wall. And in the center was his most favorite possession. His oversized bed was one of the few that could accommodate his long and broad frame. He shook his head at his longing to climb under the pile of furs and on the stuffed mattress that beckoned him. He took in the chair placed before the fire where he longed to sit now with a cup of warm mead. It had been two months since he slept in his own bed, and he looked forward to nothing more than pulling the furs over his head and sleeping until he could no longer ignore his hunger. Alas, he would not be crawling into his bed again for several more hours. A feast awaited him to celebrate his and his crew's return from their latest expedition to explore the isle of Britannia. He bathed and wore fresh clothes, so he had no excuse for lingering other than a bone weariness that set in during the last storm at sea. He was eager to spend time at home no matter how much he loved sailing. Their last expedition had been profitable with several raids of monasteries that yielded jewels and both silver and gold, but he was ready for respite.

Leif left his chambers and knocked on the door next to his. He heard movement on the other side, but it was only moments before his sister, Freya, opened her door. She, too, looked tired but clean. A few pieces of jewelry she confiscated from the holy houses that allegedly swore to a life of poverty and deprivation adorned her trim frame.

"That armband suits you well. It compliments your muscles," Leif smirked and dodged a strike from one of those muscular arms.

Only a year younger than he, his sister was a well-known and feared shield maiden. Her lithe form was strong and agile making her a ferocious and competent opponent to any man. Freya's beauty was stunning, but Leif had taken every opportunity since they were children to tease her about her unusual strength even among the female warriors.

"At least one of us inherited our father's prowess. Such a shame it wasn't you."

Freya **BOOK 2**

Tyra & Bjorn **BOOK 3**

Strian **VIKING GLORY BOOK 4**

Lena & Ivar **VIKING GLORY BOOK 5**